SISTERS
OF THE
WOLF

PATRICIA MILLER-SCHROEDER

SISTERS
OF THE
WOLF

DUNDURN
PRESS

Publisher: Scott Fraser | Acquiring editor: Kathryn Lane | Editor: Susan Fitzgerald
Cover designer: Laura Boyle
Cover images: wolf and moon: istock.com/cirodelia; mammoths: istock.com/Daniel Eskridge
Printer: Marquis Book Printing Inc.

Library and Archives Canada Cataloguing in Publication

Title: Sisters of the wolf / Patricia Miller-Schroeder.
Names: Miller-Schroeder, Patricia, author.
Identifiers: Canadiana (print) 20200368168 | Canadiana (ebook) 20200368214 | ISBN
  9781459747524 (softcover) | ISBN 9781459747531 (PDF) | ISBN 9781459747548 (EPUB)
Subjects: LCGFT: Novels.
Classification: LCC PS8626.I45 S57 2021 | DDC jC813/.6—dc23

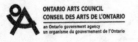

We acknowledge the support of the Canada Council for the Arts and the Ontario Arts Council for our publishing program. We also acknowledge the financial support of the Government of Ontario, through the Ontario Book Publishing Tax Credit and Ontario Creates, and the Government of Canada.

Dundurn Press
1382 Queen Street East
Toronto, Ontario, Canada M4L 1C9
dundurn.com, @dundurnpress 🐦 f 📷

I wrote *Sisters of the Wolf* to introduce
young people everywhere to our fascinating
prehistoric past. This story is fiction but all the
people and animals in the fossil record have
their own tales to tell.

I dedicate this book to my grandchildren:
Aurelia, Leona, Owen, and Anneke. May you always
follow your hearts, your interests, and your own
path, no matter what age you are or where you go.

CAST OF CHARACTERS

Shinoni: A thirteen-year-old Kula girl, the daughter of a shaman and granddaughter of a healer. She resents the growing restrictions placed on her as a girl that boys don't have. Most of all, she longs to hunt and paint animals in the sacred cave.

Keena: A thirteen-year-old Krag girl. Her life changes one day when she's caring for the young children and a lion kills a young boy. Then her uncle, Haken, comes visiting with a nasty proposal.

Tewa: A large silver-grey female wolf with mesmerizing green eyes. She might be Shinoni's spirit guide, but is also a real wolf.

Haken: A fierce Krag hunter and warrior who spreads fear and destruction wherever he goes. He hates Kulas with a passion, but at the same time covets what he believes is the magic they have used to become superior hunters.

Kreel: A good-natured Krag youth who has been close friends with Keena from early childhood.

Sabra: An arrogant young Kula hunter who lived with Keena's family one winter when he was lost from his people. He taught the Krags to speak some of his language and has learned theirs.

Atuk: Keena's aging father and the leader of their band of Krags for years. Keena idolizes him, but even he thinks it might be time for a new leader.

Ubra: Keena's mother and Haken's sister. She is the reason Haken visits Keena's group.

Shazur: Shinoni's father, a powerful shaman of their band of Kulas. He paints animals and symbols in the sacred cave and speaks to the spirits.

Reza: Shinoni's grandmother, a healer, and the most powerful woman in their band of Kulas. She is teaching Shinoni to be a healer.

Leeswi: The Krags' Earth Mother. A spirit whose voice

is the wind, who often causes bad things to happen, and can decide to give breath or take it away.

Teenoni: Shinoni's mother, who is in the spirit world after being killed by a snake while protecting Shinoni as a baby.

Tat: A four-year-old Krag boy who Keena watches.

Teal: Tat's mother.

Esel: A young Krag woman in Keena's band who has lost her mate.

Caster and **Bardak:** Two Kula hunters.

Gorda: A Krag girl.

Dakur: Keena's uncle, who had his arm ripped off by hyenas.

Shad: A Krag hunter who was gored by a woolly rhinoceros.

Sate: Kreel's father, a bad-tempered and lazy Krag hunter.

Wenzel: A Kula girl.

Etak: A young Kula woman in Shinoni's band, pregnant with her first child.

Najka: An older Kula woman in Shinoni's band.

Sakat and **Berdat:** Two Kula boys. They are Shazur's helpers and are learning the secrets of painting in the sacred cave.

Gandar: A Krag hunter.

Ardak, **Rena**, **Tark**, and **Bril:** A Kula family outcast from their band.

Dak: A young Denisovan hunter.

Deka: A young Denisovan woman and Dak's mate.

Fadin and **Seezel:** Two grey-haired elder Kula women abandoned by their band.

Ruppa: The leader of a Kula band of mammoth hunters.

Grey-Haired Crone: The leader of a group of Krag women fishers.

Luka: Sabra's father and leader of their Kula band.

40,000 YEARS AGO, ICE AGE EUROPE,
PYRENEES

1

NEANDERTHAL (KRAG)
MOUNTAIN CAMP

"STAY AWAY FROM THE BUSHES!" Keena's warning echoes across the clearing.

The children jerk their heads up, eyes wide like startled deer, before returning to their task of gathering wood. Keena clutches her father's spear in one hand and scans the forest edge. Atuk gave her the weapon this morning before he left camp with the other hunters to kill the beast terrorizing their band. Father trusts her to protect the young ones. She'll do her best, but she wishes he were here with her now. Her legs tremble as she sniffs for danger. Only the children's familiar scent and the smell of pine needles reach her nostrils.

"Keena, let go." Tat tugs at her other hand, struggling to break free of her grip. "I'm big and strong. I can help." His chubby body wriggles with excitement.

"You're growing up, Tat." Keena smiles at his toothy grin and big brown eyes. "You can help pick up firewood, but you have to stay close." She releases his hand.

"Whoohee!" Tat races toward the others, his tangled curls barely visible above the swaying grasses.

Keena tracks his movement until he reaches the group. A queasy feeling settles in her gut as she returns to her vigil. Tat has only lived through four snow times. He shouldn't be here. Not today, when she's the only one watching the children. She told that to his mother, but Teal was giving breath to a new small one and the women were helping her. Tat's a handful, but everyone says Keena can handle him.

Clouds cover the sun and a breeze stirs the trees. Keena pulls her furs tight against the biting wind. There's a movement in the shadows. A flash of gold in the greenery? She blinks and strains her ears, but hears only the rustle of leaves. Then a sudden shift in the wind from the forest slaps Keena's face. Her nostrils flare. There it is. The smell of death.

Caw, caw. Crows take flight, their bodies black against the sky.

"Run! Drop your wood. Run to the cave." Keena rushes to gather the children. Where's Tat? He's not among them. "Tat!" Her scream mingles with the cries of the crows and the children's shrieks. Then she sees Tat, following a hare into the tall grass at the forest's edge.

The bushes explode as a giant tawny shape bursts from the undergrowth and seizes Tat. The pungent odour of lion mixes with the scent of terror heavy in the air.

"No, no! Not Tat." Tears stream down Keena's face. This can't be happening. She can't let this happen. "Eeeyaaa. Drop him!" She advances on the cat with her spear raised. "Let him go!" What would Tat's mother do? What would Atuk do? Her father trusted her to keep the children safe.

Keena scoops rocks from the ground and hurls them at the beast. The lion snarls and backs away, shaking Tat's lifeless body, sending his blood splattering over her. She sinks to her knees, spear pointing at the lion, waiting for the fatal spring.

"Eee-yii-yi!" The children have reached their mothers. Teal's screams rise above the rest, mingling with the wails of her newborn. "My boy! Tat, Tat!"

The big cat's fierce amber eyes glare at Keena, mocking her, before it disappears into the bushes with its prey.

That evening, in the high country near the glacier, a silver moon shines in the sky. Ice crystals ride the breeze, stirring the trees that blanket the slope near the Krag cave. The deep, throaty cough of a lion echoes in the valley, wakening Keena from the most troubled sleep of her thirteen snow times. She hugs herself, trying to shake the blood-filled nightmare from her mind. Ominous figures cast by the firelight loom on the stone walls all around her.

Keena pushes back the bison-hide cover and rises from her bed of dry grasses. She's careful not to wake her parents sprawled on one side and her aunt and cousin on the other. All around are shadowy lumps and muffled snores. She picks her way to the entrance, where a row of fires protects her people from the night hunters outside.

Keena stares beyond the flames. Two pairs of orbs glint in the dark outer camp. She throws more brush onto the fires, and sparks shoot high into the night.

"They're only foxes." Ubra emerges from the dimness behind her.

"I know, Mother, but they're not the only ones out there," Keena whispers. The distant call of the lion floats on the wind. She shivers. Even the heat of the flames can't warm her. "I was there when the lion took Tat." Keena squeezes her eyes shut to block the horror from her mind.

"It wasn't your fault, child." Ubra hugs her. "No one could've saved Tat."

Mother's right. Little Tat wasn't the first of their band to be taken by the great cat. Uncle Orak, already crippled by a charging muskox, was killed at the stream several suns ago. Keena's friend Morda was taken three suns ago while gathering plants in the forest. And now sweet, playful Tat is gone. Keena shudders. None of their bodies or bones have been found. The hunters searched for the lion, but it was like a spirit and left no trace. Perhaps Leeswi, the Earth Mother, had sent it. If she had, nothing could stop it.

2

CRO-MAGNON (KULA)
SPIRIT QUEST CAVE IN THE VALLEY BELOW

I N A CAVE IN THE VALLEY, under the same silver
moon, Shinoni of the Kula people trembles in her
sleep. She teeters on the edge of a jagged cliff, unable
to move, as a mighty eagle with flaming wings swoops
overhead. Below her, a silver-furred wolf leaps over a
twisting stream that turns into a coiling serpent with
blood-red eyes. Screams, snarls, howls, and hisses com-
bine in a swirl of sounds until the clear keening wail
of the wolf rises above the others.

The rock surface of the floor is hard and cold against
Shinoni's cheek as she forces her eyes open. Total blackness bears down on her, sharpening her hearing. The
howl of the wolf still echoes, soon answered by another,

and another. These aren't the calls of wolves in the dream world. These are real wolves, a hunting pack, and she's prey. She's stayed in the dream world too long. The night, with its predators and swift death for the careless, surrounds her. Shinoni's survival depends on fire, and she gropes blindly, searching for her firestones.

An icy wind shakes the treetops at the forest edge, where a large silver she-wolf sits, watching the cave at the foot of a hill. Movement and the scent of human coming from the crevice promise an easy meal. The other wolves of the pack crowd behind her, brushing against each other, whining in anticipation of the kill. She starts down the hill and the others glide out of the shadows, following her lead. A sudden spark of firelight flashes in the cave. The alpha female skids to a stop and paces back and forth in front of her pack. Hunger gnaws at her gut as she studies the scent. Her nose tells her this human is young and alone. Still, she's cautious of these creatures. Her mate died under their spears in the last snow time, and she bore no pups after the snow melt. She flashes her teeth, warning the pack to stay, then turns and lopes silently toward the cave, alone.

Shinoni, now wide awake, sits cross-legged on a deer-hide mat. Her bronze skin glows in the warmth of the flames as she adds more branches to the fire. On the cave floor, a puddle of water from a spilled water bag reflects her muddy image: thick black hair pulled back with a hide thong, and long arms and legs covered by a deerskin tunic and leggings. Drawings of animals are scratched into the earth all around her.

Shinoni shakes her head to clear her thoughts. The sun has risen twice since she broke the taboo and entered this place where no Kula girl should set foot. Her stomach rumbles in the stillness. She's remained here without eating, only taking sips of water from a skin bag, drifting into and out of the dream world several times. She's never been this late starting her fire.

Shinoni's heart pounds against her breast bone like a hunter hitting a drum. The howling has stopped. Is the pack coming for her? She picks up a stick and sketches the outline of a face with pointed ears and snout and slanting eyes in the dirt beside her. A low growl reverberates from the other side of the fire.

She springs to her feet and clutches the stick like a club. Something's moving on the other side of the flame.

"Who's there? Have you come for me, wolf?"

Shining green eyes peer through the smoke, closer than any wild creature should come to a fire. Shinoni blinks. Perhaps she's still in the dream world and this is a vision. No, the sharp scent of wolf floats in the air, and she hears panting as the creature moves slowly back and forth in front of the entrance.

With her free hand, Shinoni grips the pouch of animal bones and dried plants she wears at her hip. Grandmother Reza made the medicine bag for Shinoni's mother and gave it to Shinoni for protection when her mother died, many snow melts ago. She moves her hand to clutch the amulet hanging round her neck. It's carved from antler in the shape of an eagle, the powerful totem of her father's clan.

The wolf stops pacing now and sits across from her. Flickering flames reflect in wolf eyes and girl eyes, locking the two together.

"Shinoni!" A distant shout breaks the spell. The wolf turns and snarls, then leaves as silently as she appeared. Lights move in the darkness beyond the fire. Shinoni recognizes them as torches. The voice rings out again, closer now. "Shinoni, are you there?"

"Yes, Father, I'm here." Shinoni scrambles to erase the animal images in the dirt. Shazur will be angry she's broken the rules once again. Will he punish her for seeking visions like a Kula boy who's becoming a hunter?

"We've been searching for you since last sun time, girl." Shazur's large frame fills the entrance. "You could've been killed. There are fresh wolf prints out here." The fierce tattoos of a Kula shaman can't hide her father's relieved smile. He moves inside, followed by two hunters, Caster and Bardak. The men squat by the fire to warm up.

"We saw the Strange Ones hunting not far away," Shazur says. "Who knows what would happen if they caught you. Some say they eat children. What are you doing here alone, girl?"

"I'm on a spirit quest, Father. I've seen a wolf through the fire." Shinoni clamps her lips shut, but it's too late. The words hang in the air as the three men stare at her.

"You'll find your spirit guide at the women's celebration. Not now," Shazur says.

Shinoni knows that after the snow time the grandmothers reveal the women's secrets to the girls, who then find spirit guides to help them become strong Kula women. But Shinoni wants to be a strong hunter.

"I'm not a child. I've seen spirit animals." Shinoni lowers her gaze but her words are clear. She's seen thirteen snow times. Father knows if she were a boy she'd be on a spirit quest.

"Eat now," Shazur says. "We have a long walk back to our camp when the sun rises." He offers dried deer meat from his pouch to her and the hunters.

"Why is she doing the quest a boy does after he's been initiated in the sacred cave?" Caster scowls and points to remnants of Shinoni's animal drawings still visible in the firelight. He traces the outline of a deer antler with his spear tip.

"Do you want to anger the spirits, girl, and ruin the hunting?" Bardak spits into the fire. "Shazur, what'll you do about this?"

"We'll see what can be done when we're back at camp." Shazur lies down with his back to Shinoni. "Now we need rest."

Shinoni hugs her knees as she curls up by the fire. The wolf's glowing eyes seem to stare back at her from the flames. She drifts into the dream world, relieved it was the wolf that came to her — and not the snake with its blood-red eyes.

3

NEANDERTHAL (KRAG) CAMP

THE MORNING AFTER THE LION ATTACK dawns cold and cloudy. Keena hesitates at the mouth of the cave. Normally the outer camp bustles with Krags going about their chores. Today it's empty. Bone and stone tools lie where their users dropped them when the beast killed again.

Caw, caw.

Keena stumbles backward as a crow flies up from feeding on scraps. Yesterday she helped the women butcher a deer there, before she took the children to gather wood. Keena presses her fist to her eyes, blocking tears. The crows had warned her, but she wasn't quick enough to save Tat.

It was her fault he died.

Keena's band clusters beside her, but no one ventures outside. Their familiar scents mingle and envelop her in a thick cloak. Krags are powerful and her father's their leader. Still, all around her men, women, and children hang back, shifting from one sturdy leg to the other, unwilling to leave the group.

"Good morning, daughter." Atuk walks past Keena, then steps out of the shelter. "We're Krags," he shouts, raising his spear above his head. "We're hunters."

Some of the band members shuffle and mutter beside Keena. No one moves out of the cave. Her father's hair is grey and his pale skin furrowed with wrinkles, but his eyes are still piercing under their heavy brow ridges. He scans the group and focuses on Keena. Heat spreads across her cheeks.

"We must destroy this beast before it kills more Krags," Atuk says. "We can't hide here. We need to bring in food before the snows come."

Atuk's right. Keena takes a deep breath and joins her father. The wind whips her flame-red hair across her eyes, blocking her view of the band clinging to the safety of the cave. She smells her people's fear.

Keena avoids looking at Teal, cradling her newborn small one. "Come out. We're safer together," Keena calls. Ubra steps out and joins arms with her daughter. The warmth of her mother's touch flows through

Keena's body. Soon all the band members join them and spread out to begin the day's work.

Keena thrusts a torch into one of the fires by the entrance and transfers the flames to a hearth outside the cave. A fire roars to life. Others collect wood or water, but whatever they do, they do it together. Keena knows, as they all do, that a lone Krag is often a dead Krag.

The icy breath of Leeswi, the Earth Mother, shakes the trees surrounding the camp. Keena looks up. Have they displeased her in some way? What had they done or left undone that angered the spirit enough that she sent the lion?

Older women and mothers with small ones squat by the fire, drying strips of deer meat. They work side by side in a circle, facing the forest in all directions. The smallest children play inside the circle, protected by the women's bodies. Keena's mother chants as she takes precious strips of meat and throws them into the fire. The smell of burning flesh fills Keena's nostrils and rises on the wind. Will Leeswi accept the offering?

Keena joins her friend Gorda and the older children gathering kindling to keep the fires burning. She shoos them into a huddle. "Do you want to be lion food?"

"Lighten up, little mother Keena." Gorda moves to the other side of the group. "We have to spread out to find wood," she says. "We're close to the hunters."

In an open area, Atuk has gathered the men and the boys old enough to hunt. They are planning the best way to track and kill the lion. Keena breathes easier with Atuk so near. Stories of her father's skill and bravery as a hunter are often shared around their campfires. As a young one, she would snuggle on his lap and touch his scars. She loved hearing about his battles with powerful predators like hyenas, wolves, and bears.

Keena waves at her father as she moves on with the children. She remembers the story of his first hunt when he was about her age. He was trampled by a woolly mammoth but survived and gained honour for helping with the kill. She's proud to be Atuk's daughter and she won't let him down again.

"Do you think they'll be able to kill this lion?" Gorda asks.

"Of course. Atuk's killed many lions. He'll kill this one and wear its teeth." A shiver runs down her spine even as she speaks. This beast, which strikes without warning and disappears without a trace, isn't like other lions.

Keena bends to pick up a large branch, then turns to watch her father. Atuk paces back and forth in the clearing, limping as he talks to the men. Two suns ago, when she walked with him in the forest, she heard and smelled a wolverine long before he did. Just last night, when Atuk thought she was asleep, he told Ubra the lion might be a messenger from Leeswi, a sign that it's time to choose a new leader.

Keena flares her nostrils. Her sharp eyes rake the forest fringe. She'll help her father kill this lion. More than anything, she wants to make Atuk proud of her. It's too bad she's not a son.

Keena and Gorda herd the children away from the forest and closer to the men. The hunters clutch heavy spears with sharp stone blades the size of their fists. Keena helped Atuk bind his blade onto its thick wooden shaft with rawhide and pine resin after the first lion attack. He let her take it to protect the children last sun time, but she still couldn't save Tat.

Keena tries to remember a time when Atuk wasn't their leader. Would any other hunter in their band do a better job than her father? Two are grey hairs like Atuk and have hunted with him since they were boys. Three others are younger and stronger, but one of them, Keena's uncle Dakur, had one of his mighty arms ripped off by hyenas. Another, Shad, is still recovering after being gored in the ribs by a woolly rhinoceros. The third, Sate, is bad tempered and lazy. Keena doesn't see a leader among them. None is as smart or strong as her father.

The remaining two are young, more boys than men. Each has only recently become a hunter after killing an animal large enough that they could share meat with the band. They've only killed deer or ibex so far. They haven't faced the most dangerous creatures; certainly not a lion.

One of the boys, Kreel, steps away from the other hunters. He grins and waves at Keena. Her lips twitch but she turns back to her task. Now isn't the time to fool around. She and Kreel, who is Sate's son, have played together since they were young ones wrestling over bone playthings. It's strange to think of him as a hunter now.

Thunk. Keena jumps as a stone lands at her feet. She turns in time to see a smiling Kreel rejoin the group of men. She scoops up the rock and returns it with a direct hit on his backside.

"Has Kreel spoken to Atuk about you?" Gorda asks.

"Why should that poor shot of a boy speak to my father about me?"

"He's killed an ibex and shared meat. Soon he'll have his own hearth. It's obvious he wants you as his mate. You're lucky."

"Lucky? He's a child, always playing. He should be listening to Atuk, not throwing stones."

"You'll see. Atuk likes Kreel. Soon they'll talk, and then you'll go to Kreel's hearth." Gorda hoists her load of kindling onto her back.

Keena bristles. "I'll decide whose hearth I'll go to. Maybe I'll go with Kreel, maybe I won't."

"*You'll* decide?" Gorda smirks.

Keena clenches her fists as Gorda hustles the children toward their mothers. She grasps part of a lichen-covered tree trunk broken by the wind and braces her legs as she hoists it onto her shoulders. Gorda's always sticking her big nose where it doesn't belong. Sure, she likes Kreel, but he needs to grow up. She's stronger and smarter than he is, and she's not leaving her father's hearth until she decides to. She looks back at Kreel, who's still watching her. He waves and a smile spreads across his face like sunshine warming the hillside. His eyes sparkle under the ridge of his brow. She can't resist a small grin and returns his wave. They're still friends, after all.

"Kreel!" Atuk's raised voice refocuses Keena's attention on the men's group. What's caused her usually patient father to shout? She drops the log and moves closer to the group, gathering brush as she goes. Kreel's annoying, but she doesn't want him to be in trouble because of her.

Kreel's friend Sabra pulls him into the group of hunters. "Atuk's talking to you, brother, and your father's angry, too."

"What do you think, Kreel? Should we dig a pit to trap the lion?" Atuk nods encouragement. "Bait it with fresh deer meat?"

"This lion likes Krag meat, so it might be hard to trap that way." Kreel's voice squeaks, and he scans the faces of the more experienced hunters.

"Then we should use the most useless Krag in the band as bait," Sate snarls. Keena holds her breath. Why does Sate say things like this about his son?

"There aren't any useless Krags in this band," Atuk says. He turns his attention to Sabra. "What would the Kula do? Have your people tracked a lion such as this?"

Keena's concern for Kreel turns to annoyance at Sabra. "Of course the Kula knows what to do," Keena mutters. "Doesn't he always?"

Sabra stands a head taller than even her father, and his skin is brown like the earth. His black hair is adorned with hawk feathers and pulled back into a tail, which bobs up and down as he talks.

"Our hunters wouldn't use spears such as you carry." Sabra holds up Kreel's spear. "You have to get too close with these. The lion will kill or injure you before you thrust into its heart and kill it."

"What would you use, then?" Atuk asks. "We've killed many mighty beasts with our spears."

Keena clenches her teeth and snaps a dead branch from a tree, breaking it with her knee. Ever since Sabra stumbled into their camp, frozen and starving during the last great snow, he's been the centre of attention.

Crack. Keena stomps another limb. They saved Sabra's life and let him stay in their camp. When the ice melted he returned to his Kula people, but he often comes back to visit, and sometimes his father, Luka, visits them, too.

Crack. Whenever Sabra visits, he shows off his superior Kula way of doing things.

"You've seen my smaller spear." Sabra holds up his own weapon. "My people use a stick that helps us throw our spears so they fly through the air like a bird. I can show you how to make this stick, but it'll take practice to use it."

"Krags aren't afraid to get close to beasts." Dakur laughs, raising his arm stump. "We've always hunted and killed this way." Many of the Krag hunters nod agreement.

Sabra shrugs. "As you wish, Dakur, but you wouldn't lose so many parts of your body with a Kula spear."

"Perhaps you can teach us to make these throwing sticks later, but we have no time now. We have to kill this lion before it takes another from our group." Atuk raises his own sturdy spear and the hunters gather around him.

Keena heads toward camp with her kindling. She's heard enough from Sabra. How can his bragging draw her father's attention and Kreel's friendship?

As the men talk, Keena stands on the ridge near the cave and looks down into the valley. The bushes sway far below, but the movement isn't like that caused by the ever-present mountain breezes. It's more like movement caused by a large animal travelling up the hillside toward the camp. Is the lion coming to attack them once again?

"Father, come quickly. Some beast's approaching." Keena's shout freezes in her throat when a long, mournful sound trumpets from the bushes. *Bleeepp, bleeepp*. This is definitely not the call of a lion.

She gapes at the sight of the creatures emerging from the shadows below, their backs humped, covered with fur. "It's not the lion. It's strange hunters covered with fur."

"They're worse than the lion," Atuk growls as he reaches the ridge.

Keena gasps. "What can be worse than the lion?"

"Your uncle Haken, girl." Atuk's grip on her shoulder tightens and sweat glistens on his brow. "You must stay away from him."

Keena peers over the ridge. How can this be? Her father, who's faced rampaging mammoths and charging bears, is afraid of this hunter and his men struggling up the mountain.

4

CRO-MAGNON (KULA)
CAMP

HONK, HONK. A large flock of geese rises from the water, blocking the sunlight and throwing shadows over Shinoni and Wenzel, who are gathering reeds in the marsh. They gaze skyward, following the birds' V-shaped flight toward the horizon, away from the coming snow time and its icy grip. Cold water splashes Shinoni as more geese fly up around her. Since returning to camp with Shazur this sun time, she's been trying to stick to her chores and please her father, but it's hard when there are so many other exciting things to do.

"We should take some of these fat birds, Wenzel." Shinoni rushes to the shore and drops her reeds. She whisks the sling from her pouch and scoops stones from the ground.

"The men can kill some when they return to camp." Wenzel makes no move to leave the water and continues to pick reeds.

"They've been gone many suns and might be gone many more. We don't have to wait for them." Shinoni fits a stone into the sling and twirls it around her head, sending it whizzing toward a group of geese.

Honk, ho-o-n-nk. Feathers fly and the birds scold as they rise into the sky.

"You're no hunter," Wenzel says.

"I can hunt. I've been on a vision quest and I've seen spirit animals." The words tumble out before she can stop them. She puts her sling away in her pouch.

"That's not possible. Only boys do that," Wenzel scoffs and returns to her work.

Shinoni balls her hands into fists and grinds her teeth. In the distance, Grandmother Reza approaches from the camp. Shazur didn't punish her for going to the vision cave, but Shinoni is sure Grandmother would if she knew. Better put some distance between herself and Wenzel. Secrets have a way of popping out of Wenzel's mouth.

Shinoni joins several women farther down the shore. Etak's there. Only a few snow melts older than

Shinoni, she's heavy with her first child. She shifts her weight from one leg to the other.

"Take it easy or you'll give breath to the new one right here in the water." Shinoni pats Etak's swollen belly and takes her load of reeds.

"When will the men return?" Etak clasps Shinoni's arm. "The sun's risen many times since they left."

"They're likely enjoying themselves, knowing we'll do all the work here," Shinoni says. She helps Etak sit on the shore as the other women join them, spreading their reeds to dry.

"You know the men must find a cave for us before the snows come," an older woman, Najka, scolds Shinoni. "They might have to travel far to find one that isn't used by Strange Ones or bears or hyenas. Maybe they'll have to fight for a good one."

"Can't we stay in the sacred cave this snow time?" Etak points toward the rock wall behind the camp. The other women gasp and she lowers her voice.

"Perhaps the spirits wouldn't mind if we stayed in the outer area —"

"Enough. Such nonsense," says a firm voice.

Shinoni knows that voice, and she knows Etak's in big trouble. Grandmother Reza, standing on the bank behind them, frowns down at the women. The lines on her face show her age and wisdom. She carries a carved walking stick to get around — and to make sure she's listened to. Shinoni also knows the range of that stick. She hauls Etak to her feet, pulling her out of Reza's reach.

Bone and shell decorations adorn Reza's long grey braid, and ornaments made of otter and fox teeth and deer antler line her tunic. An ivory amulet in the shape of an eagle hangs around her neck. Shinoni watches the eagle fly from side to side as her grandmother hops from one foot to the other.

"You bring shame to Kula women. You know we must honour the animal spirits in the sacred cave if we're to live here," Reza snaps.

"I'm sorry, Reza. I meant no disrespect," Etak says. "I do know that, and I know the hunting's been good."

"Would you have the animals hide from our spears? Would you have the hunts fail and our people go hungry?" Reza shouts. She swings her stick in an arc, pointing it at the women. "The sacred cave can only be entered by the shaman and the hunters. To live in there would anger the spirits and turn them against us." Reza stops to catch her breath, sides heaving.

Najka intervenes before the medicine woman gets any angrier. "We know it's important to honour the spirits, Reza. We're just worried because we have young ones and Etak will soon give breath to a new one. We need shelter from the snows." Najka lowers her head. "Mother Reza, can you tell us if the men will find a new home for us soon?"

Reza throws back her head and closes her eyes. "Hahaahaahumm," she chants as she rocks on her heels. Shinoni rocks with her, mouthing the sounds. She's watched Grandmother use her inner sight many times. An uneasy prickle runs along Shinoni's spine as she waits for Reza to answer. Finally the medicine woman's eyelids flutter open, but her words bring no comfort to the women. "Shazur has asked the spirits to help the men in their search. If we haven't angered the spirits, the men will find a cave and return."

Reza dismisses them with a nod of her head. The women return to their work, not daring to question the medicine woman further. Shinoni slips away along the shore, putting distance between herself and her grandmother.

If Reza can see things, perhaps she already knows Shinoni has been on a vision quest. Perhaps Grandmother knows she's broken an even larger taboo and been in the sacred cave and seen the painted animals on the walls. Perhaps she knows the animal spirits are calling Shinoni, drawing her there once again.

Shinoni quivers and rubs her icy palms together. Should she go? She holds her breath, then releases it with a whoosh. The pull's too strong. Her face flushes and her chest pounds as she turns her footsteps toward the rock wall and its hidden secrets.

— 5 —

NEANDERTHAL (KRAG)
CAMP

H AKEN AND HIS HUNTERS struggle up the steep
path toward the camp. They're still far below, but
even at a distance they remind Keena of predators re-
lentlessly stalking their prey up the hill. She presses
close to her father's side as their faces come into view
through the trees. Black patterns cover the hunters'
cheeks and brow ridges. The teeth of bears and wolves
around their necks and woven into their hair clatter in
the wind. Skin bags loaded with furs are slung across
their shoulders, giving them the look of a pack of wild
beasts advancing on Keena's camp.

"Which one's my uncle Haken?" Keena whispers.
Atuk points to a hunter who wears a cave bear skull

as a headdress. A vivid red scar slices across one side of his face from eye to chin. He raises an ibex horn to his lips and blows another strident call to announce their arrival.

"What does that bloodthirsty bear want with us?" Atuk mutters.

Ubra joins them and turns Keena away from the ledge. Her mother's cheeks have flushed red as her hair. "Take the young ones to the cave, daughter."

"Why do you call him a bloodthirsty bear?" Keena looks from her father to her mother. If Haken is family, why must she stay away from him? What terrible thing has he done to upset her parents? She's full of questions, but Atuk and Ubra aren't listening. They've turned their attention back to the hunters in the valley.

Keena gathers the youngsters playing nearby and shoos them toward their mothers. Once they reach the women, she heads back to the ledge to ask more questions about her dangerous uncle.

"Atuk, he's my brother." Ubra's voice, high and anxious, reaches her ears. "I'd rather he kept on going, but we must welcome him."

Keena slows her steps. Perhaps now isn't the best time to rejoin her parents.

"Keena, wait up." Keena jumps at her friend's voice. Kreel and Sabra join her, and Kreel holds out a pendant made from an ibex tooth. "From my first kill. It's for you." He beams proudly as she takes it.

"It's nice, Kreel." Keena has never had an ornament before. She smiles and slides the cord holding the tooth over her head.

Her mother's shout breaks the spell. "Sabra must leave before Haken arrives!"

Keena whirls around to see her father hurrying toward them. Atuk brushes past her and hands Kreel a spear, then pulls both boys toward the open meeting place and the forest beyond. Keena rushes to follow them, mouth gaping. What's possessed her father? Atuk is always calm and in control. She's never seen him behave this way before, not even with the lion.

"Ubra's brother, Haken, is coming. He's powerful and he hates Kulas," Atuk says through clenched teeth. "I won't be able to protect you, Sabra."

The boys try to pull away, but Atuk's like a charging muskox and they can't stop him.

"I'm not afraid of this Haken. I can defend myself," Sabra protests.

"He can't tell us what to do here, Atuk," Kreel says. "You lead this band."

"He's Ubra's brother, but he cares for no one." Atuk pulls them to the forest edge. "Haken's killed many Kulas. And Krags, too, who stand in his way." He pushes them toward the trees. "Our band has trouble enough now. We don't need more."

"You think Sabra's safer in the forest with the lion than here in our camp?" Kreel shakes his head in disbelief.

"Stay together and go to Sabra's band." Atuk turns back toward camp. "You are hunters," he calls over his shoulder. "Keep your eyes sharp and your spears ready. Thank Luka for letting Kreel stay with him awhile."

Keena gasps. What is her father thinking? He knows Krags are safer together.

"How tough can this hunter be that he has a man like Atuk so worried?" Kreel clutches his spear firmly and slings a stout wooden stick from the forest floor over his shoulder.

"I'd like to meet this Haken someday. Then he won't be so tough," Sabra growls.

"Be careful in the forest, Kreel," Keena says as she fights back tears.

"Don't worry, we can take care of ourselves. You be careful with this Haken." Kreel's smile is the last thing Keena sees before she rushes back to camp.

Haken and his hunters emerge from the bushes at the top of the twisting path. Keena moves closer for a better look. His scent comes to her, familiar but troubling.

She shivers and her skin prickles as it does when a predator is near.

Atuk approaches Haken and his men, Ubra behind him. Keena has seen rival wolf packs approach each other this way near her camp, their leaders, stiff-legged and with teeth bared, sniffing each other for signs of weakness.

Her father stands his ground. Relief floods through Keena's body as Atuk's hunters form a tight line behind him, still clutching their spears intended for the lion hunt. She'll be safe here, close to her parents. No need to join the women and children clustered by the cave. This is her uncle. Still, the hairs along her spine bristle, warning her to flee and hide.

Atuk and Haken now stand face to face. Keena holds her breath, trying not to draw attention to herself. Atuk raises one hand in greeting but clutches his spear in the other.

"Welcome, Haken. Much time has passed since we stood together."

"Yes, much time. I thought you might be dead, Atuk." Haken's eyes wander over her father's bent body and his grey hair. Keena seethes at the insult. She's never heard anyone speak to her father this way.

Ubra steps protectively beside Atuk. "Why have you come, brother?" Her red hair dances like sparks and she clutches a spear, which she points toward Haken.

Keena glares at Haken. She can be brave like her mother.

"You were just a girl when you left our hearth to follow this one." Haken spits in Atuk's direction. His hair, red as Ubra's, falls around his shoulders. The bear- and wolf-teeth ornaments gnash together, hurling a threat in the wind.

"I'm not here to talk about old times." Haken faces Atuk. "We have furs for you."

Atuk pulls back suspiciously. "You bring us furs? Why?"

"We'll give you the furs in exchange for females." Haken watches her father closely, like a forest cat playing with its prey before eating it.

Keena's jaw drops. Surely her father won't do this.

"Many from our band have died because the brown devils kill our animals," Haken snarls. "They take our food with their magic, and our young ones starve." He shifts his gaze around the group and points at Keena. "We need females like this one to give breath to small ones." He smiles and the scar on his face wrinkles and puckers, obscuring his eye. "She'll give us strong hunters to crush the brown ones."

Run! The urge is strong, but there's no place to hide. Keena locks her knees and meets Haken's smirk with a scowl. Ubra steps in front of her, blocking Haken's view.

"She's my daughter. Keena's grown since you last

saw her, but she's my blood and Atuk's blood. She belongs here."

"We don't need furs and we have no females to spare." Her father also moves in front of her. "We lost one to a lion only a few suns ago. It was full daylight when the beast took her from our camp."

Haken squints his good eye at Atuk. "Has this lion taken others from your band?"

"Two others, one a child just last sun time. The creature comes and goes like a spirit."

Haken throws back his head and howls. He brings his face close to Atuk. "It's no spirit. I saw lion spoor on the trail in the valley. I saw its tracks." Haken thumps his chest and raises his spear. "I can solve your lion problem for you."

"My hunters were about to track the beast when you arrived." Atuk stands firm.

"You said it's a spirit, so how will you hunt it?" Haken sneers. "I know it's an animal and I'll kill it." He pounds his chest.

Atuk's band members draw closer.

Haken motions to his men to drop the skin bags from their shoulders. Lush furs of fox, otter, lynx, wolf, and even bear spill out on the ground. He raises his spear in the air, then circles round the furs, thrusting the blade deep into the pile, skewering the pelts, tossing them into the air.

"I'm Haken, killer of beasts and men. No beast can survive if Haken's on its trail," he shouts. "I'll go now and track this lion for you and kill it. I'll bring you its head and you'll give me the females I choose to take to my camp."

Keena gasps and backs away into the group of Krags. Many of their faces shine with hope at this offer to rid them of a dreaded threat.

"Agreed?" Haken eyes Atuk impatiently.

Atuk looks at the faces of his people. He avoids looking at Keena or her mother.

"Agreed." Atuk sighs. He and Haken lock muscled forearms and bring brow ridges together to signal agreement, then spring apart as if they'd embraced hot embers.

Haken and his hunters disappear into the forest at the edge of camp. Startled crows fly from the trees. *Caw, caw.*

Another warning, but Keena has no more power to stop Haken now than she had to stop the lion last sun time.

—— 6 ——

CRO-MAGNON (KULA) CAMP

SHINONI CROUCHES on a rock ledge deep within the recesses of the sacred cave. She shouldn't be here, but the dancing light beckons her on. She hears a rustling in the stillness. Are the spirits whispering her name? Are they angry? If so, why do they keep calling her here?

She bends her legs and wiggles in among the rocks, behind a row of stalagmites pointing upward to the roof of the cavern. Her hair comes loose from its leather tie and falls around her shoulders like a cloak, obscuring her view. She pulls it back and slides along the stone wall, hiding in the shifting shadows. Faint drumming from the floor below vibrates in her chest.

Barely daring to breathe, Shinoni leans over the edge of a stalagmite and peers down on a wondrous scene. Bathed in the glow of a bear-oil lamp, paintings of animals live on the sleek rock wall below her. Mammoth and reindeer, horse and ibex parade before her eyes, bursting with life and energy. She's been in the forbidden cave before, but she's never dared come this close to the images.

A tall figure draped in reindeer skins and antlers carefully applies red pigment to the belly of a pregnant horse. On the wall, his shadow looms over those of two smaller figures mixing pigment on bone plates at his feet. The murmur of their voices rises in the stillness. Shinoni strains, trying to catch the words. Words a girl is not supposed to hear. If only she could touch the images, feel if they breathe.

She squirms closer. Sharp rocks scrape her arms and legs. A stone slips under her foot and clatters into the space below. She ducks as three startled pairs of eyes search the ledge. Did they see her? Surely they can hear the wild hammering of her heart.

Shinoni slithers with practised speed down the narrow tunnel leading to the cave's back entrance. She scrabbles through a hole hidden by brush, high on the hillside. The cool autumn breeze licks sweat from her face. Sunlight stings her eyes.

Below her, the camp sprawls in a grassy clearing near the dense forest. She hurries. No one must see her.

She leaps, nimble as an ibex, down the rock-strewn hillside. Fox and otter teeth sewn onto her tunic jingle with each bound.

Shinoni skirts the edge of the camp and ducks behind some shrubbery to catch her breath. She peers through the rustling grasses, then drops to the ground, pulling in her arms and legs, making herself as small as possible.

High on the rock face near the hidden entrance, the shaman in the reindeer-skin robe emerges. Shazur removes his antler headdress and searches the clearing below.

Father has the eagle eyesight of his clan. Shinoni lies still as a fawn hiding in the grass.

— 7 —

NEANDERTHAL (KRAG)
CAMP

THE RAYS OF the late afternoon sun filter through the trees, sending shadows into the outer camp. Keena and Ubra tend the line of fires at the cave mouth, as they often do. Keena loves these times when her mother shares stories and lessons. This time, though, silence thick as mammoth hide lies between them. Questions buzz in Keena's mind, clamouring for attention. Finally she can't contain them.

"Why do you and Father fear him, Mother?" Keena asks.

"Haken? He takes what he wants. He uses others for his own purpose."

"He said he wants *me*," Keena whispers. "You'll

stop him from taking me, won't you? Father will stop him?"

"I'll try, my girl. I can't say what Atuk will do." Ubra looks away.

"Maybe he won't kill the lion," Keena persists. "Maybe the lion will kill him."

"They're good trackers and hunters. You saw their furs." Ubra hugs her.

Keena nestles in her mother's arms. "Why does Haken hate the Kulas?"

"Fewer animals come to our spears now and many Krags are hungry. Haken blames the Kulas."

"You don't hate them and you're his sister. Father and Kreel like Sabra."

"Long ago your father tried to stop Haken from killing a Kula mother and her small one. He thrust his spear between Haken and the little one just as Haken lunged forward. He couldn't save the child, but Haken's face was torn on Atuk's spear and he wears the mark to this day."

A queasy wave of vomit churns in Keena's gut. How could this happen? Her band protects small ones and mothers. They don't kill them. She wants to ask Ubra more questions, but the sound of shouts and breaking branches at the forest's edge interrupts them.

The mournful call of an ibex horn announces the arrival of Haken and his hunters. They emerge triumphantly, crashing through the bushes, carrying the large and bloody carcass of a lion.

Keena and Ubra join other band members gathered in silence around the beast's body. Even in death the giant cat is fearsome. Keena shudders. Its blood-spattered fur is golden, mottled with darker splotches to blend into the woods and grasslands where it hunted and killed her people. Stretched out full length, the lion is longer than Atuk and Ubra together, and it would've eaten both her father and mother if it could have. If it were to stand up on all four legs now, Keena would have to look up into its eyes.

She shivers, remembering how those yellow eyes watched her, challenged her, as she ran to rescue Tat as he hung lifeless in the lion's jaws. She half expects the beast to leap up now and drag her into the forest. The great jaws lie empty and open, the long pink tongue draped over dagger teeth waiting to sink into her.

"It can't hurt you now, Keena." She jumps as her father touches her shoulder.

A small boy standing beside them overhears Atuk's words. He pushes forward and kicks the lion's lifeless body. "You can't hurt me now," he hoots gleefully. The boy winds up for another whack, but Atuk pulls him away from the carcass.

"The lion was a great hunter. If you disrespect it, you'll anger Leeswi and then others of its clan might come to seek revenge." Atuk lets the boy go.

Keena tries to stop the shakes wracking her body. She wants to kick the lion herself or stab it with her father's spear.

Haken swaggers around the carcass, his face and hands smeared with the lion's blood. He throws back his head and howls into the wind.

Atuk approaches him warily. "You're a mighty hunter, Haken. You've killed the lion, a great and fearless hunter, too."

"Yes, I've killed the lion for you." A smirk wrinkles Haken's face, as nasty as it is triumphant. "Now I claim my reward. Three strong young females." He whirls around and points at Keena, who is backing toward the safety of the cave. "She will be one of them."

--- 8 ---

CRO-MAGNON (KULA)
CAMP

SHINONI CRAWLS ON HER STOMACH, intent on closing the gap between her and the two red-coated foxes she's stalking. They're young, likely hunting on their own after leaving their mother. No match for such a mighty hunter as her. Thistles stab her hands as she creeps forward. No matter. Her hair falls across her eyes, blocking her view. She brushes the strands away.

Her movement in the grass isn't lost on the ever-present crows. *Caw, caw.*

The foxes raise their heads and squint suspiciously in Shinoni's direction. She lies still. The wind blowing in her face brings their musky smell to her and hides her scent from them. They resume searching for mice among the bones and other debris of the Kulas' refuse pile.

Shinoni draws her sling from the pouch at her hip and reaches for stones on the ground beside her. What's this? She freezes as the stones begin to move. She's not alone. A large snake coils its grey-and-brown-dappled body upward, the black slits of its pupils unwavering in the red ovals of its eyes. The serpent's black forked tongue flicks, just a finger's length from Shinoni's face.

All thoughts of the foxes disappear. Shinoni gasps, her eyes wide with fear. Sweat slithers from her brow and drips off her nose.

The snake draws back its head, ready to strike.

"Don't move," a calm voice whispers behind her. "It won't harm you if you stay still." Shazur slowly reaches into the grass, grips the snake behind the head, and flings it away. The serpent swiftly disappears into the bushes. "Snakes don't hunt us. They'd rather hide in the grass or between the rocks, but they'll hurt you if you threaten them."

Shazur extends his hand but Shinoni can't control her trembling legs. Her strength has wriggled away with the snake.

"I know, Father. I could've handled it." She plucks a thorn from her thumb.

"You're supposed to be with Reza at the lake." Shazur pulls Shinoni to her feet.

"I was practising my sling. I almost had a fox, and soon I'll bring down a deer. I'm getting better every —"

Shazur interrupts her. "Someone came into the sacred cave today and watched while I instructed my helpers."

Shinoni bends down to retrieve her sling from the grass, avoiding her father's gaze.

"They'll soon go on their quest to become hunters. Nothing must go wrong to anger the spirits."

"It was me in the cave," Shinoni admits.

"I know. Why were you there? You know it's forbidden."

"I want to make the animals live on the cave wall," Shinoni says. "I want to honour the animals and be a hunter like you."

"Females don't do these things," Shazur insists.

"I'd be a better helper to you than Sakat or Bardat," Shinoni pleads. "I can make the images in the dust. I'll show you." She drops to her knees and an antler forms in the dirt under her fingers.

"Stop!" Shazur cries. He pulls Shinoni up and scrapes the image away with his foot. "I know you'd be a good helper, even a hunter, but we mustn't anger the spirits. No good will come of it." He frowns. "Promise you won't go into the sacred cave again."

"Father, the animal spirits call me. I've seen the eagle and a great wolf in my dreams. The eagle was on fire and the wolf jumped over a river that turned into a snake."

Shazur's brows furrow, and his lips press together as they do when he's preparing for a dangerous hunt. He lets go of Shinoni and steps back, searching her face. Shinoni clenches her jaw, fighting the urge to speak. Silence hangs heavy and unmovable between them, like the brooding rock face in the distance.

Shazur finally nods his head and strides into the grass. "Come with me. Now."

"Are we going to the cave?" Shinoni scrambles to catch up.

"You've already gone in and we can't change that," Shazur says. "No female but you has ever been in there. I fear the spirits' anger."

The rock wall looms ahead of them, full of secret spaces. Shinoni slows her pace. Whispers carried in the wind ruffle the grass. Are the spirits welcoming her or threatening her?

"You're my daughter," Shazur whispers. "I'll ask the spirits to forgive your intrusion and allow you to be my helper."

"What if they don't forgive me, Father?"

"Then they'll punish us. It's too late to go back."

Shazur pushes through tangled brush at the base of the hill, revealing an entryway that Shinoni's never seen. He holds a finger to his lips for silence and beckons her to follow as he disappears through the opening.

Blackness deeper than a moonless night envelops Shinoni. The earth beneath her hands and knees is hard and smooth as she crawls through the narrow passage. How many other spirit seekers have polished these stones? None of them could have wanted to be here as much as she does.

A rush of cool air, soft and moist as moss on her skin, greets Shinoni. The passage widens, and her nostrils quiver at the smell of wet earth and decaying leaves. A steady trickle of water thunders like a waterfall to her straining ears.

Out of the darkness one flame begins to flicker, then another. Shazur appears from the shadows with two bear-oil lamps. Shinoni starts to ask a question but swallows her words as Shazur shakes his head. He hands one lamp to Shinoni and beckons her to follow him. Their lamplight reveals a stack of unlit lamps and flints by the entrance. On one side of them paintings of horses gallop into the gloom of a dusky corridor, but her father turns into another, narrower hallway that leads into blackness. The warmth of her lamp's flame fans Shinoni's face as they venture into the passage. Their shadows tower above them. Are they protectors in this spirit world where she's an intruder?

The corridor soon empties into another chamber, small enough that they can see all its walls in the glow of their lamps. There are images here Shinoni recognizes, but she's never seen them painted on a cave wall. She gapes in wonder at shapes that resemble many things familiar to her: the sun, the moon, paths, rocks, footprints, streams, shelters, spears, and antlers. There are also lines, squiggles, squares, triangles, circles, dots, and handprints. The symbols, painted with red and yellow ochre, appear singly or in clusters on the walls. Shinoni feels their pull as they flicker with a life and meaning of their own in the lamplight.

Shazur beckons her to the wall and sets his lamp on the ground beside her. Standing in the dancing circle of light, her father places his hands on Shinoni's head and chants in a high singsong voice. "Hi-hee-hai-haa, hii-hee-hee-hai."

Shinoni shivers, and the hair on her arms rises in response to this eerie wail. It's unlike any sound she's ever heard. Her father's usual deep, booming voice has transformed into a throaty bird call that vibrates in her ears.

"Spirit guardians, we ask forgiveness for my daughter's intrusion into your sacred home. She has spirit dreams and hears spirit animals calling her. She's young and female, but she has the heart of a shaman and a hunter. My blood flows in her." He begins the call again. "Hi-hee-hai-haa, hii-hee-hee-hai."

Shinoni trembles and her throat vibrates as her father's wail surrounds her. She squirms with the effort to remain silent. "Heeee-haaaaa-ayiippp —" Shinoni chokes off the squealing wail coming from her lips. Her father's fingers drum on her head and she stands still.

"She wants to become a keeper of the sacred ways," Shazur continues. "Soon she'll go on her spirit quest and become a woman and a healer. You can test her to see if she's worthy."

Shinoni shivers. Will the spirits accept her? How will they test her?

Shazur leads her to a part of the wall near the entrance to the chamber and across from the flickering symbols. There on the floor in a shallow stone bowl rests a mixture of crushed ochre and melted bear fat, red as blood. Several clumps of solid ochre lie nearby with a stone plate and hammer stone for making pigment.

Her father spits into the mixture to make it more liquid, then takes a blade from his pouch and pricks his thumb. Shinoni stretches out her hand and winces silently as Shazur pierces the skin of her thumb with his knife. Crimson drops of her blood mingle with her father's in the bowl, joining their spirits in the swirl of the sacred pigment.

Shazur places the palm of his hand in the mixture, coating it with colour, then presses it against the stone wall. He motions Shinoni to do the same. The pigment feels warm, alive under her hand as she dips it into the bowl. Then she stands side by side with Shazur, father and daughter, shaman and helper. Will the guardian spirits accept them? They step back, and their two red handprints, one higher, one lower, pulse like heartbeats in the fading lamplight.

9

NEANDERTHAL (KRAG)
CAMP

BEHIND THE FIRE BARRICADE, the cave is alive with Krag voices celebrating the victory over the lion. Keena, filling skin bags with water from a pool near the rear wall of the shelter, watches Haken and his hunters bask in a place of honour by the fires. Their teeth glint in the light of the flames as they slice chunks of meat from a deer haunch, jostling each other for the choicest cuts. Keena imagines them as wolves fighting for position at a kill. She shudders at the thought. As if taunting her, a howl echoes from the dark forest beyond the fires.

Atuk, followed by two young women, approaches Haken. Keena strains to hear their words.

"Haken, these women, Esal and Teal, have agreed to go with you. You're a great hunter and they choose to follow you."

Keena draws into the shadows and holds her breath. Perhaps she won't have to go with Haken after all, if other women want to go with him. Haken rises and walks around the women, silently nodding.

"Teal gave breath to the child that was killed by the lion. She wants to go with the hunter who avenged her son." Atuk points to the bundle under Teal's cloak. "She'll bring another small one to your camp." Haken still circles without speaking. Atuk keeps his eyes on him, turning as he does. "Esal is strong and works hard. She lost her mate in the last great snow and wants to leave the mountain."

Haken stops and glares at Atuk. "Where's your daughter, old man?"

"She's getting water for your hunters," Atuk says. His gaze doesn't waver.

"She'll come with us, too." Haken swaggers toward Atuk, closing the distance between them.

"Please, Leeswi, no," Keena whispers.

Ubra pushes between Atuk and Haken. "She's my only child, brother. I need her here." Keena's mother points at Esal and Teal. "These strong women want to follow you."

"I'll take these women." Haken waves his hand, dismissing them. He faces Atuk. "I'll take your daughter, too. You gave your word."

"Keena's already promised to a young hunter in our band. She can't go." Atuk draws himself up as straight as possible. He folds his arms across his chest.

"Kreel wants me to go to his hearth?" Keena drops the water bag and clasps her hands over her mouth to muffle her words. She doesn't want to leave her parents, but Kreel would be better than Haken.

"Where's this hunter? Has he killed a lion for you as I did? Is he brave enough to fight me?" Haken vibrates with fury. He throws back his head and howls, his rage echoing off the cave walls.

Atuk holds his ground. "He's away from camp. She goes to his hearth when he returns."

Keena nods. Yes, she'll gladly go to Kreel's hearth. But she doesn't want him to fight Haken. That wouldn't end well for her friend.

"I'll wait and kill this pup. I'll still take your daughter, and you'll lose a hunter." Haken raises his spear, the bloodstained blade pointed at Atuk's throat.

Atuk pushes the spear aside, but his gaze wavers. He looks from Haken's menacing scowl to Ubra's stricken face, then to his people sitting round the fire with Haken's men.

"Do you want it said that Atuk's word is like dust

in the rain? That Atuk is full of wind? Such a man doesn't deserve to lead a band." Haken sneers.

Keena stands by the pool in the shadows. She holds her breath, waiting for her father's answer that will decide her fate.

Atuk sighs heavily and nods. His words slice through the stillness, a flint blade piercing Keena's heart. "I'll keep my word."

Keena drops to her knees, faith in her father dissolving into the puddle of water spreading around her.

Morning dawns cloudy and cold as Leeswi sends her icy breath into the camp. Keena's band mills around the cave entrance as Haken and his hunters prepare to leave. Teal and Esal stand together, wrapped in warm furs, as Haken's men place supply packs on the women's backs.

"You're strong, Keena. You know how to survive." Ubra hugs her daughter close.

"I'll return, you'll see." Furs and tears muffle Keena's voice. She pushes away from her mother's embrace. She doesn't want to go with this hunter they all fear. Being wrenched away from her family is like getting ripped apart by an eagle. Keena wipes the tears from her cheeks with her fur cape. Father said she must go, so she will. She buries her anger and pain deep in her belly and faces her mother with a wobbly smile.

"Remember all that I've taught you, and don't anger Haken," Ubra says. "He's dangerous, like a woolly big horn." She pushes a small hide-covered package wrapped with a tendon into Keena's hand. It lies hard and unyielding in her palm.

"What's this, Mother?" A chill runs through Keena's body.

"It's a claw from the lion. I cut it from the beast last night while Atuk slept."

Keena imagines Ubra bending over the lion carcass in the dead of night, sawing its claw with a bone blade as the night creatures circle beyond her torch.

"Why, Mother? You could've been killed." She tries to drop the claw, but Ubra catches her hand and closes her fingers around the package.

"It's powerful and it'll protect you," her mother says.

"Why protect me? The lion would kill me if it could, like it killed Tat and the others."

"Keep it with you." Ubra hugs Keena. "The lion hates Haken more, and the claw can protect you from him. Keep it close to your body."

Keena ties the tendon to a strip of fur inside her cloak.

Atuk approaches, his face grey and drawn, his eyes shadowed. "I'm sorry, daughter."

Keena turns away to hide her tears. How could her father have allowed this to happen? She used to sit on his knee and listen to his stories. He'd always protected her.

"You're the leader. What's the life of a daughter compared to that?" Keena flinches as Haken forces a pack on her back.

"Your daughter belongs to me now. She follows a new path." He smirks at Ubra. "She'll take the place you left when you followed this one." He spits at Atuk, then takes Keena's arm and drags her toward the mountain path.

"Keena," Ubra calls after her. "You carry my breath and my mother's breath."

"I'll come home, Mother." Keena stumbles as she looks back, but she's pulled into line and supported by Esal and Teal as they move down the mountain path. Her mother's voice disappears into the wind.

10

CRO-MAGNON (KULA)
CAMP

SHINONI EMERGES WITH SHAZUR from the darkness of the sacred cave into dazzling sunshine. She turns slowly, much more aware of her senses as she takes in the familiar surroundings. The calls of birds are clear and piercing as they flock in the trees, and the rustle of small animals travelling through the grasses and bushes throbs in her ears. The distant bellow of a rutting deer far in the forest sounds as near as the crackling of the smoke fires and the children's voices rising from the camp. Are the animal spirits talking to her?

Shazur rubs his hand with moss and gives Shinoni a clump.

"I'd like to wear it for awhile." Shinoni admires her red palm.

"No one must see it," Shazur says.

Shinoni wipes her palm clean and follows Shazur down the hillside. His long legs eat up the ground, and soon the cluster of deerskin shelters looms ahead. She tugs on his tunic. "Have the spirits forgiven me? Have they accepted me as a helper?"

"I don't know. You must be patient." Shazur sighs.

"Will I be able to talk to my mother's spirit as you do?"

"Your mother's spirit will speak to you when you're ready to hear her."

"Will you teach me what the symbols in the cave mean?"

"We have to wait and see if the spirits accept you as a helper before you can learn the symbols' meaning." Shazur hesitates. "They may test you."

"I'm ready to be tested," Shinoni says.

"There's danger near," Shazur cautions. "When the sun rose, I saw the eagle fall from the sky in flames. I don't know if it was a warning or a threat from the spirits."

Shinoni shivers as a cloud covers the sun and the animal voices ring louder in her ears. "Our hunters will be back soon. You see, someone's coming now." She points to where the bushes are swaying, but when they part it's her grandmother who pushes through.

Reza drops her load of reeds and stands, hands on

hips, frowning at Shinoni. "There you are, weasel girl. Always slinking away when there's work to do."

"Let me help you, Grandmother." Shinoni picks up Reza's reed bundle and carries it into one of the skin shelters.

"You must do something with your daughter, Shazur." Reza's words reach Shinoni's ears, and she peers out from the shelter. Surely Father won't tell her what they've done.

"She's a lot like you, Mother. Neither of you listens to anyone." Shazur touches his tattooed chin to Reza's wrinkled forehead. "I feel the spirits warning of danger. It's strong." Shazur scans the silent forest like a man waiting for the charge of a wounded bear.

"So you've felt it, too. Then it's a powerful warning," Reza says. "The spirits spoke to me at the lake."

"I fear for Shinoni," Shazur says. "The spirits whispered her name in their warning."

Father never mentioned that to her. Shinoni leaves the shelter and joins Shazur and Reza, standing uneasily between them.

"My granddaughter's strong, but she must find her own spirit helper. The eagle may not be able to help her." Reza hugs Shinoni. "I'll keep her with me."

"Perhaps I already have a different spirit helper," Shinoni says. Good thing the wolf came to her in the dream world and visited her fire.

"I've something for you, daughter." Shazur opens his deerskin pouch and takes out a beautifully worked flint knife. It's the one he used in the cave to prick their thumbs. The sharp blade, slender and fluted, has been wiped clean of their blood. "I made this for you to use when you go on your real quest for a spirit helper at the women's celebration," Shazur says. "Take it now. You might need it."

Shinoni takes the knife and holds it gingerly, balancing it in her hand as the sun glints off the sharply angled marks on the blade.

"Thank you, Father. I'll use it often." She places it in her pouch beside her sling, stones, and rope.

Reza snorts. "It's a fine blade, but really a boy's gift."

"You've much to learn and a long way to travel, Shinoni," her father says. "The blade will serve you." He strides down the path to the camp before she can answer.

"Come, girl, you can help me pick medicine plants." Reza hands Shinoni a woven grass basket and leads her into a tangled patch of berry bushes and small trees near the marsh.

"Remember, you're the shaman's daughter," Reza scolds. "Even though you're female, you might become a leader. You'll be medicine woman to our people."

"I know this, Grandmother," Shinoni says. "You tell me all the time."

59

"To lead you must follow the Kula rules," Reza says. "Stop hunting and fighting with the boys and act like a woman of our tribe. Be an example for others."

"Shouldn't a girl who might someday lead her tribe be able to hunt and fight? I'm better than most of the boys, anyway." Shinoni moves into the bushes to avoid Reza's scowl.

"Pick medicine plants, then. Berries and leaves from the belly plant to help Etak push her little one out quickly when she gives it breath. Fever plant, too. Take it all — leaves, stem, roots. You remember?" Reza says, her voice shrill. "We might need them to take poison from wounds the men have when they return."

"Do you think the men will be injured, Grand-mother?" Shinoni shifts uneasily from one foot to the other.

"I don't know, girl, but medicine women must always be prepared." Reza rubs her back, then points to a scrubby tree, its needles yellow among the green blanket of the taller conifers. "My back is sore from cutting reeds and that tree's sap helps ease the pain. Look for the other plants and bring them to me." Reza stamps down the trail, leaving Shinoni alone in the shadows.

11

NEANDERTHAL (KRAG)
HAKEN'S CAMP IN THE VALLEY BELOW

K EENA SITS BY HERSELF in a small recess at the back of Haken's cave. The rhythmic drumbeats echo deep in her chest. She loves drumming, but this time it's different. Her shoulders sway, but this is no joyful celebration. A crackling fire dances and leaps high, throwing monstrous shapes onto the stone walls around her. Krag women and children sit in the shadows. Teal sits among them, nursing her small one.

"Hiyaa, hiyaa, yip, yip, yip!" The women and children watch as Haken and his men stomp and chant fiercely. Their faces and bodies, painted with red ochre and black pitch, glisten with sweat from the heat of the fire and their feverish dancing. Most wear headdresses of antlers or tusks pulled over their heavy brows.

Haken, wearing his headdress made of the skull and upper jaw of a cave bear and brandishing a wooden club over his head, is working himself into a wild frenzy. His bloodcurdling howl echoes from the stone walls. "Destroy the brown-skinned devils. They take our animals and leave our people hungry." Haken's club smashes against a stalagmite on the floor, shattering it. A shower of jagged rock splinters flies over the dancers. Pain from their cuts only increases their rage. This, too, is the Kulas' fault.

Haken throws a fine grey powder into the fire, causing the flames to shoot higher and sending sparks into the dome of the cavern. The glow illuminates a giant log painted with black lines that stands propped against a side wall. Haken grabs a spear, its heavy stone point coloured with red ochre. He charges the log.

"Eeeyaaa!" His thrust pierces deeply, the blade embedded in the gut of the log. "Death to the Kulas. Destroy them all," Haken screams.

Other men take up the cry, attacking the log, the symbol of their enemy, with spears, clubs, and hand axes.

Keena pulls a tattered deerskin shawl over her head, covering her ears and hiding the bushy, flame-coloured braid on her shoulder, separating herself from the raw fury pulsating around her. *I hope the Kulas can fight.* She's a female of Haken's band now, but she's still Keena, daughter of Ubra. The long treacherous journey from her mountain home was exhausting and took many sun times, but Keena knows in her heart that nothing can keep her from going home.

12

CRO-MAGNON (KULA)
CAMP

SHINONI PEERS INTO the matted undergrowth on the forest floor. Where are the barbed leaves of the fever plant hiding? Where are the tart red berries of the belly plants? They'll be dry now and harder to see among their hairy leaves, but she'll find them.

The earthy smell of rotting plant debris tickles her nose as she pushes aside some fern fronds. *Aha, there.* Nestled among the pine needles on the ground are several small fever plants. She wraps a layer of moss around them to protect her hands from their stinging leaf barbs, as Reza has shown her. An uneasy breeze ruffles her hair as she plucks the plants and places them, moss and all, into her pouch.

Buzzzzz, buzzztt. Buzzz.

Shinoni cocks her head, locating the droning bees. "Hey, little stingers, do you have honey to share?" Her mouth waters at the thought of the sweet liquid oozing onto her tongue. She moves farther into the bushes, trying to spot the hive.

Stay close to camp, Shinoni. Her father's warning intrudes into her thoughts. Why must there be so many rules?

You'll be medicine woman to our people. Reza's words prod her on. She still has to find the belly plants. *Ah, there they are.* Red berries swaying waist high on prickly stems deep among the brambles. Yes, she's a medicine woman like her grandmother. Shinoni carefully plucks the berries, wraps them in their own toothed leaves, and adds them to the treasures in her pouch. Reza will be proud of her.

The shadows of the berry bushes lengthen as Shinoni steps back onto the trail. Now where *is* her grandmother? Has she gone down the slope to the marsh where women are still cutting reeds and setting fish traps? It's not likely Grandmother would return there with her sore back.

Shinoni looks up the slope toward the camp, where everyone else is busy going about their tasks. Old women hang fish to dry on the smoke racks, and scrape hides. Children wrestle with each other and play with scraps of hide and bones. Old men test their skill rolling stones in the shade. Her father instructs his helpers, Bardat and Sakat, under a tree. Not likely Grandmother went back to camp, either. She's probably still picking medicine plants.

Everyone but me is happy doing what they're supposed to do. Shinoni closes her eyes and sighs. It would be fun to explore the valley beyond with the men.

"Arrrgh! Yeee yip! Raahhrr!" Beastly roars slash through the stillness of the camp. Shinoni's eyes fly open.

Screams of the children mingle with the murderous snarls. "Help! Ma! Nooo!"

Shinoni drops to the ground and rolls behind a bush, nostrils flaring. What kind of predators are terrorizing her people? Drawing a deep breath, she creeps forward and peeks through the branches. Her neck hairs bristle in terror. Strange Ones! Father said they eat children.

Shinoni sobs as the Krags charge among her startled band. One runs through the group of children, smashing them with his club. The old women rush forward but are met with the Krags' spears. Within moments, the ground is littered with bodies.

The marauders light torches from the smoke fires and throw them into the shelters. Their faces, painted with ochre and pitch, glow in the light of the flames.

They wear the skulls, antlers, and teeth of beasts on their heads, and their animal snarls drive a wrenching shaft of terror deep into Shinoni's belly.

She gags as smoke fills her nostrils, choking her breath. As the flames lick at her home, the heat and ashes carried on the wind sting her throat and eyes, temporarily blinding her. By the time her vision clears, her family's shelter has disappeared.

Shazur rushes forward with Sakat and Bardat, leading the old men and boys in a counterattack, armed only with sticks and rocks. "Father, nooo!" Shinoni cries.

"Eeeyaaa!" A Strange One wearing the jaw of a cave bear on his head meets her father head on, impaling him on his spear. "Hiiii yiiippp!" His victory howl pierces Shinoni's ears as she collapses on the ground.

"No, no. Father!" Rough hands grab her from behind and pull her into the brambles. She struggles wildly and tries to scream, but a hand clamps over her mouth. Needle thorns rip at her arms as a frantic hiss coils in her ear.

"Shhh, quiet." It's Reza. Shinoni stops struggling as her grandmother hugs her tightly. "You carry our people's knowledge, girl. You must protect it. Run. Hide."

"Come with me, Grandmother," Shinoni pleads. "We'll hide together."

"I'm old, Shinoni," Reza says. "You're our medicine woman now. Run."

"Eeeyaaa!" A Strange One yells. Shinoni and Reza turn and see some of the Strange Ones pointing toward the lake. They must have seen the women there. Shinoni and Reza watch in horror as they crash down the slope.

Shinoni freezes, but Reza pushes her into the trees. Shadows close around her as her grandmother's words trail behind her. "Run like a deer. I'm always with you."

Shinoni races blindly into the twilight world of the great forest. She runs along game trails, deeper and deeper into its dappled depths. Her chest feels like it'll burst, and she can no longer breathe when at last she falls on the leaf-strewn earth.

"Father ... Grandmother ... don't leave me alone," she whispers. Her mind flies to the sacred cave. She sees her father's face, lined and serious, telling her that the spirits had warned him of danger, that he'd seen their mighty clan eagle fall from the sky in flames. She'd also seen an eagle on fire in her own dream.

Had the spirits warned Shazur of danger, or had they threatened him because his daughter had been in the sacred cave? Are the spirits protecting her now or punishing her? Had her behaviour angered the spirits so much they punished her people? She forces the painful thoughts from her mind and pulls herself up.

Shifting patterns of light and shade filter through the oak and evergreen canopy. The forest spins around her. Tree tops tower above her. Everything looks the same.

Croak. Craat. Bizzzt. The deep voice of a frog, the raucous calls of a jay, the drone of insects — the muted calls of the forest surround her.

A twig snaps in the undergrowth, then another. Something's moving stealthily toward her through the tangled shrubbery. Shinoni rises, her senses jangling with alarm.

She detects movements around her in several places. The bushes tremble here; leaves rustle there. A low growl rumbles in the sudden stillness.

"Who's there? Show yourself." No human voices answer Shinoni, but the sound of breathing is all around her. She backs against a large tree, feeling behind her for the solid trunk. Sweat drips from her brow and trickles between her shoulder blades.

A large grey she-wolf moves out of the shadows and approaches Shinoni. Her eyes gleam in the dim light, and her white fangs flash. The wolf sits down, cocking her head and staring at Shinoni.

The rest of the pack glides out of the twilight, and now six wolves form a circle around her. The other wolves aren't as calm as their leader. Some snarl, and a young wolf leaps forward, teeth bared. The large female steps in front of him, knocking him aside. She growls and snaps at the youngster, and he backs off submissively. The pack settles down around Shinoni.

Why don't they attack? What do they want from me? Shinoni tries not to move. She struggles to keep her voice calm as she addresses the pack leader. "Thank you, mother wolf — or are you saving me for yourself?" Shinoni shudders at the thought. She slowly slips the rope out of her pouch and glances up at the overhanging branches.

She looks back at the wolf. "Perhaps you've been sent to be my spirit helper, my tewa." She speaks slowly and calmly, never taking her eyes from the she-wolf. "Stay calm, mother."

As she tosses the knotted end of the rope over an overhanging branch in one quick, smooth motion, Shinoni begins to sing softly, a wordless lullaby chant her mother had sung to her when she was a frightened small one. "Aaii, aaii … um, um … he, he."

A wolf snarls and stands up.

Shinoni gulps and continues to sing shakily. "Aaii, aaii … um, um … he, he. Aaii, aaii … he, he … he, he …"

The wolves whine, heads tilted, as Shinoni reaches up and pulls on the rope to test it. The coil falls limply back on her shoulders. She wills herself to keep singing calmly. "Aaii, aaii … You don't want to eat me … aaii, aaii … I taste bad … um, um … C'mon rope, hold …"

Again she throws the rope over the branch above. She catches the knotted end and jerks it. This time it holds. She scales the tree, pulling herself up, then swings her legs up over the branch as two wolves rush toward her, growling and snapping. Shinoni clings precariously to the limb as the pack mills and leaps below her. The big she-wolf still sits, watching her.

"Are you my tewa?" Shinoni murmurs. She can't look away from the wolf's eyes.

A sudden commotion along the trail breaks the spell. Shinoni gasps as loud voices and harsh laughter swell from the forest depths. She's sure these are the Strange Ones, and the last time she heard them, they were killing her people. Tremors shake her body as the sounds of crashing footsteps and breaking branches draw nearer. The wolves snarl and disappear like wraiths into the undergrowth.

The boisterous Strange Ones burst into the clearing carrying loads of skins, food, and tools taken from Shinoni's camp. To her horror, they flop on the ground near her tree. She blinks back tears as they laugh, pass around a stash of finely chiselled Kula blades, and chew on dried meat from her people's fires.

Their leader glowers under his bear-skull headdress. His fierce face is smeared with red ochre and streaks of sweat. A puckered scar runs across his cheek, partially closing one eye.

This Strange One stabbed her father with his bloody spear. She wants to leap on him and slit his throat with the knife Shazur made for her, but there are too many of them. She wills her body to be still and clings to her perch.

Several of the Strange Ones approach the leader, holding out their hands and calling him something that sounds like *Ha-ken*. He shoves them and spits on the ground. Shinoni strains to hear what they say, but their words are gibberish to her ears, like the grunts of beasts. The hunters keep their distance, and she senses they fear him.

"Hoo-yeeeaa." Shinoni cringes at the leader's ferocious howl. He reaches under his cloak and pulls out an eagle-shaped amulet and swings it in the air.

"Nooo," Shinoni moans. Her father's amulet. She chokes back a sob, but her movement shakes the branches.

The startled hunters jabber and point at Shinoni. Haken's face twists into a triumphant leer. These Strange Ones swarming below her are far more dangerous than the wolf pack was, but her fear erupts into fury. "Stay away from me," she screams. "You'll be sorry if you bother me."

A hunter below her swaying perch scoops a stone from the ground. He takes aim and sends the rock flying into the branches. The stone hurtles through the leaves. An excruciating pain explodes in Shinoni's head, and she falls from the tree. Darkness closes over her as she hits the ground.

Her eyes flutter open. A circle of Strange Ones bends over her. One of them raises a club and she braces for the killing blow, too weak to move.

Haken shouts and grabs the hunter's arm. He lowers his face to hers and lifts the eagle amulet tied around her neck. Shinoni gags at his animal smell and sinks into blackness, the the image of her amulet and her father's amulet, gleaming together in Haken's blood-stained hand, seared into her mind.

13

NEANDERTHAL (KRAG)
HAKEN'S CAMP

S HINONI AWAKES IN AN ALIEN WORLD. How did she get here? Her eyelids, heavy as flint, refuse to lift, but her nostrils recoil at the earthy animal stench surrounding her. This was the last thing she smelled before losing consciousness. Strange Ones.

Shinoni shakes her head groggily, wincing as pain shoots down her neck. She opens her eyes and the cave spins wildly. Sinister shapes prowl the walls around her. A woman of the Strange Ones pulls her to a sitting position and unties the strips of sinew that bind her hands. She holds a skin pouch to Shinoni's lips. The liquid is warm and as bitter as reindeer bile. Shinoni sips a little, then spits it out. The woman persists, speaking to her in that language she can't understand.

Suddenly it all comes back. "Father, Grandmother," Shinoni whispers.

She struggles to stand but doesn't get far. She falls back to the ground, her ankles bound together with sinew. Her vision clears, bringing into focus firelight licking the stone walls and dancing over the faces of the Strange Ones watching her. Their eyes glitter below heavy brow ridges, hostile and suspicious.

"Leave me alone, monsters," Shinoni shouts.

The strange woman pushes aside a bearskin that covers the cave entrance and bellows into the night. Heartbeats later, she leaps aside as Haken bursts through the opening.

Vomit rises in Shinoni's throat as his scent overpowers her. The hands that killed her father pull her to her feet. He babbles in the Strange Ones' language. His rasping words are meaningless in her ears but the threat is clear.

"What do you want, disgusting creature?" Shinoni says.

Haken shakes her angrily. He lifts her close to his scarred face and stabs his finger at her amulet swinging on the cord around her neck. Shinoni struggles, tugging his fur cloak off his shoulders. There, hanging around this hateful Strange One's neck, is her father's amulet. Firelight glints off the polished ivory eagle.

"That belongs to Shazur, thief. You killed my father." Shinoni grabs for the talisman.

Haken roars in surprised rage and snatches a club from a nearby henchman. Shinoni squeezes her eyes shut, unable to move. Quick as a flash, two hands jerk her backward out of Haken's reach. The club crashes on stone.

"If you do that again, he'll kill you." The voice hissing in her ear is speaking her own language, the Kula language.

Shinoni turns and stares into the green eyes of a girl about her own age. She's a girl of the Strange Ones, short and heavy, with fair skin on her broad cheeks and brow ridge, and red hair pulled back in a braid. Their eyes connect and hold.

The girl releases Shinoni's arm and shrugs. "It doesn't matter to me if he does kill you."

"Kee-na," Haken shouts. He kicks the girl and she withdraws into the shadows.

Shinoni glares at Haken and holds her hands over her ears.

Haken shakes her like a fox with a vole, then points at her amulet. The woman who untied Shinoni's hands whispers to him. He releases Shinoni and motions to Keena, speaking to her and gesturing toward Shinoni.

"Haken wants the hunting magic your people use. He thinks you know it." Keena points to the amulet around Shinoni's neck. "He thinks there's magic in that."

"My father asked the spirits to help our hunters. But I don't know how," Shinoni says. "Women can't see the ceremony."

"You'd better tell him what he wants to know, Kula girl."

"I can't." Angry tears well in Shinoni's eyes.

"Haken has no patience. He'll kill you. If you tell him what he wants, he might let you live as a captive."

"Tell him he's ugly and stupid and I hate him." Shinoni swallows hard. "He's too stupid to learn Kula hunting magic."

"He'll kill us both if I tell him that," Keena says. She speaks to Haken, who grunts impatiently. "I told him you're trying to remember but you're weak and need food." Keena's lips twitch in a grin. "After all, you're scrawny and don't have the strength of a Krag."

The hunters grumble and move back, watching Shinoni warily. The woman brings her a slice of deer haunch from the fire. She hasn't realized how hungry she is until now. She wolfs down the hot, dripping meat.

"Haken's losing patience." Keena nudges her. "You'd better tell him what you know."

Suddenly, all around her, Shinoni hears rustling, whining, sighing, moaning. Her body vibrates with the sounds. The girl, Keena, doesn't seem to hear it. None of the Strange Ones do. Are the animal spirits talking to her? Are they guiding her — or tricking her? Shinoni takes a deep breath, and the spirit messengers fade away. But now she knows what she must do.

"Tell him there's a special cave where my father painted pictures of the animals we hunt," Shinoni says. "That's where he must go to get the hunting magic." She hesitates. "Spirits dwell there, and they won't let him enter unless he carries my father's amulet." Is she betraying her people?

Keena tells Haken, and he shouts to his hunters, gesturing at Shinoni. The men watch her suspiciously. Haken growls orders to Keena, who turns back to Shinoni. "He wants to know where this cave is and what he has to do."

"It's on a rock ledge above my people's camp, the camp he destroyed." Shinoni scowls at Haken through eyelids half-closed with revulsion. "It's hidden by bushes, but the amulet will lead him. He must enter alone or the spirits will be angry." She watches Haken's reaction as Keena translates.

"He says he's not afraid of spirits." Keena grins slightly. "But I think he's afraid."

"There's a special rock in the cave that looks like a deer," Shinoni continues. "He must touch it with the amulet."

Keena speaks to Haken, who nods and grunts.

"He must bring this rock back to his camp and throw it into his fire," Shinoni says. "Only then will the spirits help him." She pauses, looking around the circle of hostile faces. "If he doesn't do exactly as I say, the spirits won't help him. They'll destroy him and his men."

Keena tells this to Haken, and he leaps over to Shinoni. Thrusting his face close to hers, he snarls a threat that Keena translates. "He says if the hunting magic doesn't work, they'll throw *you* into the fire."

— 14 —

NEANDERTHAL (KRAG)
HAKEN'S CAMP

SHINONI WAKES IN THE EARLY MORNING, stiff, shivering, and alone on the cold rock floor. Her hands, retied last night, are now so numb she can hardly feel them. The bearskin partially covers the opening, but she can see Haken and his hunters walking toward the forest on their quest to find her people's hunting magic.

"I hope the spirits keep you in the cave forever," she whispers.

Shinoni desperately searches for some means of escape. There's only that one entrance, with Strange Ones on the other side. If she's still here when Haken returns, she'll certainly die.

Shinoni begins to wiggle the thong around her waist, slowly bringing her pouch closer to her tied hands. She works it open, grasping her father's gift, the flint-blade knife, between her numb fingers. *It's lucky the Strange Ones didn't have enough sense to see what a Kula girl carries in her pouch*, she thinks.

Shinoni rubs the sharp blade against the sinew holding her wrists. "Ow—" She bites off the cry as blood drips from her thumb, sliced by the knife. No matter. She keeps hacking at the bonds until the tough sinew finally gives way and her hands are free.

She begins to slice through the bonds on her ankles, quickening her work as footsteps clatter on the loose stones by the entrance. The same Strange One girl who had spoken to her at Haken's fire enters the cave carrying a drinking pouch. Better not to trust her. Shinoni backs up against the rock wall, pretending her hands are still tied.

The girl shrugs. "You can't fool me, Kula girl. I see you've freed yourself. You're bleeding." She pulls the bearskin over the entrance and offers the pouch to Shinoni.

Shinoni hesitates. She takes the bag and pours water on her bloody thumb, then wipes it on her leggings before drinking thirstily. She watches the Strange One carefully. This girl looks more like a bear than a person, with her short, squat body and muscular arms.

Her head is large, with a brow ridge above her green eyes and a broad nose. Shinoni wants to touch her pale skin to see if it feels cold, like ice. The girl's hair is the colour of fire, as is the hair of that hideous monster, Haken.

Shinoni catches her breath and stops drinking. The girl helped her, but she's still a Strange One.

Keena takes back the water bag. This Kula girl has the same brown skin and dark hair and eyes as Sabra. She has the same gangly arms and legs, and she's reckless like him, too. The girl would likely be dead now if Keena hadn't been there to help her last night. Still, she was brave standing up to Haken the way she did. But she's not Krag, so she might not be trustworthy.

"You lied to them, didn't you?" Keena asks.

The Kula girl hesitates. "There's hunting magic there, but it won't help them."

"They'll kill you, then," Keena says. "It's better than living as their captive, anyway."

"No, Krag, they won't kill me, or keep me captive. I'm leaving." The girl moves toward the entrance, but Keena blocks her way.

"There are women working outside. Why shouldn't I sound the alarm?" Keena takes a step toward the entrance while the girl watches helplessly. Keena stares back at her and makes a decision. "All right. I'll distract them so we can crawl down the far side. It's steeper but hidden."

"We?" the Kula girl stammers. "You're a Krag. Why do you want to leave your people?"

"These aren't my people." Keena's face clouds and she stamps her foot. "Haken took me from my people in the high country." She sits down in front of the entrance, blocking the way out. "I go with you, or you don't leave."

The Kula girl sits on a rock across from Keena and studies her warily. "How is it you speak my language?"

"A Kula hunter spent last snow time at my family's hearth." Keena frowns. "He was a know-it-all like you."

"How do I know I can trust you? You're a Strange One." The Kula returns the frown.

"My people are Krags, not Strange Ones," Keena growls. *How rude and snotty this Kula girl is.* "You're strange — and you need me." She stands and crosses her arms. "I don't like Kulas much, but I hate Haken."

"Well, come if you must, but don't slow me down," the Kula girl snaps. "The hunters of my band were away searching for shelter when Haken attacked. Maybe I can find them." She chokes back tears. "Perhaps some of the women and children survived and are hiding in the forest. Maybe my grandmother's with them."

"Slow you down?" Keena ignores the tears and bristles. "My name's Keena, swift mountain bird. My father's Atuk, a great Krag leader, far greater than Haken."

"I'm Shinoni. My father, Shazur, is a mighty shaman of the Kula Eagle Clan." The Kula wipes away her tears, her lips quivering. She sits up straighter and holds her chin high. "My grandmother, Reza, is a powerful healer. One day I'll lead my people, too." The girl gets up and rushes toward the entrance.

"Wait." Keena stands in her way. "Sit and look like you're still tied. I'll distract the women, but be ready to come quickly when I call. And don't you slow me down, Kula."

Keena walks out of the cave. A woman scraping a large bison hide calls to her. "Where've you been, Keena?" She holds out the scraper. "I've work for you."

Keena walks past her. "I have to get more water for the prisoner. She's very weak."

"That Kula brat? Let her be. She can drink from the puddles on the floor."

"She's weak," Keena says. "What'll Haken do if she dies before he returns?"

"Be quick, then. I've lots of work for you." The woman frowns and waves Keena on.

Keena scrambles down the steep slope and walks briskly toward the nearby stream before. She enters a stand of willow trees, out of the women's sight. As the branches close silently behind her, Keena splashes mud on herself, rips her tunic, and messes her hair. She waits a few heartbeats, then bursts wild-eyed out of the bushes.

Caw, caw. Crows explode into the air, their warning cries ringing as Keena runs toward the camp, screaming. "Kulas! They're hunting Krags. Run for the forest. Hurry! The Kulas will eat your children."

The Krag women shout in panic. "Iii-yeee!" They scatter, terrified, grabbing their children as they flee toward the safety of the forest.

Keena quickly climbs to the cave mouth. "Kula, move," she calls.

Shinoni appears at the entrance. Both girls drop to their knees and crawl along the rock face, hidden by boulders. Keena leads the way, and soon they reach a steep side trail behind tall bushes. They slip and slide down the path. Loose shale crumbles under their feet, making the going treacherous.

"Hurry! I told them your people were attacking," Keena says. "They'll soon discover there aren't any Kula hunters."

Shinoni pushes her aching legs to go faster. Her secret forays into the shaman's cave have given her a great deal of practice scrambling on slippery slopes, but who would think that this squat Krag girl could move so fast and be so sure-footed? She pauses momentarily to catch her breath. "What'll they do when they find we're gone?"

"You're not too bright," Keena says. "What do you think they'll do?"

"They're women. Will they come after us? Kula women wouldn't."

"I don't know. There aren't many children in the band to slow them." She pauses for breath. "But Haken will come after us."

"We've got a good head start." Shinoni's sides heave with exertion.

"You don't know how powerful an enemy Haken can be." Keena gulps. "We'll be safer facing the forest beasts than him."

They slide and stumble on the slick shale, splash through wet clinging fingers of marsh grass, then reach the trees. As the girls enter the shelter of the forest, an angry chorus of shouts from the Krag women follows them. The din disappears as they move into the green half-light world where both sight and sound are muted.

Shinoni and Keena fall into each other's arms, gasping with relief, then push away when they realize what they're doing.

"We're free. We did it. We've outwitted the Krags," Shinoni crows triumphantly.

"*Some* Krags, Kula girl. We've outwitted *some* Krags," Keena comments with a half smile.

Shinoni points at the seemingly endless stands of conifers intertwined with thickets of poplar, birch, and willow, her eyes wide. "Now all we have to do is find my people. How hard can that be?"

Skreeeiii. Shinoni and Keena look up. An eagle soars, lazily circling above them.

"I think my father is saying goodbye," Shinoni says, wiping away tears. A wolf howl echoes in the stillness.

— 15 —

SHINONI'S EYES FLY OPEN as she's jarred awake from an uncomfortable sleep. Something is tickling her cheek! She squints and tries to focus on an ant meandering across her face. Shinoni lifts her hand to brush it away but smacks a hard surface above her head. Faint light filters in from a small opening near her feet. Where is she? The smell of rotting wood and rodent droppings surrounds her.

Memory floods back. She and the Krag girl stumbling out of the forest at twilight, desperate for safety. The ancient, hollowed-out log by the stream bank offering them shelter.

Something hard pushes into Shinoni's spine. "Wake up. Your fat knee's in my back," she says, and she pushes Keena. "You smell bad, too."

"I smell?" Keena yawns. "You must've eaten too much meat at Haken's fire. You passed stink winds all night."

Arms and legs thrashing, they struggle to put distance between themselves in the cramped space.

"You're the one who insisted on coming with me," Shinoni says. "I'd have more room in this log and could travel faster without you." She pushes Keena out of the opening and tumbles after her. They unfold their stiff bodies on the damp earth and stare at the icy blanket of greenery surrounding them. Frost-tinged boughs of spruce and pine trees sway in the wind. Tendrils of ice fog caress a small stream, and ducks escaping the snows in the high country splash down in the water.

A flock of ghostly white swans swims in the mist. "Perhaps my father sent the white long necks," Shinoni says. They bring good luck."

A breeze rattles the dry leaves on the willow trees by the water's edge. Keena points, her voice low. "Leeswi's warning us. Haken must be on our trail."

Shinoni squints at the swaying trees. "There's no one there."

"You aren't Krag, so she doesn't speak to you," Keena scoffs.

"Maybe I can't hear this Leeswi, but I can catch a deer. I could eat a whole one right now."

Keena turns over a dead log and picks fat white grubs off its underside. "Will you use your little knife? Better have some of these first." She tosses a handful of thick wriggly grubs into her mouth. They crunch between her teeth.

"Ugh." Shinoni gags. *How repulsive this ugly Krag girl is.* "That's food for wild beasts and Krags, not Kulas."

"You think so?" Keena grins, her mouth full of half-chewed grubs. "You'll starve before you catch a deer."

"How would you know? You're not a hunter," Shinoni snaps.

Keena practically chokes on her grubs as a sudden rustling shakes the bushes at the forest edge. "What's that?" She gulps. An enormous grey she-wolf steps into the clearing. "Aaaaaiii!" Keena shrieks, scrambling toward the stream. "Run!"

Shinoni recognizes the wolf! She's the leader of the pack that treed her in the forest. The wolf steps closer, never taking her fierce golden eyes from Shinoni's face. "It's all right. I know her." Shinoni speaks softly, calmly. "She won't hurt us."

"Yeah, right. You know a wolf devil." Keena doesn't sound reassured. She picks up a stout branch. "Keep away," she says to the wolf and backs frantically into the muddy water. She stumbles backward. "I can't feel the ground," she cries. The mud crawls up to her ankles, then past her calves, as the quicksand sucks her body slowly downward. "Help, I'm sinking. Help me, Kula!"

Shinoni stares in disbelief, the wolf forgotten. The Krag girl, covered in slimy grey mud, sinks even deeper. Her body has disappeared up to her waist. Shinoni runs downstream to where a low-lying tree limb juts out over the water.

Sluurrp. Keena frees an arm and looks around frantically. "Come back. You can't leave me!" Keena shouts. "I should've known not to trust a Kula." She struggles and sinks deeper.

Shinoni climbs onto the branch and her weight bends it low over Keena. "Grab on. Grab it. Hurry!"

"I can't reach it. Lower, lower!" Keena's eyes bulge. The mud now sucks at her shoulders. Shinoni bounces hard and the limb dips over the water. With a final lunge, Keena grips it. The limb bounces back, partially yanking her from the quicksand. Keena clings precariously, her legs still trapped as she fights against the downward pull. The muddy depths won't let go of their prize.

Shinoni grasps the heavier Krag girl's hands and pulls until her own arms feel like they'll pop out of their sockets. Slowly Keena's legs emerge from the quagmire. She wraps them around the limb and hoists herself up. Shinoni pulls her backward along the branch and both girls fall exhausted onto the ground.

"You're pretty strong for a Kula," Keena gasps.

"Good thing. You're heavy as a bear." Shinoni gets shakily to her feet.

The wolf trots toward the girls, ears forward, tail high. She nudges Shinoni with her snout, then brushes her body against her. Shinoni is startled but thrilled at this physical contact with the big wolf. She places her hand on the coarse silver-grey fur, feels the panting breath, and smells the strong scent of the beast. *This is a real wolf and she's chosen to come to me.*

The wolf then moves to Keena, looking into her terrified face. The wolf's pink tongue lolls over her dagger teeth, only a finger's length from the girl's throat. She cringes and backs away, but Shinoni puts a restraining hand on her arm.

"If you fall in that mud trap again, you're on your own. I won't pull you out twice." Keena's body shivers as Shinoni squeezes her arm. "She won't hurt you. I think she's my spirit guide. My people call them tewa, helper. You and I can call her Tewa and maybe she'll help us."

"She doesn't look that friendly." Keena gasps as Tewa growls and grabs Shinoni's tunic, pulling her toward the bushes.

The sound of crashing in the vegetation announces intruders on the game trail. The earthy scent of Krags wafts on the breeze. Tewa melts into the bushes.

Panicked, Shinoni and Keena roll into the dense undergrowth. A heartbeat later, Haken and his hunters break into the clearing.

Haken sniffs the air. "They've been here not long ago."

The girls peer through the bushes, trembling.

A hunter points to tracks in the mud near the water. "A wolf's stalking them." He bends to look more closely. "There was a fight here. See how the ground's trampled?"

"They're mine. I'll kill them *and* the wolf." Haken snarls.

Shinoni and Keena cower in the bushes, barely daring to breathe.

Hissss. They aren't alone in the undergrowth. They've unwittingly invaded the resting place of a large adder. It slithers by them, sluggish from the cold, its brown and grey scales barely visible in the shadows. The snake stops and coils near Shinoni, who backs away, rustling the bushes. Keena clamps a hand over Shinoni's mouth as a deadly spear plunges into the undergrowth.

"You can't fool me, brats. I've hunted bigger game than you." The girls can see him staring intently at the shrubs as he moves ever nearer.

Suddenly, a grey streak leaps from the undergrowth. A snarling Tewa knocks Haken to the ground, then jumps over him and runs into the forest. The hunters take off in pursuit. Haken roars an angry oath. He glances back suspiciously into the clearing before following the others on Tewa's trail.

Keena takes her hand from Shinoni's mouth, then picks up a rock and smashes the snake's head. She offers the dead serpent to Shinoni, who backs away.

"They're good eating." Keena looks at her quizzically. "So, the great Kula hunter is afraid of a snake?"

"A snake crawled into my bed when I was a young one." Shinoni relives the terrifying memory that never fades, her voice shaking. "It coiled beside me like this one here. It hissed, and I reached to see what it was. My mother threw herself over me and the snake killed her." Tears roll down Shinoni's cheeks. "It's my fault she died."

"It wasn't your fault, if you were a young one." Keena wraps the carcass in leaves and slings it on her back. "A snake took your mother's life and now this snake gives it's life to feed us. No one knows when Leeswi the Earth Spirit will take our breath."

Shinoni's stomach lurches at the thought of eating the snake, but she follows Keena into the forest. A wolf howl quavers nearby.

"Hoo hooo!" Shinoni responds. *Tewa made it.* The wolf avoided Haken's spear.

16

AFTER THEIR ESCAPE FROM HAKEN, Shinoni and Keena spend the dark time in a dead tree trunk in the forest. They leave when the sun wakes, and by the time she rides high in the sky the trees have thinned into a broad plain. The girls walk through waist-high grass that sways as the wind whistles down from the glacier. They clutch their cloaks tight against the biting cold. Keena swivels her head from side to side, peering into the foliage and testing the air. *Surely there are predators lurking here. How can the Kula girl stride ahead, so unconcerned?* Keena catches up and pokes her.

"We should walk on the forest edge." Keena's voice is low, almost lost in the rustling of the grass. "My people would cross a place such as this in a group."

"My people are braver than yours. Our hunters fear nothing." Shinoni glances over her shoulder without slowing her pace and grins at Keena. "You can stick behind me if you're scared."

Keena plants her sturdy legs firmly on the game trail and spins Shinoni around. "Ah, I forgot you're a hunter. I feel better already." She glares into Shinoni's amused face.

"Calm down, Krag. We've come too far to turn back now," Shinoni says. "We need to get across the grasses to find shelter before the sun sleeps."

Keena's no longer listening to Shinoni. She stretches as tall as she can, neck and ears straining, nostrils flaring as she sniffs the air. "Shhh. Did you hear that?" She clutches Shinoni's arm, her muscles tensing for flight.

"Stop fooling around. You can't frighten me, Krag."

"Can't you smell it?" Keena stares into the grasses ahead. "Laugh devils. Close, too."

The wind blows the hair back from their faces, bringing with it the faint but distinctively musky smell of hyena. Keena points with her free hand. "Come on, we passed some trees. Let's hide in there. They'll smell us soon."

"Relax, we're upwind of them." Shinoni shakes off Keena's hand. "Let's get closer. They may have a kill."

"You're kidding, right? *We'll* be their kill." Keena's voice is high and squeaky, like a mouse with no place to hide. "Before the last snow they carried off two boys from my camp."

"Aren't you hungry, Krag?" Shinoni persists. "Maybe we can scare them off. Take some of the meat."

"Are you kidding? They bit off a hunter's arm who tried to save those boys." Keena is horrified. *How can this Kula be so stupid?*

"It's not like they're lions," Shinoni coaxes.

"They're worse than lions when they're in a group." Keena has had enough. She turns to retrace her steps along the path, but when she looks back her breath freezes in her throat.

"Come on, shadow." Shinoni waves to Keena as she disappears into the grass in the direction of the hyenas.

Sweat rolls down Keena's face. Her terror at being alone on the open plains struggles with her fear of the laugh devils. *A lone Krag is a dead Krag,* as her father often says. She forces her numb legs to move and follows Shinoni into the grass.

Several heartbeats later Shinoni and Keena, lying on their bellies, part the grasses just enough to peer onto a savage scene. A clan of six fearsome cave hyenas snarl and snap over the torn and bloody remains of a deer.

Keena's never been this close to laugh devils before. She gags at their smell but can't tear her eyes away from their kill. The hyenas' faces, crimson with blood, push deep into the belly of the deer, ripping out entrails and snapping bones from the carcass.

The strong breeze blowing toward Keena and Shinoni carries the heavy smell of blood and death to them but keeps their scent from the hyenas. Shinoni fits a stone to her sling and starts to stand up. Keena grabs her ankle and yanks her back. Does the foolish Kula really want to be torn to pieces like the deer? Keena frantically shakes her head and makes a slitting motion across her neck.

"I've seen our hunters do this," Shinoni says. She jumps to her feet shouting, "Yah yah! Run, cowards. Eeiiyaaa!" She twirls her sling, letting the rock fly, and then scoops more stones from the ground. She advances on the hyenas, yelling and hurling rocks.

The startled beasts leap backward, tumbling over each other. Suddenly the wind shifts. The hyenas sniff the air and turn menacingly toward Shinoni and Keena. They lower their heads. Saliva drools from their heavy jaws, their lips pulled back over sharp, powerful teeth.

Hahahahahahaaa. The laugh devils' chilling hunting cry swells in the air.

"Run! Head for that tree." Keena leaps to her feet, grabbing Shinoni and pulling her back into the grass. They race full speed for a solitary tree in the distance.

Hahahaaa. Crying loudly, the hyenas take off in hot pursuit, rapidly gaining on their prey. Keena's short legs can't keep up with Shinoni's ground-eating strides. She stumbles as the lead hyena leaps.

"Leeswi, spare me!" Keena screams. She looks back in horror.

A spear is thrust up from the grass and strikes the lead hyena, killing her instantly. The seemingly empty savannah explodes with activity as Krag hunters spring from the grass on all sides, wielding spears and heavy clubs. They charge the hyenas as Shinoni and Keena scramble up the tree and watch the battle unfold.

The hyenas circle around their dead leader and pull a hunter down.

"Aiiiieeee!" The sound of the hunter's screams and cracking bones fill the air.

"Arrrgh. Rraaagg." The other Krags growl and roar ferociously as they move in with clubs swinging to save the injured hunter. The hyenas break and run. The Krags run after them, brandishing clubs and throwing stones. Two hyenas lie dead on the ground near the injured Krag hunter.

The Krags turn back to their companion, who moans as they examine his ripped and bloody leg. Almost as one, their heads turn toward the tree, and toward Shinoni and Keena high in its branches. They congregate below and glare up at the girls. One who appears to be the leader gestures for them to come to the ground.

"Do you know them? They're like you," Shinoni says.

"They're not from Haken's group or mine," Keena replies.

The leader continues to gesture for them to come down. The other Krags join him and call noisily in the Krag tongue.

"They want us down there and we'd better do it." Keena shifts her weight nervously, awkward and uneasy in the treetop.

"No way. I've had enough of Krag monsters already." Shinoni hangs on tighter to the swaying branch. Keena frowns at her and descends.

Shinoni watches as the angry hunters surround Keena and babble questions at her. Their leader looks up at her in the tree. He shakes his spear, then spits into the grass. His voice rises as he points from the injured man to her.

Keena cups her hands and shouts above the din. "His name's Gandar, and he's upset that they've lost a good hunter for a Kula girl. He's even more upset because it's his brother."

Shinoni eyes the wounded Krag rolling on the ground. "He isn't dead yet."

"He will be soon. Even if he lives he'll be a burden."

Shinoni remembers the last time Krags treed her, how they knocked her down with a stone. It's probably best to come down by herself. She watches the hunters warily as she descends to the ground.

"Tell them I can help. I need to look at his leg."

"How can you help?" Keena scoffs.

Shinoni tries to approach the injured Krag, but the others block her path. "My grandmother was a healer. She taught me to treat wounds," Shinoni whispers to Keena, who translates Shinoni's message to Gandar.

The Krag leader's brows lock in a solid ridge above his eyes as he studies Shinoni. She stands her ground and returns his stare. Gandar then snorts and motions to the others. They back off just enough to let Shinoni through. She squeezes past them, gagging as the stench of Krag blood and sweat engulfs her. She can feel the hunters' glares boring into her back as she kneels beside the injured man.

Shinoni searches for Keena's face in the crush of Krag bodies surrounding her. "Tell them to give me more room," Shinoni says. Keena calls to Gandar, who again motions to the others to back up. They sit in a semicircle watching her every move.

Keena sits close to Shinoni, hardly daring to breath. The young hunter writhes in pain as his blood flows into the ground. Can the Kula girl help him? He reminds her of Kreel. She clutches the ibex-tooth pendant he gave her as she feels the sting of his loss. She wonders if he is still alive.

Shinoni squats and opens her pouch. She takes out the small moss-wrapped yellow fever plants and carefully crushes them between two rocks. Reza's wrinkled face flashes before her eyes. She places the mashed plant material back onto the moss and spits on it several times to moisten it. She feels Reza's hands guiding hers as she spreads the mixture on the wound and covers it with more moss from her pouch.

"Thank you, Grandmother," Shinoni murmurs, grateful she'd paid attention to the lesson.

The injured Krag moans and Shinoni chants the same soothing sound that calmed the wolf pack. "Aaii, aaii … um, um … he, he. Aaii, aaii … he, he … he, he …"

The hunter seems to relax. She covers the poultice with a layer of dry grasses, then cuts some strips of hide from her cloak with her knife to bind it to his leg. Finally she breaks two stout branches from the tree and binds the hunter's leg from knee to ankle between them.

"I've done what I can." Shinoni stands up shakily. "If his spirit's strong, he'll recover. If not, he'll die."

"If not, he won't be the only one who dies," Keena says.

The Krags move forward, pushing past Shinoni and examining their companion, who's now unconscious. They begin to speak rapidly, their voices rising.

"They think he's dead, Kula. Is he?" Keena whispers.

"Why are Krags so stupid?" Shinoni sighs. "He has breath. He moves."

Keena scowls and steps back.

The unconscious Krag begins to stir. Gandar speaks to Keena gruffly, then gives orders to the others.

"He says they need to find shelter before dark. We have to go with them."

"Tell him we can't. We aren't going in the same direction."

"We don't have a choice. He's in charge," Keena points out.

Two hunters lift the injured man and support him between them. Keena and Shinoni find themselves in the middle of the group. Spear butts nudge them into a brisk trot as they silently move into the tall grass. A lion's deep cough echoes in the distance as the first flush of sunset traces a warning in the sky over the open grassland.

Shinoni feels the rumble of hunger as they move farther and farther through the swaying grass. She moves closer to Keena, drawing unexpected warmth and security from her presence, even if she is a Krag. *Maybe she can be a friend.* Shinoni blinks back tears, realizing that her Kula friends are dead. Storm clouds blow in and a chill rain begins to fall. Gandar's hunters pick up their relentless pace in the growing twilight.

Keena sighs. It's good to feel safe in a group as she trots, surrounded by burly Krag hunters. She looks across at Shinoni, who worked so hard to help the young hunter. Their safety will swiftly disappear if Leeswi decides to take his breath. None of this would have happened if she hadn't been so reckless. Still, she's not too bad for a Kula.

Keena moves closer to Shinoni until they are shoulder to shoulder, facing the dangers of the coming night together.

— 17 —

SHINONI AND KEENA crouch under the rock over-hang where Gandar's hunters have set up camp. The injured man lies by a glowing hearth, moaning feverishly. The other hunters mutter and grumble as they watch him.

Shinoni examines the darkness beyond the fire, looking for some way to escape. The rain still falls, and the shrill hunting cries of the hyenas echo in the distance. Better to stay here until the light returns. She shivers and moves closer to the protection of the firelight.

"Why did they help us if they now take us prisoner?" she asks Keena.

"I'm a Krag," Keena says. "Perhaps they thought you were one, too, before they got a good look at you."

"What will they do with us if he dies?" Shinoni asks.

"They might take us with them — as mates or captives."

"Both of us?"

"I don't know." Keena throws a stick into the fire, avoiding Shinoni's eyes. She nods toward the injured hunter. "He'll likely die soon."

"Do these hunters carry water with them?" Shinoni asks. "He needs to drink."

Keena approaches Gandar and speaks with him. He takes a skin bag from around his waist and tips it upside down before handing it to her.

Keena gives the bag to Shinoni. "They collect water in this, but it's empty. He says you can fill it."

"Me? I'd be dead before I ventured very far."

"He says you caused his pain, you should get the water. If you're smart enough to heal him you can find a way."

Shinoni takes the skin container and stands at the edge of the rock outcropping. The damp stone presses cold and hard against her back as she stretches her arm into the night, holding the bag open to the lifesaving downpour. Over the sound of the rain, she hears rustling in the brush nearby. She peers into the darkness. Yellow eyes reflect the flames and move stealthily toward her.

Shinoni gasps, pulling back into the safety of the overhang, the circle of hunters watching her every move. She shakily places the bag on the ground, careful not to spill the precious liquid. She rummages in her pouch for remnants of the fever plants, then mashes them and scrapes them into the water. The fire crackles as she props the bag near the edge of the flames with a stick.

Gandar and the other hunters move closer, muttering among themselves. As the brew heats up and begins to simmer, a pungent odour like rotting earth rises from it. Shinoni uses her stick to move the bag away from the flames, holding her breath, willing the brew not to spill. She places her fingertip in the water to test the heat and inhales the rich aroma of the herbs, as she's seen Reza do. She cups the bag in her hands, wincing from the heat. Her singsong chant swirls in the overhang as she stands and heads toward the injured Krag.

One hunter snarls and lunges to stop her, but Gandar pulls him back. He nods at Shinoni and leans forward to watch her.

She cradles the hunter's head in her lap. Sweat beads glisten on his face as he struggles to breathe. He's young — maybe on his first hunt. She holds the potion to his lips. He sips and coughs, then sips some more as she chants softly.

As Shinoni tends to the injured hunter, Keena sits by the fire and watches the rowdy and arrogant Kula girl gently comfort and care for this young hunter. She imagines how it would feel if it were Kreel lying there. It would be nice to know how to heal.

Shinoni looks up and meets Keena's eyes. Keena moves beside her. "Your grandmother taught you well."

"Yes, but she made me work hard." A tear slips down Shinoni's cheek. "I wish I had a lion or bear claw to help this hunter," Shinoni whispers.

"Why, Kula? How would that help?" Keena's breath catches in her throat.

"I'd ask the spirit of the lion to enter him and make his spirit strong enough to fight the laugh devil spirit that's killing him." Shinoni glances over her shoulder at the hunters moving restlessly behind them.

Keena places a hand on Shinoni's shoulder and fumbles under her own fur cape. She withdraws the hide-wrapped, bloodstained packet and unwraps the lion claw her mother gave her for protection. She hesitates as she sees Ubra's face and hears her plea that Keena keep the claw close to her body. Keena knows the risks her mother took to keep her safe. She smiles sadly, then hands the claw to Shinoni.

"How did you come by this?" Shinoni murmurs as she fondles the deadly curve of the giant claw. It glints ominously in the firelight. Without waiting for Keena's answer, she stands up and circles the claw several times over the injured Krag's head, chest, and leg.

"Heee-hiiiya hee-haaa." She chants vigorously, then lays the claw on the hunter's chest and sits by Keena.

Gandar and the other hunters come over to look at their wounded companion, who is now sleeping with the claw gleaming on his fur-covered chest. They shake their heads and move into the shadows to sleep. Gander lingers by his brother's side before rejoining the others.

As she and Keena settle close to the fire, Shinoni repeats her question. "How did you come by the lion claw?"

"My mother gave it to me. She cut it from the paw of a dead lion that had stalked and killed my people." Keena chokes back tears. "She wanted it to protect me when Haken took me away. She said the lion hated Haken because he killed it."

"Your mother sounds like a brave woman."

"She's brave. It'll be good to see her again when I return to my hearth." Keena hesitates. "You think each animal has a spirit?"

"Of course. You really don't know this, Krag?"

"You can talk to them, get them to help you?" Keena persists.

"It's easy if you know how," Shinoni says.

"You're strange, Kula." Keena rolls up in her cloak and turns her back. The girl reminds her of Sabra when he brags about Kula ways. She closes her eyes and falls asleep.

Shinoni sits watching the young Krag hunter through the smoky haze of the fire as the animal spirits battle for his life. The call of a lion echoes faintly in the distance.

Reza always did the healing in their camp. This is the first time Shinoni has attempted it alone. This time, she is the medicine woman. Grandmother would be proud.

Finally, exhausted by the events of the day, Shinoni can stay awake no longer. She lies down next to Keena and falls instantly to sleep.

Early morning mist is rising over the Krags' camp when Shinoni awakes to excited shouts. She bolts upright, confused at where she is. Keena is shaking her by the shoulder.

"Look, Shinoni! The lion spirit won."

Shinoni rubs the sleep fog from her eyes and looks around the rock shelter. The injured Krag is sitting up, smiling with the others gathered around him. They gabble excitedly and point to her.

Gandar leaves the group and hurries over to Keena and Shinoni. He brings the lion claw and squats beside them, smiling from ear to ear. His words tumble out in a relieved torrent as he points from Shinoni to the injured hunter and back to her.

"He says you look like a skinny Kula girl, but you're a great healer. He thanks you for saving his brother's life."

"Tell him I'm glad his brother's better. His spirit must be strong, or the lion spirit wouldn't have helped him."

Keena translates for Gandar, and he holds out the claw.

Shinoni makes no move to take the claw. "He can keep it, in case they need its help again." She looks at Keena. "Unless you want it back, Keena? It's yours."

"The claw already kept me safe by helping the hunter survive. It's done what my mother wanted. I will tell him he can keep it." She turns to Gandar.

He beams, then hands Shinoni a deerskin pouch. She opens it and finds it's filled with strips of dried deer meat. Then he hands her two hide bags filled with water and secured with wooden plugs to keep the water inside. Gandar makes a sweeping gesture toward the open plains beyond the rock overhang as he speaks.

"He's happy about the claw and he wants us to take this meat to help us on our journey," Keena translates, although the meaning's clear. "He says we're free to leave if we want — or we can travel with them."

"The less time I spend with Krags the better," Shinoni says. She looks at Keena closely. "Perhaps you should go with them."

"I suppose you'd like that, but I think I'll stay with you." Keena chuckles. "Someone has to keep you out of trouble."

"That's your choice," Shinoni says, but a pleasant warmth spreads through her body at Keena's words.

Keena picks up her fur cape from the ground, where it served as her sleeping mat. She takes the precious pouch of dried meat and the water bags from Shinoni and secures them in a fold of the cape close to her body. Then Shinoni and Keena plunge out into the tall grasses to continue their journey.

18

T HE SUN RIDES LOW in the sky when Shinoni and Keena carry brush up a rocky slope to a small cave. Their perch overlooks the surrounding plains and hills. They stack the brush waist high in a semicircle around the opening. Once the kindling's in place, Keena settles wearily inside their shelter.

Shinoni lingers by the entrance, testing the wind for danger. The undulating grasslands sprawl below their shelter in every direction. Clusters of woodland dot the plains, good hiding places for predators. Hills rise in the distance at the foot of the glacier. That's where the Krag girl says she lived with her family. What family would send her so far away with such a dangerous man as Haken?

Sunset turns the sky to crimson and violet as the cool evening breeze shakes the bushes below them.

Keena joins Shinoni at the entrance and peers into the dusk creeping over the land. It sneaks up the hillside to the open mouth of their refuge.

"Hurry and light the fire, Kula. It's getting dark."

"You know Haken can see the fire. And so can the beasts."

"If you don't light it soon, they'll only find our bones in the morning."

"You really don't know how to start fire?" Shinoni teases, but she hurries to unpack her flints and firestones.

Keena chafes at Shinoni's words. "I can move flames from one fire to start another. I just can't start a flame where there isn't one burning nearby."

"What happens if your people travel, as we're doing?" Shinoni asks.

"Krag women don't often travel without males. With my people, men start new fires and women tend them. We're the protectors of fire." Keena fidgets in the deepening gloom.

"I can do both." Shinoni puffs up her chest proudly and takes Keena's arm. "Come here. You'll be the first Krag female to learn to make fire."

Keena moves slowly toward Shinoni. Her breath catches in her throat and she gasps. *Is Leeswi warning me*

that I must not do this? What if the temperamental Earth Mother snatches away my breath? No! If a Kula girl can do this, so can she. Keena sits beside Shinoni.

Shinoni positions Keena's hands on the flint and firestone and shows her how to strike sparks into the dry tinder grass. "Now you try," Shinoni says.

Keena fumbles with the flint and firestone. Nothing happens. But she is determined. She thinks of her mother cutting the lion claw in the dark and tries again. Finally, after several tries, a tiny flame sparks in the hearth.

"I did it," Keena gasps. The spark grows as she and Shinoni gently fan it. Keena's cheeks redden and her eyes grow wide. *She* made this fire where there was none before.

"Don't spend all night admiring your fire. Spread it around." Shinoni chuckles. They put branches into the flame and spread it along the brush pile until they have a glowing barrier to protect them from the terrors of the night.

Keena's stomach rumbles. "Let's eat," she says.

Shinoni and Keena finish eating most of the meat Gandar gave them, then spread their cloaks on the ground to sleep.

Suddenly, Keena dives behind Shinoni, digging her fingers deep into Shinoni's shoulder. "Look. Something's coming," she whispers. She peeks over

Shinoni's shoulder. A glowing pair of eyes reflects eerily from the bushes at the base of the rock slope.

"Whatever it is, it won't come through the fire." Shinoni's words are brave, but her voice shakes. She picks up a burning stick and stares out of their shelter warily.

"It's coming closer. *It is!*" Keena screams.

A grey shape hurtles over the flames and knocks Shinoni to the ground, causing her to drop the burning torch. Tewa licks her face. Shinoni sits up and retrieves the torch, laughing with relief.

Keena slips out of the crevice where she'd crammed her body. "Can't you stop her from jumping at people?"

"You were happy when she jumped Haken." Shinoni rumples the wolf's thick fur.

"I thought you said beasts wouldn't come over the flames." Keena creeps closer and cautiously strokes Tewa's fur.

"Tewa isn't like other beasts."

The girls lie down with the large wolf between them and drop into a deep sleep, feeling a little safer in the night.

19

"OW, KULA, WHAT'RE YOU DOING?" Keena shouts as a stone thuds off her head. "That's not funny. See how you like it." She scoops up a rock to retaliate, but Shinoni lies snoring on her sleeping mat.

Thunk. Thunk. Thunk. Keena scrambles to her feet as more stones land beside her. She shakes Shinoni. "The Earth Mother's angry. We can't stay here."

"What? Stop it, Krag, I'm getting up." Shinoni coughs as dust swirls in the early morning half-light. Tewa sinks her teeth into Shinoni's tunic and pulls her off her sleeping mat.

Shinoni's fully awake now. "Come on, let's go!" She scrambles to pack her firestones and throw her cape over her shoulders.

"It's getting worse. Leeswi will take our breath." Keena stamps out the dying embers of the fire.

The roof of the cave starts to crack as Shinoni, Keena, and Tewa slide down the loose shale on the slope outside the entrance. A herd of horses gallops across the plains below. They snort and neigh in terror as the ground under their hooves shudders and groans.

A short distance away from their shelter, Keena turns and faces the rock slope. She takes the remaining meat from the pouch and lays it on a flat rock. She touches her forehead to the earth and shouts in the Krag tongue, "Ka-kwa-rau-set, Leeswi. Leeswi. Krag-nu-kik-kwac."

"Come on, Krag. What're you doing?" Shinoni screams.

A deafening boom rips through the air, and an avalanche of rocks and boulders thunders down the hillside. The cave where they just slept disappears in a hail of debris.

Keena ignores Shinoni and shrieks above the din. "Ka-kwa-rau-set, Leeswi. Leeswi. Krag-nu-kik-kwac."

Tewa cocks her head and whines, then steps over Keena's prostrated form. She snaps the meat off the rock and chews it with relish. Keena leaps to her feet, her face twisted in horror, as Shinoni laughs out loud.

"Eeeeee-yaaaaa!" Keena's wail echoes over the sound of the earth's rampage. "Fool! Don't laugh. That was an offering to Leeswi, the Earth Mother, so she'll spare us."

"Sorry, Krag." Shinoni chokes back her laughter. "Your face is as red as your hair."

"Stupid wolf. We're doomed," Keena moans. "It was too small an offering, anyway. Atuk would've given an ibex or a deer."

"Come on." Shinoni tugs on Keena's arm. Dust and debris fall around them. "If this Lee Swee, or whatever her name is, is so powerful, she'll know you tried. That was tonight's food, by the way."

"You don't understand. Leeswi will be very angry."

Tewa hightails it into the grass. A large rock crashes beside Shinoni and she follows the wolf, dragging Keena with her. "Calm down, Krag. If she's mad at anyone, it's me, right? I'm the one who laughed."

Suddenly the ground around them buckles and groans with the force of an earthquake. A split yawns open in front of them. Keena is flung backward, but Shinoni is sucked into the rent in the earth. She frantically claws at branches and rocks to break her slide, but she disappears over the edge of the jagged hole.

"Aaaaaaeeeee!" The earth's rumble drowns out Shinoni's scream.

"Shinoni, nooo!" Keena shouts. *Leeswi has devoured the foolish Kula.* Keena crawls on her stomach to the edge of the pit. A steamy sulphur odour, like

119

a thousand stink winds, billows up, making her roll backward, gagging.

"Help, I can't hold on. Keena, help me!" Shinoni shrieks from below.

Keena forces herself back to the edge and peers over the rim. Shinoni dangles precariously, clinging to roots in the crumbling soil. She kicks her feet, trying to get a toehold.

Keena reaches down and grasps Shinoni's wrists. "Come on, Kula. Don't give up. Fight!" She inches backward, flat on her stomach. Her muscles are straining and sweat runs from her brow. Her arms are too short and she's losing her grip. But she has to keep trying. She pulls harder, hauling Shinoni closer to the surface. Shinoni finally reaches the top, where she's able to throw her elbows over the edge and drag herself out.

The earth shudders one more time, and with a dull belch the crevice closes. Shinoni and Keena lie on the still-moving ground, clinging to each other, dirt-smeared and exhausted. They stare at each other in horror.

"You Krags have a pretty mean earth mother."

"I thought you were really gone, Kula."

"I would've been, if you hadn't come." Shinoni manages a wobbly grin.

"Leeswi spared you," Keena says. "Don't laugh again."

"I don't feel much like laughing."

The girls get to their feet, nerves still jangling. Their legs wobble as they set off to continue their journey across the quake-ravaged plain. Evidence of the disaster is everywhere: rock slides, uprooted trees, boulders strewn about. They walk gingerly, expecting the earth to heave up again.

Shinoni stops and turns in a circle, scanning their surroundings. "It's too quiet, Krag. Where are the birds and animals?"

"They're smarter than you," Keena replies. "They know the Earth Mother's still angry." She jumps at an ominous rumbling in the earth. In the distance, a horse neighs frantically.

Shinoni swivels her head, trying to locate the sound. "It's over there." She leaps up and down, pointing to a distant rock outcropping sticking above the grass. "Come on."

"We've got to keep going." Keena points in the opposite direction, toward the line of hills. "My people are that way, in the high country."

"Aren't you curious? It sounds like it's in trouble," Shinoni wheedles.

"We've enough trouble of our own." Keena digs her heels into the earth and refuses to budge.

"My people call them ulu, wind runners. I'd like to see a live one up close. Wouldn't you?" Shinoni coaxes.

Keena shakes her head. "If it's injured, it'll attract predators." Why does this Kula girl have to be so curious all the time? Who cares about a horse? Keena just wants to find her family — and Kreel.

"Perhaps your Leeswi wants us to go that way. Maybe she doesn't want the ulu's breath and is sending us a message to go there."

Keena ponders this unlikely possibility as Shinoni watches her closely. "We eat horses. Leeswi wouldn't send us to help one." She frowns at Shinoni. "You're not Krag. Why would Leeswi send you a message?"

"Perhaps the message is for you," Shinoni says. "Since Leeswi spared me, perhaps she wants us both to go to the horse."

Keena sits on the ground, torn between her desire to return home and the need to listen to the bidding of the unpredictable Earth Mother. "Maybe Leeswi wants to provide us with food." She turns toward the neighing. "I'll go with you, but we must be quick."

— 20 —

SHINONI'S LONG LEGS clamber up the rock outcropping, sending loose shale raining down on Keena, who is struggling up the slope behind her. When Shinoni reaches the top, she looks down on a young horse, alone and trapped in a tangle of willows that toppled in the earthquake. Clumps of branches and roots pin the little filly against a pile of fallen rocks. Her sharp-edged hooves scrabble and slip on the rubble as she works to free her legs. Her barrel-shaped chest and rib cage heave with exertion, and sweaty white foam lathers her reddish-brown coat and the black stripe down her back. Her soft brown eyes are glazed with fear.

"She's not full grown. She's calling for her family," Shinoni says.

"Families don't always help you," Keena says, her voice tight.

"She won't last long making such a racket. Something will kill her."

"We could kill her while she's trapped. We need food."

"Look, Krag, she's a wind runner. I saw a hunter ride one once."

"You were in the dream world, surely."

"No, it's true," Shinoni says. "Let's see if we can free her."

She slides down the rest of the hill without waiting for Keena but slows as she nears the trapped horse. The filly trembles, eyes wild with fear, as Shinoni pushes aside some of the tangled branches. Shinoni reaches past an upturned tree root to touch the velvety nose. The horse snorts at the human scent, laying back her ears, squealing and clapping her teeth.

"Hey, Ulu, little sister. I want to help you." Shinoni stands very still and speaks softly. She takes off her cloak and covers the horse's eyes. Ulu calms down immediately. Shinoni sings her soothing chant as she takes the rope from her pouch and slips it around the wind runner's neck.

Keena keeps her distance from the horse. "Be careful," she says. "She's so big, even if she's young. Why are you covering her head?"

"Maybe if she can't see the ugly Krag, she won't be so frightened." Shinoni grasps a branch and works it out of the tangle. "Can you help me?"

"If that wolf comes now, she'll make a meal of her." Keena tugs a twisted tree root from the pile.

"Tewa won't bother her if she's mine," Shinoni says. She scans the surrounding plain. The wolf's nowhere in sight.

"The horse isn't yours, and the wolf only knows she's hungry," Keena says.

"It's no use arguing with a Krag. You know so little about animals."

"You think you know animals, Kula, but I know how to use them to feed myself." Keena sits down, arms folded, as Shinoni pulls away more of the branches. At last there's just one large tree root blocking the horse's path, and Keena joins Shinoni in hauling it away.

Ulu, her eyes still covered, turns and lashes out with her hind legs.

"Duck, Krag!" Shinoni grabs Keena's arm and yanks her down as a hoof whizzes past her ear. Shinoni gets up, dusting herself off. "You should be more careful. You almost had your head knocked off." She pulls Keena to her feet, then moves closer to the horse. "She doesn't seem to be too badly injured. Just some scratches."

"She almost injured *us*, Kula." Keena hangs back, anxiously eyeing the horse. "Why doesn't she run?"

"She'll run like the wind once she can see." Shinoni speaks softly as she nears the horse. She climbs on a large boulder beside the twitching filly and beckons Keena.

"Climb up here and we'll throw our legs over her back at the same time."

Keena squeaks in disbelief. "You're the reckless one, not me. I'm not doing that."

"Of course, you don't know how. Only Kulas ride wind runners," Shinoni says. "I'll show you how, then we can ride and Haken will never catch us."

Keena jumps to her feet. Her jaw drops and her eyes bulge in their sockets. "Surely not even you would do such a foolish thing."

Shinoni brushes away Keena's doubt. She has always longed to ride a wind runner, and she won't let the Krag's fear stop her. She swings a leg over Ulu's back and hooks her heels around her belly. The horse flinches. Her chest heaves and Shinoni can feel her powerful leg muscles coil to spring. Shinoni rubs the filly's neck, still lathered with sweat.

"Take it easy, wind runner. We're just going to have a little ride." She grabs the scruffy mane and the rope before pulling the cloak away from Ulu's eyes. The horse stands perfectly still for a heartbeat. Then, with the energy of pure panic, she rears up high, slams her hooves down hard, and twirls around, bucking.

Shinoni sails through the air, landing against the tree stump with a thud. Ulu gallops off, snorting and squealing, into the swaying grasses.

"It's good you showed me how to ride a wind runner." Keena helps Shinoni to her feet. "Can you walk? We must get going before Haken finds us."

"I'll know how to do it better next time," Shinoni gasps, winded and bruised. She takes one step, then another. Her legs seem to be working, but her ankle twists under her and pain shoots up to her thigh. She shakes her head to clear her vision and wipes the blood dripping from her nose with the back of her hand.

"Come, Kula, we've wasted too much time here." Keena begins to walk briskly away, and Shinoni hobbles behind her. Keena turns and offers Shinoni her sturdy shoulder for support as they head back in the direction of the foothills.

Before long there's a rustling in the grass behind them.

"Something's following us. Head for that tree." Shinoni points toward a scraggly pine standing solitary in the distance. They quicken their pace, chests pounding.

"We won't make it. Can you run?" says Keena.

Pain shoots up Shinoni's leg. "You run. I can't." She ducks behind a boulder and takes out her sling. Keena crouches beside her.

The rustling gets closer. Shinoni raises her sling. A wedge-shaped head with flicking ears and soft brown eyes appears above the vegetation. Shinoni and Keena gape in surprise as Ulu steps out of the tall grass with a chortling whinny.

"I think Leeswi really does want us to eat her," Keena mutters, putting the boulder between herself and the horse. Ulu takes a few steps closer and nickers plaintively. "Come on, we have to go." Keena pulls Shinoni back into the grass.

"Wait, maybe she's thirsty." She hands her drinking bag to Keena and cups her hands together. "Here, pour some water into my hands."

"We need the water, Kula," Keena protests, but she does what Shinoni asks.

Shinoni offers her outstretched hands with the precious water to the horse. Ulu cocks her ears forward and comes to Shinoni. She dips her velvet nose into Shinoni's cupped palms and drinks. She licks Shinoni's palms, and Keena pours the rest of the water into Shinoni's hands. Ulu drinks again, then moves back into the grass.

"Kula, come on." Keena offers Shinoni her shoulder and they resume their course for the foothills. "Let's hope there's a stream on the way. The wolf ate our meat and you gave our water to the horse."

Shinoni limps heavily as her ankle swells and

throbs. They stop to rest briefly, plopping down into the grass.

Keena suddenly sits up and points into the tall, swaying grass. "Look, Kula, something's moving there in the grass."

Shinoni stands as tall as she can, wincing against the pain, and shades her eyes. "It's Ulu! She's following us."

"Why would that foolish beast follow us when our people hunt them?" Keena snorts.

"She's lost her family like we have, Keena."

As the girls walk on, the horse continues to follow them. She stops now and then and looks over her shoulder, as if she's not sure what she should do, but she shortens the distance between them. At last she's only a neck's length behind, and her continuous nickering murmur soothes the girls.

Shadows are lengthening when they stop to rest. Ulu halts beside them, lowering her head and nibbling gently on Shinoni's hair.

"Ho, Krag, she likes me." Shinoni stands and rubs her fingers in Ulu's stiff mane.

"You know, we won't reach shelter before the dark time unless we move faster." Keena cautiously moves beside Shinoni and whispers, "Perhaps you'll have another chance to ride."

"Would you ride, too?" Shinoni tries to keep her voice soft and calm.

Keena nods. "It would be better to fall off a horse than be eaten by a lion."

Shinoni's rope still dangles from Ulu's neck as the horse grazes beside them. Shinoni wraps her fingers in Ulu's mane and puts her good foot in Keena's cupped hands. With a burst of pain, she throws her injured leg over Ulu's broad back as Keena boosts her up. Ulu tosses her head and neighs shrilly, stamping her feet but staying put. Shinoni reaches down and pulls Keena up behind her. Ulu's ears go back and her teeth chatter while her body trembles.

"Hang on, Krag. She's going to run." Shinoni clutches the rope and works her fingers tightly into Ulu's mane. Her knees clasp the horse's heaving sides, her injured ankle flopping below.

"You hang on. You've got the rope." Keena's muscular arms wrap around Shinoni's waist, her stubby fingers interlocking in a death grip. She clings like a bramble as the horse gallops toward the hills. But Shinoni doesn't mind. She's riding a wind runner!

The sun hangs low in the sky when Ulu slows to a walk. Shinoni relaxes as Ulu stops to examine a mound of steaming dung. She pushes her nose close to the pile and she snorts in excitement. The filly bobs her head and Shinoni grabs her mane just in time as she takes off running. Keena tightens her hold around Shinoni's middle.

"She's found her family's scent." Shinoni is excited, despite the pain in her ankle and her hands, now blistered from the rope and Ulu's stiff mane.

"Good. If we fall off there's a hill with caves nearby."

At last Ulu slows to a walk and lowers her head. Finally, exhausted, she stops. Keena tumbles off her back and helps Shinoni slide down the horse's rounded belly. Their legs are unsteady after the unaccustomed horseback ride.

"I don't think I'll ever sit comfortably again." Keena winces and rubs her backside.

"We rode!" Shinoni laughs. "It was like flying. I told you they're wind runners."

Keena looks at the deepening shadows. "The sun's going down. We need to start a fire."

"There are caves above." Shinoni points at openings in the pale limestone rock.

Keena nods at the horse. "What about her? Can she climb?"

Just then Ulu snorts loudly, throwing back her head with fear. Shinoni grips the rope tightly and swivels to see what's spooked the horse. A short distance away, Tewa sits on her haunches, head cocked, eyes glinting, watching them.

"Tewa, the wind runner is a friend." Shinoni moves between the wolf and horse.

Keena moves beside her, spreading her arms to

help block the view. "I don't think she has a problem eating friends."

Tewa gets up, stretches, and picks up a dead hare lying beside her in the grass. She ignores the frightened horse and bounds up the hillside toward the caves with the bloody hare swinging in her jaws.

"Ho, Ulu. Tewa won't try to eat you. She has food already." Shinoni rubs the horse's neck.

Keena stands on her tiptoes and points to the valley. "Look, there's a herd of horses down there." The sound of neighing carries on the evening breeze. Ulu turns her head and nickers longingly.

"Thank you, wind runner. Go, your clan is waiting." Shinoni removes the rope.

Ulu races toward her family. She whinnies excitedly and the herd answers. A small stallion gallops to meet her. He sniffs her, then chases her in among the other mares.

"At least she's home." Shinoni sighs. "I'd like to ride her again."

"We could've eaten her, you know." Keena's voice is gruff, but she smiles.

Shinoni throws an arm across Keena's shoulder. "Looks like Tewa has brought tonight's meal. Maybe she's sorry about eating your offering to Leeswi."

"The wolf's sorry for filling her belly?" Keena laughs. "Your foot looks as big as your head." Keena offers her arm to Shinoni as they climb the hill toward Tewa and their shelter.

"Do you think Leeswi's sorry she filled her belly with me?" Shinoni chuckles. "She did spit me out."

Keena gasps and shakes Shinoni. "Kula, never question what Leeswi does. She gives breath. She takes breath." Keena scans the hillside, her eyes anxious, as an icy breeze rustles the shrubbery. "Don't make her angry again, or we might never see our people."

21

SHINONI HOBBLES UP the hillside beside Keena, both of them gathering kindling in the growing dusk. Every step sends barbs of pain shooting into her ankle, but she knows they must start a fire to protect themselves. Soon the four-legged hunters will prowl, looking for meat. She gulps, then sees Tewa lounging near an opening in the rock, calmly licking the dead hare. One of the hunters is already here, and luckily they are members of her pack. Tewa has brought them food and she'll keep them safe.

"Tewa's chosen a shelter for us." Shinoni moves to the cave mouth, then stops so suddenly that Keena crashes into her and drops her load of firewood.

"Oh, you're clumsy, Kula."

"Shhh." Shinoni points. "Someone lit a fire here

recently." A blackened hearth lies near the entrance, its hollow filled with charred wood and ashes.

"Could it be Haken?" Keena clutches her shoulder.

Shinoni looks at Tewa nibbling on the hare. "Tewa wouldn't be so calm if it was Haken or some other danger. It's too dark to search for another place now. Whoever was here has moved on." She enters the shelter and begins striking her firestones to start a flame.

Keena fumbles in the twilight, collecting her dropped kindling.

"Come inside, Keena. Whoever was here left enough wood for our fire."

"I don't want our flames to burn low before the sun wakes the sky." Keena hauls her wood into the cave. Tewa follows her and drops the half-eaten hare beside the hearth. The wolf yips and disappears into the night. "Do you think she's afraid to be here?" Keena asks.

"Tewa left us food and went to hunt for her own supper. She wouldn't leave us if it wasn't safe."

"How do you know that? She's a wolf after all."

"Tewa's a wolf, but she's my spirit guide. I trust her." Keena thrusts a stick into the growing fire and spreads the flame into the brush and kindling stacked near the entrance. "Does your leg hurt you?" she asks. "It looks bad." Keena settles beside Shinoni and pokes her in the ankle, which has swollen to twice its normal size and is the colour of overripe berries against her brown skin.

"It burns like sparks." Shinoni slaps Keena's hand away.

"Will you be able to walk next sun time? We don't have the horse, you know."

"I'll look for the swelling plant when we leave here." Shinoni chooses two short sticks from the kindling and places one on either side of her ankle. "Hold these, Keena, while I tie them. They'll keep my ankle straight." She uses her knife to cut strands of deerskin from her cloak and binds the wood to her leg.

Keena explores the shelter as Shinoni tends to her injured ankle and starts to skin and gut the hare. The cave is larger than it looks from outside, and the far wall is cloaked in shadows. Keena lights a torch from the fire and looks around. "Better be sure nothing's hiding in the gloom," she says. She walks toward the back of the cave. "Hey, Kula, there are marks on the wall. Do you know what they are?"

Shinoni skewers the hare on a stick and places it over the fire, then turns her attention to the wall. Red and black symbols are spread along the rock surface, dancing before her eyes in the flickering light. "I've seen those marks before, in our sacred cave. Kulas were here."

"Your people make those marks? Why? What do they mean?"

"Shazur showed them to me, but Haken killed him before he could tell me their meaning." The pain of losing her father masks the pain in her ankle. She limps to the wall and examines the marks. "No Kula woman has seen them but me."

The smell of charred meat rises from the fire, and Keena hurries to turn the hare. "Come, Kula, our meal is too important to burn because of some marks on the wall."

Shinoni lingers, examining the symbols. She traces their outlines with her fingertips. There is a cluster of red dots off to one side and, at a distance from the others, four dots, two large and two small, near a long wavy line. She points excitedly at a mark higher on the rock wall. "Look! I've made a mark such as this with my own hand." She reaches up and places her hand beside the much larger red handprint. "The hunter who made these other marks left this here. Perhaps it's his message to the spirits."

"What spirits, Kula? Is that why you put your hand mark on the wall?"

"My father and I both put our hand marks on the wall in the sacred cave." Shinoni hobbles back to join Keena at the fire. "He asked the spirits to forgive me and accept me as a spirit helper."

"Why forgive you? What did you do?" Keena takes a bite from a hare leg. "Do you annoy the Kula spirits, too?" she jokes.

But Shinoni doesn't laugh. "I entered our sacred cave and watched my father make animals live on the rock walls," she whispers. "Only the shaman and hunters are allowed in there — not women."

"How did he make animals live on the walls?"

Shinoni picks up a pointed stick from the kindling and smoothes the dirt on the floor between them. Slowly and carefully, without saying a word, she draws the form of a horse with a rounded belly and then a deer with forked antlers. Finally, the pointed face, eyes, and ears of a wolf appear under her stick.

"What magic is this?" Keena marvels. "You can make spirits of the beasts come to life?"

"Well, the ones Shazur made on the walls were bigger and had colour, which gave them life. But they were like this." Shinoni flushes with pleasure at Keena's reaction.

Keena hands Shinoni a chunk of meat from the fire. "You'd better eat some of the hare unless you can bring that deer to life."

Shinoni and Keena finish their meal and settle down by the fire. Keena soon falls asleep, but Shinoni stares at the flickering symbols on the wall far into the night. Will she ever be able to decipher their meaning?

22

$\int$ HINONI AND KEENA leave the rock shelter and its mysterious symbols and travel along a game trail, past hills cloaked in conifers. Leeswi swoops low, ruffling Keena's hair. The crisp scent of pine needles fills her nostrils. It smells like home.

"There must be a path along here leading up to the high country where my family lives." Keena hurries ahead, searching for a way through the forest. But soon, as the trees thin out and dip into a ravine, her shoulders slump. Tangled bushes and scattered willows follow a meandering stream. It seems there is no path home here.

"Come on, we can fill our water bags." Shinoni leans heavily on the stick she's using as a crutch. "There could be swelling plants here." She parts the vegetation.

Keena joins her. "What do they look like?" she asks.

"They have small leathery leaves and thick stalks," Shinoni replies. "The flower petals are tiny and gold, but they'll be shrivelled and brown now, so they won't be easy to find." She gasps as she steps down too hard.

"Does it hurt a lot?" Keena asks.

"It throbs like stepping in a nest of fire ants."

They double their efforts to find the right plants.

"Ah, there they are," Shinoni says. A patch of the plants spreads along the shoreline under the reeds. "Thank you, Grandmother," Shinoni whispers. She up-roots several herbs with her crutch and places them in her pouch.

Keena bends to examine something in the mud near the stream. "Footprints. Two people passed here not long ago."

Shinoni places her good foot beside them. "One's close to my size and the other is much larger. Maybe a hunter and a woman." She places her hand across the width of the smaller footprint. "They aren't wide like yours, so maybe Kula." She pauses. "Maybe the hunter who made the marks in the cave."

"If they're Kula, will they be friendly?" Keena's own footprint in the mud is dwarfed by the hunter's large one.

"They won't be from my group, but I'd like to get closer for a look. Maybe I can talk to them."

"You hope the hunter will tell you what the marks mean?"

"Don't you also want to know?"

"The marks mean nothing to my people." Keena hesitates. This matters to the Kula girl. "Still, we can get closer to have a look at them."

They climb the trail out of the ravine until it opens into a grassy meadow. Two figures are barely visible in the distance, moving toward the shelter of the hillside.

By the time Keena and Shinoni peer over some scrubby bushes near the hillside caves, the sun hangs low in the sky. Ahead of them, a tall brown-skinned woman digs tubers from the ground with a sharpened stick and places them into a woven willow bag. On her back is another bundle wrapped in fur. This bundle moves and makes a high-pitched mewling noise. The woman sways back and forth chanting softly. "Aiiia, aiiaa, aaii ..."

"She's carrying a small one on her back," Shinoni whispers. "She's calming it with her song. Many Kula mothers do this."

"Where's the hunter, the one with the big footprints?" Keena cranes her neck, trying to see beyond the shrubbery.

A spear with a flint point, sharp and deadly as an eagle talon, whizzes past their heads with a shrill whistle. *Thunk*. It impales the bush in front of them. Shinoni and Keena drop to the ground.

Shinoni looks up. Their attacker stands behind them. "We mean you no harm," Shinoni says. "We're just travelling this way looking for shelter." She stretches out her hand, palm up in the Kula gesture of friendship.

The hunter towers above them clutching a curved spear thrower and two more spears. The deadly blade of one points directly at them. The hunter's face is twisted into a ferocious snarl that slowly fades as he lowers his spear. Shinoni's outstretched hand trembles as he bends over, examining the girls. "You're Kula, but you travel with a female of the Strange Ones. Why?"

Keena holds her breath, wondering what he will do with her.

"Her people are called Krags. We're both searching for our families and travel together." Shinoni stands up shakily and helps Keena to her feet.

"Two girls travelling alone, without hunters?"

The man reaches to retrieve his spear from the bush and Keena sees that he, too, carries a fur bundle on his back. As he bends, the bundle moves. The same mewling cries as those from the bundle on the woman's back tumble out. Keena stares, mouth open. "A hunter with a young one on his back?"

Shinoni shushes her as the woman approaches and stands beside the man.

"Ardak, be careful with Bril." The woman pats the bundle on his back.

"He's fine, Rena, but we need to get him and Tark to the cave." The hunter nods at Shinoni and Keena. "These girls travel alone. They need shelter, and we have room."

Shinoni puts one arm around Keena's shoulder and extends the other hand, palm up, toward the woman. "We mean you no harm," Shinoni says.

The woman hesitates but then beckons Shinoni and Keena to follow them. Shadows creep down the hillside.

"I thought they'd leave us out here for the beasts," Keena says. She supports Shinoni as she hobbles to reach the safety of the cave.

"Kulas help each other," Shinoni says. "You and I help each other, too."

Ardak pushes aside some brush and reveals the opening into the family's shelter. As Shinoni and Keena linger just inside the entrance, a wolf howls in the distance.

"What if Tewa comes? Will she eat the small ones?" Keena asks.

"I don't think she'll come," Shinoni says. "But if she does and sees they're friends, she won't harm them."

"They'd be a good meal for her." Keena shakes her head, unconvinced. "If she comes, the hunter will try to kill her to protect his young ones."

"Come inside, girls. You're safer in here than outside with the prowling beasts," Ardak calls. He extends his hand palm up. "I'm sorry I frightened you. I didn't know who, or what, was in those bushes. We have to be careful with the small ones." The firelight dances across his lined face, which breaks into a broad smile. His dark eyes are friendly. "We've food and room for you. Come and tell us where you're going."

Ardak sits down and begins skinning a fat marmot, and Rena nurses both young ones at once. Their small brown fingers clasp the fur trim on her open tunic as they suck contentedly, nestling in her lap with their legs intertwined. She smiles down at them, but her face is lined and tired.

Shinoni settles by the warmth of the hearth, but Keena sits farther back. How should she behave? She's never been with so many Kulas before. The only Kulas she knows are Shinoni and Sabra, and they both are strangers in her world. It's odd to be the stranger in theirs.

The small ones fall asleep, and Rena joins Ardak at the fire as he cuts up the marmot and gives them all a share. "Now that the small ones are taken care of, we can talk," he says. "I'm Ardak and this is Rena." He motions to the sleeping twins, their chubby bodies swaddled in fur on the grass bedding. "Our boys, Tark and Bril, came from Rena as the last snows melted."

"I'm Shinoni." Shinoni points to herself. "My father, Shazur, was a great shaman. He and others in my group were killed by a Krag hunter called Haken, who took me captive."

Ardak and Rena gasp and shake their heads sadly.

"I'm called Keena. Haken took me from my family also," Keena says. "They didn't want him to take me, but they couldn't stop him."

"We escaped together and now travel to find Keena's people in the high country." Shinoni puts her arm around Keena to help her stop trembling.

"It's hard to lose your people," Rena says.

"We have each other and our boys." Ardak places his arm around Rena. "We're travelling into the valley to escape the snows and find a new group to live with."

"Where are your own people?" Shinoni can't help probing. "Why did you leave them to travel with such little ones?"

"Our people are far from here. We couldn't stay with them," Rena says.

"Rena and I have been together a long time," Ardak explains. "We had two young ones many snow times ago, but they both died. We thought there would be no more, but last snow time Rena's belly swelled and we were happy. When the snows finally melted, it was time for Rena to give breath to our young one."

"One came out and then another," Rena says. "It was a big surprise — like our two lost children were returning."

"Our shaman said it was bad luck to have two young ones come from the spirit world at the same time. One must have slipped out by mistake." Ardak growls. "He said we had to return one to the spirits quickly before he was missed."

"They were going to take Bril and set him out in the forest so his breath could return to the spirit world," Rena says, her voice shaking. "I wouldn't let them take him."

"Rena refused to kill our son, so they sent her from our camp with the two young ones. She became an outcast and no one could speak to her or help her." Ardak hugs Rena. "I couldn't do that, so I followed her and became an outcast, too."

"It's terrible they sent you away." Keena turns to watch the twins. Her father had sent her away, too, but she could take care of herself.

Tark begins to squirm and fuss, sucking on his tiny fist. Rena takes tubers from the embers by the fire and mashes them between two rocks, then takes some in her mouth. She picks up Tark and settles him on her knee, then lowers her face close to his and transfers the chewed mush into his tiny open mouth. She coos softly and feeds him another mouthful of mush.

"Kula mothers often feed their young ones this way." Shinoni's voice startles Keena, who's absorbed in watching the mush flow from Rena's lips into Tark's mouth. "The young ones are usually older though, not as helpless as these."

Rena overhears and nods. "My milk isn't enough for two hungry young ones. We have to travel, so they must be strong." She looks down at Tark, who has fallen asleep in her lap. "Back at our camp, women nurse each other's young ones if a mother needs help. It's good to be with other women." Rena places Tark on the grass bed and picks up Bril, who's now calling for food.

"I've never seen this way of feeding young ones. Perhaps I'll feed my young one this way when I have one." Keena moves in closer, watching carefully as Rena begins feeding Bril the mashed tubers.

"You must also feed them milk if you want them to grow strong," Rena says.

After Rena has finished feeding Bril, she and Keena continue talking quietly. Shinoni doesn't have as much interest in young ones as Keena. She sits by the fire melting leftover fat from the marmot and mixing it with some of the crushed roots of the swelling plants. She unwraps her ankle and rubs the mixture over its swollen, bruised surface. Tingling warmth spreads along her injury as she replaces the wood supports and bindings.

Shinoni turns her attention to Ardak, who's sitting at the back of the cave, busy with something on the floor. He lifts his hands in the air, then dabs and presses his fingers on the rock wall. What's the hunter doing? Shinoni moves closer. Her legs begin to shake and her stomach lurches. He's placing red dots and lines on the wall. Ardak is making sacred symbols, messages to the spirits. Most amazing of all, he's doing it here, in the cave with his family. In a cave with females watching.

Shinoni barely dares to breathe. What if Ardak becomes angry and makes her leave? What if the spirits become enraged? Her whole body trembles when Ardak turns and sees her. He beckons her to come closer.

Shinoni hesitates, then sits down beside him. "Won't the spirits be angry if I watch?"

"Why would the spirits care, girl?" Ardak says. He turns back to the wall and places two red circles near a cluster of four red dots, two large and two small. He looks over his shoulder as he finishes the second circle. He points toward her, then at the red rings. "Shinoni and Keena." He motions to the larger of the four dots. "Ardak and Rena."

"Tark and Bril?" Shinoni excitedly points at the small dots.

Ardak nods. He begins adding other symbols: a curved line, a four-sided figure, several small forked lines.

"I saw marks like these in another cave last dark time. Did you make those marks, too?" Shinoni tries to hide her excitement.

"I tell our story so others can see we were here," Ardak says.

"My father made these marks and other ones in our sacred cave. Some were like animals." Shinoni jumps up, flailing her arms wildly. "Women weren't supposed to see them and my father didn't tell me their meaning." She takes a deep breath. "Can you tell me what the other marks mean?"

"I don't paint the animal spirits on the wall, but our shaman did and I've seen them. Women didn't paint them in my group, either." He studies the wall again. "I've told you some symbols, but others would take more time."

"I want to learn the symbols, if you'll teach me," Shinoni says.

"Some symbols are meant to send messages to the spirits. You have to learn and perform rituals." Ardak stands up and smears his palm with ochre, then places his handprint on the wall.

Shinoni waits, breathless. Will he say more?

"We must rest now." Ardak wipes his hand carefully on his tunic. "When the sun lights the sky, we'll leave here and travel into the valley. It'll be a long journey, and Rena could use help with the young ones. If you come with us, I'll teach you once we find a safe place to stay."

Shinoni lowers her head to hide her disappointment. She follows Ardak back to the hearth, where he and his family fall asleep on the grass bedding. Shinoni and Keena curl up on their cloaks on the far side of the hearth. Keena drifts into a restless sleep, tossing fitfully. Shinoni lies awake long into the night, listening to Keena's snores and the crackling fire as she ponders the decision she must make by morning's light.

23

SHINONI AND KEENA stand outside the cave where Rena and Ardak are packing up the twins and their belongings. Cries and coos drift outside from the entrance.

"It's a lot of work to care for two little ones," Keena says.

"Yes, a lot of work. Come, we have to talk." Shinoni pulls Keena toward the nearby trail, which rises to a ridge above them. Her ankle feels better this morning and she walks without her crutch. They climb to the hilltop. On one side of them they see plains, and on the other a broad plateau leads toward distant hills that blend into jagged mountains.

The sun disappears behind grey clouds scudding across the sky, and snowflakes begin to fall. "I'll have to travel up there to find my people," Keena says, pointing toward the hills. "They don't travel far from camp when the snows come."

"My band never travels this far into the high snow country," Shinoni says. "The men always find a warm cave and we stay there during the snow times." A thrill of excitement rushes through her body, squashing the tremors of fear burrowing in her stomach. She'll be the first Kula girl to make such a trek.

"Perhaps it's time to part," Keena says. "Any of your people that survived will be in the valleys. You can travel back with Ardak and Rena." She hesitates. "I heard Ardak ask you to go with them."

"He offered to teach me about the symbols he makes in the caves," Shinoni says. "But Haken's not far behind us. If I go back now, I'll likely meet him."

Keena nods toward the herd of wild horses they can make out grazing below them on the plains. "Maybe you could ride Ulu again. Then Haken would never catch you."

"It'd be fun to ride Ulu again," Shinoni says, "but I think I'll travel a little farther with you. To be sure you don't become lost."

"I'll have to keep *you* from getting lost." Keena laughs with relief.

"I wouldn't like to think of you being eaten by cave bears or mountain cats."

"That's more likely to happen if I'm with you," Keena says. "Still, if you want to come, I'd like your company."

"That's good, because I told Ardak and Rena this morning I'm staying with you." Shinoni joins arms with Keena as they look out over the frigid expanse of steppe and hills rolling into the distance.

"You do know how to find your people, don't you, Krag?" Shinoni asks.

"Many paths lead into the high country," Keena says. "I can't tell if this is the way Haken took me. There wasn't snow then, and we travelled quickly. That was the first time I ever came down from the high country. We went through a snow passage in the mountains, and I know my home's beyond that."

"I hope all paths into the high country lead to that snow passage, then." A chill runs down Shinoni's spine.

"I'll ask Leeswi to help us find the right path," Keena says.

"If Haken's still tracking us, perhaps she can lead him to the wrong one."

"Haken's still after us. He'll never stop until he catches us. And no one knows who Leeswi will choose to help."

Shinoni and Keena look back on the plains one last time. Ardak and Rena travel at a fast pace through the grass toward the valley. They stride side by side, each with a small one strapped to their back.

"Goodbye, friends." Shinoni calls and she waves, but Rena and Ardak keep walking.

"They're too far to hear you, Kula, and they need to be on their way quickly."

"I know, but I wanted to warn them again about Haken."

As they turn to leave the hilltop, faint shouts and screams draw them back. There on the plains below, a murderous pack of predators emerges from a thicket and advances on the family.

"Arrrgh. Rahhrr. Hiii-yiiii." Threatening roars pierce Shinoni's heart, and the memory of the slaughter of her band replays in her mind.

"No, monsters!" Shinoni screams.

"Quiet. We can't help them." Keena clamps her hand over Shinoni's mouth and pulls her to the ground. "We can't let Haken see us."

They lie on the hilltop, hugging each other in sorrow. "Little Tark and Bril," Keena whispers, her eyes filling with tears. "Why, Leeswi? They're just small ones."

Shinoni and Keena creep on their stomachs to the ridge and peer over. Ardak and Rena stand back to back, bravely protecting the twins as Haken and his hunters close in with spears drawn and clubs raised. It's over in moments. Rena's and Ardak's death cries mingle with the victorious screams of Haken's hunters.

Haken's own savage howl rises above the others. "Hiiii-yeeee-yipppp."

Shinoni and Keena back away from the ridge. Shinoni forces her injured ankle to move, wills her thoughts to focus on flight and not the horror on the plains below. Keena doubles over and retches. Then, clutching hands, they run for their lives, heading for the refuge of the distant hills.

24

THE SUN IS SINKING LOW, smearing tears of blood across the sky, when Shinoni and Keena finally reach another row of hills. Icy winds howl along the upland trail, biting through their leather clothing with glee. The grass here is dryer and shorter than on the plains. A herd of steppe bison grazes a short distance from the side of the trail, their shaggy heads lowered as they wrench stalks of dry grass and twigs from low-lying shrubs.

The pungent smell of bison surrounds Shinoni and Keena as they come alongside the herd. Keena pulls Shinoni to a standstill. "We should move up the hill before they see us," Kenna says. "These thunder hooves move fast when they're scared."

"Wouldn't you like to have one of their warm coats right now? This wind doesn't bother them at all."

Shinoni takes a step toward the massive beasts that graze so close to them. "See, they're not afraid of us."

"We should move off the trail before they realize we're here," Keena hisses. "Many mothers have young ones from the last snow melt."

The herd clusters together. Their heads rise, stems dangling from their mouths as they crunch the tough stalks. The mothers scan the steppe for danger to their young ones. *Oh no*, Keena thinks as an old cow spies them backing up along the trail. The cow snorts a warning. Other horned heads whip out of the grass. Soon all the mothers are snorting and pawing the ground with their sharp hooves and moving in front of their vulnerable young ones. The whole herd is now alert, scanning the grasses for a predator. One cow bellows, then another.

"You're right, better hide." Shinoni gulps. She drops to the ground and crouches in bushes near the trail.

"Too late. Climb." Keena shouts. She grabs Shinoni's arm and they scrabble up the rocky shale of the hillside. Shinoni struggles to get a foothold on the crumbling stone. She yells in pain as rocks rain down on the trail and hit her ankle. Keena lunges to boost her up the slope to a ledge and then clambers up beside her. A heartbeat later several large mothers, snorting with rage, toss and thrash the bushes where Shinoni had been hiding. The whole herd then thunders into the distance, looking for a safer place to graze with their young ones.

"That was close. You saved me from being squashed." Shinoni shudders.

"You should be more careful. Your leg's still weak." Keena offers Shinoni her shoulder as they descend from their hillside perch. They move out onto the steppe, the clatter of the bison's hooves still ringing in their ears.

"One of those young thunder hooves would've made a very good meal." Shinoni pokes at a pile of still-steaming bison dung.

"Perhaps we should eat grass and twigs as they do," Keena says.

"There's meat here. We just have to find it," Shinoni says. "See there?"

Swaying grass betrays the hiding place of a fat brown grouse. Its feathers have started to change to the white of the coming snows. Shinoni carefully draws her sling and fits a stone, letting it fly. Her deadly aim kills the bird instantly.

Shinoni limps to the place where the grouse lies, wings spread and feathers ruffling in the wind. "Ho. We'll eat tonight. Thank you, bird, for giving yourself to feed us." She picks up the bird and thrusts it at Keena. "Here, carry this so my hands are free for more hunting."

"Where's your wolf? She could've brought down one of the young thunder hooves. Won't she provide meat again?" Keena yanks the dead grouse from Shinoni's hand. *Must she always be so bossy?*

"She might, but we shouldn't depend on her to feed us." Shinoni steps closer. "What are you doing with the bird?"

Keena removes a leather tie from the top of her leg wrap and ties the grouse into a fold of her cloak, securing it to her waist with the leather strip. She rearranges her clothing to carry the bird and still protect herself from the biting wind.

"Krag, why don't you just sew your clothing to hold it closer to your body, like I do?" Shinoni says. "It's warmer if it doesn't flap in the wind."

"What's *sew* mean, Kula?" Keena looks at Shinoni's fitted leather leggings and tunic, which leave no skin exposed except her face and hands.

"Do you really not know how to sew?" Shinoni shakes her head. "We have tools that bind our clothes together around us. Krags don't have this?"

"It's not the Krag way." Keena reties the laces on her leg wrap. "Let's move on before some beast makes a meal of us." She hurries down the trail, leaving Shinoni to catch up.

159

"We need shelter and a fire. Soon." Keena glances around anxiously as shadows hide the trail and the stirrings of night hunters rustle in the twilight. "We should've taken the last cave, Kula. You're too fussy."

Shinoni sighs. The Krag girl is always worrying. "It was barely big enough for two of us, and there was no firewood nearby," Shinoni says. "The ground's rising here. We'll find something soon."

"Let's hope we find something before something finds us," Keena says.

The setting sun breaks through the clouds to throw a final splash of light onto the land before night descends. There on the hillside above them, a black crevice beckons.

"Ho, Kula, you were right." Keena whoops.

"I know." Shinoni grins.

The girls hug and rush up the slope, gathering kindling as they go. They build up a brush pile and start a fire with Shinoni's firestones. The flames grow, filling the entranceway with a protective shield of warmth and safety.

Tewa joins them, dodging the flames. She stretches out near the entrance, tongue dangling as she pants heavily. Then she begins to lick dried blood from her snout and paws.

"Looks like the wolf has no meat to share from her hunt," Keena observes. "Good thing you killed this fat bird, Kula."

Shinoni beams at Keena's appreciation of her hunting ability.

As Keena continues plucking feathers from the grouse, Shinoni picks up several of the most distinctive brown, grey, and white tail feathers. She tucks them into the thong that ties her thick hair at the nape of her neck. "Would you like me to put some in your hair?" she asks Keena. "The colour would look good in your braid."

"Why would I put the feathers of a dead bird in my hair?" Keena asks.

"Why not? You wear the skins and fur of dead animals. The feathers look nice, and maybe you'll get some of the bird's skill in hiding."

"Well, they didn't help this one much with hiding." Keena turns back to pulling the entrails out of the grouse, preparing it for roasting. Tewa moves closer to Keena and sits panting behind her, watching her every move with the carcass. When she's done, Keena places the bloody entrails on the ground by Tewa. The big wolf gulps them down with relish, then continues to watch Keena.

"There isn't much meat here to share with this big wolf," Keena says.

"I don't think she's hungry. By the blood on her face when she came in, I think she's already eaten but didn't have enough to share." Shinoni watches Tewa fondly.

Keena puts the gutted grouse on a stick and uses stones to prop it up close to the flames. She sneaks a peak at the feathers in Shinoni's hair. "If you have some of those feathers left, you can put a few in my hair if you want."

Shinoni knows she wouldn't share her prize feathers with any of the Kula girls at her camp, but she *really* wants Keena to have some. She picks out three of the largest and softest feathers from the pile and slides across the floor to sit beside Keena. She works the feathers into her thick red braid, then admires her work. "They look very beautiful. In my band, women and men often wear feathers and other ornaments."

"Like those teeth on your clothing?" Keena touches the fox and otter teeth on Shinoni's tunic. "Do they mean you've already become a Kula woman?"

"Not yet. I have to go on a spirit quest first and have my first blood. My grandmother sewed those on to show I'm the shaman's daughter and that I was training as her assistant to be a medicine woman." She fondles the teeth as Reza's proud face flickers in her mind's eye. "She sewed a new ornament whenever I proved I'd mastered a new healing skill." A tear slides down Shinoni's cheek. "I'll sew them on myself from now on. I hope someday soon I can go on my spirit quest."

"I don't know this spirit quest, but would it be harder than what you're doing now? Perhaps you're already on your quest. Surely you're learning and doing more things than you ever knew or did before?"

"Perhaps I am." She studies Keena as she pulls her braid forward to admire the grouse feathers. "When will you become a Krag woman? What must you do?"

"When I start to bleed, my band will drum and sing to welcome me as a woman." Keena selects a twig from the brush pile and chews on it. "Then any hunter who's shared meat with the band and has his own hearth can ask me to join him at his fire. He'd provide meat to my father and mother and ask them to let me come."

"Can you choose who to go with? What if you don't like the hunter who asks?"

"I'd tell my father I didn't want to go with him and he'd refuse the hunter's offer." Keena reaches under her cloak and clutches the ibex-tooth pendant, Kreel's gift to her from his first kill.

"So if you haven't started to bleed and you hate Haken, why did your father let him take you away to his hearth?"

Keena stares stonily into the flames. "Haken killed the lion that was hunting my people. Atuk promised he could take some women from our band with him. He said women who *chose* to go with Haken, but Haken listens to no one. He insisted I be one of them." Keena's voice quavers as she spits out the words. "It was hard for my father, but he had no choice."

163

"It was wrong to send you away with a man such as Haken," Shinoni says. "You still want to return to your father's hearth?"

"My father's old and Haken has many hunters," Keena says. "You saw what he does to those who stand in his way. He killed your people to get their hunting magic."

Now Shinoni blinks back tears. "It was my fault. I did something that caused my people to die. I entered our sacred cave even though I knew only the shaman and hunters were allowed to be there. My father took me back into the cave to ask the spirits to forgive me and allow me to paint the animals. Maybe the spirits are still angry with me, and the death of my people is my punishment." She sobs. "It's my fault, too, that Ardak and Rena and the small ones were killed by Haken."

Keena wraps her arms around Shinoni. Their tears glisten like broken shards of quartz in the firelight. Tewa sits up, whining and looking from one to the other.

Keena is the first to speak. "You're still alive, so perhaps your spirits are protecting you, not punishing you."

"You must have a good father or you wouldn't want to return to his hearth," Shinoni reassures Keena.

"Haken's the one who's caused our pain. He's the one to blame — not my father, not you." Keena wipes her eyes with the back of her hand.

Shinoni clears her throat, anxious to change the subject. She rummages in her pouch and takes out her sewing kit. Tewa cocks her head, and perhaps sensing the change in mood, relaxes and moves back into the shadows. She turns in a circle before settling down to resume her sleep.

Shinoni feels the spirits of her mother and grandmother beside her as she touches the soft white rabbit fur that wraps the sewing kit. Grandmother made the kit for her mother and then gave it to Shinoni after her mother died. She opens it and takes out the bone needle and stone awl. "Look, Keena, these are the tools we sew with. Come closer and I'll show you how it works."

"I'm happy with the Krag way," Keena says, but she wiggles closer to Shinoni. She leans over Shinoni's lap to get a good view of the strange small tools.

Shinoni threads one of the narrow strips of sinew through the hole in the bone needle and shows Keena how the awl punches two small holes in the leather of her tunic. She pushes the needle through the holes, attaching some grouse feathers before tying off and knotting the sinew. "It takes longer to prepare and sew clothing, but it's worth it." She shows Keena the stitches on her leggings.

Keena runs her fingers over the raised pattern of sinew that tightly holds together the two sides of Shinoni's deer-hide leggings. She fondles the ties on her own hide-wrapped legs. Her brow furrows and she purses her lips as she looks from one to the other. "I see that this sewing could be useful, but it would take a lot of time to do. Wrapping's faster, and we can change the size and shape of the hides we wear when we need to."

"Our way keeps out the wind and snow better, and once it's done, the skins stay closed around us. Rips can be fixed quickly, too."

Keena doesn't seem convinced, so Shinoni puts away the sewing kit. She pats Keena on the back. "I can teach you how to sew your clothes sometime if you want."

Keena takes the grouse from the flames. "Perhaps, but I think the way my grandmother taught me suits me better."

Shinoni and Keena settle down to their meal. A chill wind from the high country dances across the cave entrance, outside the fire's warmth. Its high wailing cry dares the girls to come out and be tested.

25

"HO, WOLF, WHAT'S YOUR HURRY?" Keena clutches her cape as Tewa pushes past her, knocking her sideways. Tewa sniffs the wind, muscles tense and tail high. Then with a yodelling yip she lopes down the hill and disappears into the steppe grass below.

"The wolf's in a hurry. Do you think Haken's close by?" Keena asks.

"She'll warn us if there's danger." Shinoni checks her pouch to be sure her sling and knife are ready if needed. "She probably smells those thunder hooves and wants to fill her belly."

Keena and Shinoni continue their journey at a brisk pace. Shinoni's ankle has almost completely healed now. She used the wooden braces as fuel for their fire last dark time. She's proud of the healing skills Grandmother Reza taught her. Maybe she *will* be a medicine woman, like Reza. Maybe a shaman, too.

The sun is high overhead when they stop to drink at a creek. The ice-cold water sparkles as it tumbles over grey and brown stones washed down from the glacier.

"Leeswi's smiling. Maybe it's a good day for us." A playful breeze ruffles the feathers in Keena's braid. "Let's follow this stream until we find the river it flows from. Maybe that river will lead us to my family."

Shinoni sniffs for danger. "It'll be a good day if we avoid Haken. Perhaps he won't follow us into the high country."

"Haken came into the high country to take me from my home. He's no stranger here." Keena scans the area and shivers. "He knows this land better than I do."

The dry grass behind them shakes ominously. Shinoni leaps over the stream, sling loaded and raised above her head. "Quick, Keena. Someone's coming."

Keena frantically sloshes through the frigid water, her short legs unable to make the leap. She crouches behind Shinoni and peers into the swaying grass. With a final crackle, the dry stems part and a large grey shape emerges.

Tewa pants heavily, her tongue lolling and sides heaving. The fur on her head is matted and blood oozes from a cut above her eye. She heads straight to the stream and laps the water in great gulps.

"It's only Tewa, and she's hurt." Shinoni jumps back across the stream and examines the cut on the wolf's head.

"You take care of her. You're the healer." Keena sits on the ground on the far side of the stream and removes her soggy foot wraps. She pulls out the wet moss lining and stuffs the hide wrappings with dry grasses. Her bare toes are freezing. She wipes her feet on her cloak before sticking them back into the grass-lined foot coverings. Keena clumsily reties the laces, her fingers numb and stiff from the cold.

Shinoni touches the cut on Tewa's head, and a growl rumbles deep in the wolf's throat. She withdraws her hand and stands up. "That's not so bad, sister, but you should be more careful." She jumps back across the stream to rejoin Keena, and Tewa follows her.

"You're a good one to give advice on being care-ful." Keena laughs. "Looks like she took on more than she could handle without her pack. Probably some big mother thunder hoof got upset when she tried to make a meal of her young one."

"We're her pack now, Keena." Shinoni places one hand on Tewa's densely furred back and the other on Keena's broad shoulder. "We take care of each other."

Shinoni, Keena, and Tewa move along a game trail within hearing of the running stream. The wind picks up, blowing their hair forward as it pushes them along.

"It *is* a good day. Leeswi's helping us move quickly," Keena says.

Tewa, who's been bounding silently through the grass ahead of them, suddenly stops. She growls a warning.

Both Keena and Shinoni sniff the air but the wind's blowing away from them. They can't detect the threat picked up by the wolf's much more sensitive nose. Tewa continues growling as she stares at a distant clump of trees.

"Something by that thicket has spooked Tewa," Shinoni says. "Let's get a look before we go any farther." Shinoni moves off the trail, circling around, trying to get a better view.

"If the wolf smells whatever's there, it can smell us, too," Keena says.

"It seems your Leeswi isn't helping us now. She's carrying our scent in that direction." Shinoni increases her stride, a deep frown creasing her brow. Keena trots to keep up.

Keena cautions Shinoni. "You shouldn't question what Leeswi does, Kula. She gives breath. She takes breath. Don't anger her again."

In her mind's eye, Shinoni sees the earth's yawning mouth opening to swallow her on the day the ground shook. She smells again the stench of the earth's bowels. "I'm sorry … I'm sorry," she mutters into the wind above her.

Suddenly, the rattle of the grass dies down and Shinoni's hair no longer blows past her face. The wind eases to a whisper.

Keena gasps. "You see, Leeswi's chosen to help us this time."

Shinoni and Keena clasp each other close in a hug before silently moving forward. They follow Tewa's tail flag until they reach a large mound of earth jutting above the grass. A perfect vantage point to view the dangerous thicket.

"Look, Krag, what beast is that?" Shinoni points to what looks like an immense grey rock moving slowly in the grass beside the thicket, munching shrubs. There seems to be a smaller grey stone between the huge beast and the low trees.

Keena raises her head, testing the wind for scent. The beast also raises her huge head. Two curved horns sit on top of her snout, the one in front dwarfing the one behind. "It's a big horn! She won't eat us, Kula, but she will chase us down and squash us like bugs."

Shinoni marvels at the size of the shaggy creature. She's more massive than the huge thunder hooves they saw last sun time. The woolly rhinoceros snorts, shaking her head from side to side as she moves away from the thicket. Does she smell them? She's wary, and Shinoni sees the reason. Following at the great beast's heels is a much smaller version of herself. The calf's tiny horn touches her mother's flank as they walk together.

"I've never seen this big horn beast before. Why would she chase us down and crush us? We mean her no harm," Shinoni says.

"Atuk says all big horns are bad tempered, and this one has a youngster to defend. My people hunt and kill them for food, but it's dangerous and takes several strong hunters."

"Well, then, it seems fair they'd see us as enemies and squash out our guts." Shinoni scans the area. "You know this land better than me. Which way should we go?"

"It's likely best to head away from the big horn," Keena says. "There's a line of hills over there and other rivers that flow from the high country."

Shinoni, Keena, and Tewa climb down from the earth mound. They travel rapidly, putting distance between themselves and the danger they know lurks in the thicket, but heading ever closer to the unknown dangers in the new line of hills.

26

"DEATH BIRDS." Keena points to vultures circling in the sky over the open grassland just ahead. They are near the crooked hills. The vultures dip and swoop, their giant wings black against the lowering sun. "Something's injured or dying over there."

"Maybe a good place to find a meal," Shinoni says. "We've been travelling too fast to look for food."

"It could be dead already." Keena slows down, worried about getting too close. "Whatever killed it might still be there, feasting on it."

"Perhaps they'll share, if it's a big kill."

"Ah, yes." Keena sighs. "Like the laugh devils did."

Tewa growls deep in her throat, then bounds toward whatever has attracted the vultures' attention.

"Come on! We didn't have Tewa with us when we met the hyenas," Shinoni calls as she charges ahead around a bend in the trail.

Keena runs to keep up. "Even Tewa won't have a chance against a clan of laugh devils or a lion. Slow down."

Shinoni skids to a sudden stop. Keena rounds the bend and crashes into her. They've run right into the kill site.

Keena gags. The sharp scent of death hangs heavy in the air. A vulture, its head and neck stained with gore, hisses and claps its hooked beak at the girls. The giant bird spreads its wings, half covering the deer it is feeding on. The deer lies on its side, head twisted back, neck broken, and throat torn. Entrails protrude from gashes in its belly. Off to one side, the deer's killer, a lion, also lies dead. A long wooden spear protrudes from its chest. Close by the lion lies its killer, a young brown-skinned man, his abdomen badly torn.

"What's happened here? They've all killed each other," Keena says. The hairs on her neck prickle at the scent and sight of the lion. An image of another lion with a child in its mouth fills her head. Tewa snarls, hackles raised, as she circles the big cat's carcass.

"They're not all dead." Shinoni moves to the young man. "This one breathes, but I don't think I can help him." She examines his wounds. His eyes are glazing as death approaches. He's not much older than the girls, but he's different from both of them.

The young man waves weakly toward the hillside behind him and struggles to speak. His voice is failing. Shinoni bends low, trying to hear his words.

"Come here quickly, Keena. He's trying to tell us something, but I can't understand him."

Keena cups her ear near the hunter's mouth. He speaks again, moving his hand weakly toward the hills. What's he trying to tell them? "His words aren't Krag. Some are like my people's, yet different."

The stranger falls silent. His eyes no longer see them. "Leeswi's taken his breath," Keena says calmly. She looks around. Tewa is pulling chunks of meat off the deer carcass. She feeds hungrily, along with some ravens and a growing number of vultures.

Keena backs away from the kill. "We should leave. Other beasts will come and add us to their feast."

Shinoni tugs at the young hunter's body. "Let's just pull him over to the hillside and cover him up. I don't want him to be torn apart and eaten by beasts."

"We must go. The beasts will find him, anyway." Despite her words, Keena hurries over and takes his arm, lending her strength.

The girls roll the body down a small incline into a depression at the foot of the hill. They quickly cover him with brush and place rocks over his head and body.

Keena stands back, confused, while Shinoni chants a song. "Why are you singing? We have to go," she says.

"This is the song Kulas sing when a hunter dies and is buried."

How odd to sing to one whose breath is gone. However, when Shinoni's done, Keena circles her hands over the rocks in a gesture of farewell to a brave Krag hunter.

"We should take some meat with us." Shinoni turns back toward the kill site, but Keena takes her shoulder and propels her away from the carnage. Shinoni struggles to pull away. "Aren't you hungry?"

"Kula, that lion was thin and young, but others could be around. We saw what happened to that hunter when he tried to take the lion's kill." Keena's grip tightens as she continues to pull Shinoni along the hillside. "Hyenas will be there soon if they aren't already. We can't fill our bellies if we're dead."

Shinoni gives in and they move swiftly through the grass at the base of the hills, looking for shelter from the night. Halfway up a rock slope, a dark opening with a solid ledge looks inviting in the twilight.

"I'd like to be farther from the kill site." Keena anxiously watches the trail, her ears and nostrils straining to detect danger.

"I would, too, but the beasts will be busy eating there. We'll be safer inside a shelter with fire than travelling at night," Shinoni says.

They gather brush and some branches from a lone tree nearby and hoist their load of firewood up the slope and onto the ledge. *What's that?* Keena freezes in fear. The sound of scraping and shuffling comes from the darkness of the cave. Keena and Shinoni recoil, stumbling backward. The cave isn't empty.

"Dak? Dak, to-taw?" a voice calls softly.

A scent wafts out on the breeze, one they've already smelled today. Then a face appears in the cave entrance, a woman's face, brown with small brow ridges and large cheekbones. Sweat glistens on her cheeks in the fading light and plasters her wavy black hair to her head.

"Dak?" she calls again, then gasps at the sight of the girls. She withdraws into the safety of the cave.

Keena exchanges a shocked look with Shinoni. Another stranger, and in *their* shelter. It's too late to find another place.

"She must be calling for the hunter that was killed. She's frightened," Keena says. The deep cough of a lion sounds in the distance.

"We'd be frightened, too, if strangers showed up at our cave." Shinoni approaches the entrance. The shadows are deepening around them. They must go inside.

The woman appears again, and this time she holds a spear like the one they saw buried in the chest of the dead lion. She shakes her head and points down the hill. Shinoni stands her ground and smiles at her. She folds her arms across her chest, touching opposite shoulders, then stretches her arms out toward the woman, palms up, showing they're friends. Keena does the same.

The woman moves onto the ledge, still brandishing the spear. She waves the girls away. It's obvious that she's carrying a young one in her belly and that it will come out for breath soon.

"We're friends. We can help you." Shinoni points to herself and Keena and to the woman, then makes a hugging motion. "We have to make her understand or we'll all die in the dark," she whispers to Keena.

Keena points to the firewood. "We can make a fire. You'll be safe." Why won't this stupid woman understand? She and Shinoni won't survive the night out here.

The terrified woman shakes her head, but then drops her spear and collapses on the ledge. Shinoni and Keena clamber up beside her and carry her limp body inside. Shinoni moves the spear out of the woman's reach and stacks the kindling on the earth by the entrance.

"Why don't you make the fire, Keena?" Shinoni says. "I'll make her comfortable and see if I can help her. The flint and firestones are in my pouch."

As Shinoni covers the woman with her cape, Keena rummages in the pouch for the flint and firestones. Can she do this? Her hands shake and sweat drips from her brow ridge. She's helped Shinoni make a fire, but she's never started one by herself. Will she remember how? She makes a small pile of firewood and brush, then strikes the firestone with the flint. Nothing! She gulps but remembers Shinoni doesn't always strike a spark the first time either. Keena steadies her hands and tries again. A spark glows in the kindling and spreads quickly as the fire springs to life. Her cheeks glow with the heat of the flame and her heart swells with pride. She, Keena, daughter of Ubra, did it! She made a fire!

A scrabbling noise on the rocks outside brings both Shinoni and Keena to the entrance. They peer over the ledge. To their relief, Tewa bounds up the hill. She drops part of a deer haunch on the ground and stands panting as Shinoni rumples her fur.

"Thank you, sister. You haven't forgotten us," Shinoni says.

Tewa wrinkles her nose at the unfamiliar scent of the woman. She jumps down from the ledge and turns in a circle, making herself a bed in the shrubbery nearby.

Keena sharpens a stick to hold the deer meat over the fire and tends to supper while Shinoni tends to the still-unconscious woman. Shinoni raises her head, bringing the water bag to the woman's parched lips. The stranger chokes and sputters, then sips the cool water. Her eyes fly open with alarm as she becomes aware of them. She looks around but seems to calm a bit when she sees the fire and smells the roasting meat.

Shinoni smiles at her and points to herself. "Shi-non-i." She points to Keena. "Kee-na." Keena smiles and gives a small wave as she turns the meat.

Shinoni points to the woman, who looks at her confused. Slowly her eyes light up. She points to herself. "De-ka."

───── 27 ─────

EARLY DAWN STREAKS THE SKY a pale pink as Shinoni and Keena lie on their capes on the earth floor near the fire. Their stomachs are full but their sleep has been uneasy.

Keena props herself up on one elbow and looks at Deka sleeping fitfully behind them, snoring in a low growl. In the flickering firelight, the strange woman's belly throws a huge shadow on the cave wall.

"We must be on our way," Keena says. She nods toward Deka. "If we're quiet we can slip out before she wakes up."

Shinoni gasps. "What do you mean? You know she won't survive on her own. She can't hunt, and her mate's dead. She'll starve or be eaten by beasts."

"We can leave the rest of the meat with her. It'll last her a few suns if she's careful."

"But you saw she has no fire for protection." *Can't the Krag girl see how helpless Deka is?* "We can take her with us," Shinoni insists.

"She'll slow us down." Keena shakes her head. "It's sad, but we can't help her more than that."

"She's young, like us. Soon her small one will have to be pushed out and she'll need help giving it breath." Shinoni knows Keena's right — Deka will be a burden. But she can't abandon her.

"I know that, but Haken's not far behind us. We must move quickly." Keena looks away from Deka and blinks back tears.

"Will Leeswi be angry if we leave her? Perhaps Leeswi doesn't want the breaths of Deka and her young one to return to her before she calls for them," Shinoni says.

"Deka's not Krag," Keena mutters, but she sounds doubtful. "One can never know who Leeswi will help — or harm."

Deka has woken up, perhaps from hearing her name repeated several times. She struggles to raise her heavy body from the floor.

Keena starts rolling up her belongings. "She won't want to come with us. She's waiting for her mate, and we can't talk to her and tell her he's dead."

"Deka, Shinoni, Keena go now." Shinoni points to herself and Keena, then points toward the entrance.

She points to Deka and then to the entrance again, taking Deka's arm and pulling her up and slowly forward.

"Deka sa ni. Dak. To-taw, Dak." Deka shakes her head, fear clouding her eyes.

"I told you, Kula." Keena sighs. "We'll build up the fire and leave her the meat."

Shinoni tries one last time to communicate. "Dak. Dak no come." She points to the entrance, shaking her head from side to side.

Deka watches, frowning.

"Dak dead." Shinoni makes a slitting motion across her neck. "Dak dead." Shinoni falls to the ground and closes her eyes. "Dak dead."

Deka continues to watch, starting to mouth sounds. "Dak matik?" She moans and tears well in her eyes.

"Help me here, Krag," Shinoni calls to Keena. "Act like a lion."

"You're unreal." Keena rolls her eyes but comes to stand beside Shinoni.

"Dak." Shinoni says loudly to Deka as she points to herself. "Quickly, leap on me, lion," she instructs Keena.

Keena makes a fierce face, opening her mouth wide and showing her teeth. She swipes with her arms and jumps on Shinoni, knocking her to the ground while growling loudly.

Shinoni shouts at the horrified Deka. "Dak dead." She points at Keena. "Lion kill Dak." She stretches on the floor, eyes closed.

Deka kneels awkwardly beside Shinoni. Tears flow down her face, and she lets out a deep, keening wail. "Dak matik."

Shinoni helps Deka to her feet and points to the entrance. "Deka come with Shinoni and Keena." Deka turns her back and continues wailing.

"Come on, Shinoni, we've done what we can. If she won't come, we can't make her. We must leave *now*." Keena packs the meat, puts out the fire, and moves outside.

"Come, Deka. Shinoni friend." She pulls her toward the cave mouth. She pats Deka's belly. "Come, help with little one."

Deka shuffles to the entrance, where she stands, moaning and wailing.

Shinoni follows Keena down the path through the vegetation to the trail by the hillside. She turns and sees Deka still standing on the ledge.

"You took the meat and fire. How will she survive?" Shinoni says. "I can't leave her."

"She won't survive, anyway. We have to go quickly now. She's free to come or not, but it's her choice." Keena firmly propels Shinoni down the trail. Tewa trots far ahead.

A few heartbeats later Shinoni looks back one more time. Her heart lifts. Deka has picked up her spear and is moving down the hill, slowly following on the trail behind them.

— 28 —

"WE MAY HAVE TO choose her life or ours. She can't travel much farther, and Haken will find us if we don't move faster." Keena scans the hills and brush around the stand of willows where they rest. "He could be anywhere. On the trail or in the grass, waiting to pounce."

Shinoni puts her hands on Deka's bulging abdomen and probes gently. "Her young one's moving low in her belly. She'll give breath to it soon, so we need to find a safe place for this to happen."

"Didn't you hear me?" Keena balls her fists and clenches her teeth. "We can't take more time. Haken will be here *soon* and there won't be a safe place for *any* of us."

"I can't just leave her. We can find a cave and hide the entrance with brush. I'll help her give breath to the young one," Shinoni says.

"We'll all die then," Keena says. "How can you help her?"

"I've watched Reza guide young ones out of their mothers, and I've helped her sometimes. I have some leaves of the belly plant in my pouch to help speed births."

"Belly plants? What *don't* you have in that pouch?" Keena scoffs.

Shinoni bristles. "I picked them to help a woman in my band who was ready to give breath to her first young one." She pushes down a lump in her throat as Etak's smiling face and big belly flash before her. "I picked them just before Haken attacked my people. We'll use them now, before he attacks us."

"Let's move, then, while she still can," Keena says. "There must be a better hiding place than this."

Shinoni pulls Deka to her feet. Deka wobbles onto the narrow game trail between Shinoni and Keena, using her spear as a walking stick.

They haven't gone far when Keena stops abruptly. "Something's moving out there. Looks like hunters, maybe two of them."

"It can't be Haken. He'll be behind us." Shinoni sniffs but catches no hint of the hunters' identity.

"Maybe they'll care for Deka if they're friendly," Keena says. "Let's get closer, but don't let them see us before we know who they are."

Shinoni steadies Deka, who clutches the bottom of her belly. The young woman begins to pant, her eyes wide with fear. Not the best time for the belly squeezes to start. Shinoni places her hand on Deka's mouth and puts a finger to her lips. Deka must be quiet.

Soon the girls have moved close enough to see the figures more clearly. There are two of them, draped in reindeer hides, the hoods protecting their heads from the wind as they bend over something in the grass. The hunters stand up, their backs to Shinoni and Keena. One holds a small animal and drops it into a bag held by the other. Their scent comes faintly on the breeze to the girls, who are crouching in bushes downwind of them.

"They're Kula. Perhaps they'll help." Shinoni jumps to her feet. The rustling from the thicket startles the hunters. They whirl around clutching stone-tipped spears. Their hoods slip back from their heads, revealing earth-brown faces lined with crevices. Their long black hair is streaked heavily with grey.

"They're women, Keena. Elders like Reza, my grandmother," Shinoni says.

"Grey hairs? Why would they hunt alone? Their band must be close by." Keena ducks behind Shinoni as the two women approach, spears raised.

"We mean no harm, grandmothers." Shinoni greets them, hand outstretched, palm up. "I'm Kula like you, and these are my friends."

The grandmothers come closer but keep their spears high. One points to Keena and Deka. "You travel with a Strange One and a Dark One. Why?"

Shinoni places one hand on Keena's shoulder and the other on Deka's. "These are my friends," she repeats.

Deka trembles and lurches sideways, dropping her spear. She falls on her knees, moaning, in the throes of a belly squeeze.

"They're just girls, Seezel," one grandmother says to the other. "The Dark One is carrying a small one in her belly." She lowers her spear and goes quickly to Deka's side. She squats beside her, feeling Deka's abdomen as another squeeze seizes her in its powerful grip.

"The young one will come soon, Fadin, and she'll attract predators." Seezel lowers her own spear. "We should take them to our hunting hearth."

Seezel and Fadin help Deka to her feet, supporting her on both sides. They begin to hurry off across the steppe, away from the row of hills. With her free hand, Fadin motions Shinoni and Keena to follow.

"Should we go with them, Kula?" Keena picks up Fadin's skin bag, opens it, and looks inside. It contains snares and two dead hares. She slings the bag over her shoulder.

"We can't just leave her." Shinoni picks up the grandmothers' stone-tipped spears and Deka's long wooden spear with its fire-hardened wooden point.

"She has help. Now would be a good time to leave, before Haken comes." Keena pats Fadin's bag. "And now we have both food and weapons."

"You wouldn't really take their food and spears?" Shinoni says. "How can you even think of such a thing?"

"You're right. I'm just worried about getting back to my people." Keena sighs, then claps Shinoni on the back. "We've brought her this far. It would be good to make sure she's safe."

They turn and follow Fadin and Seezel as they half drag and half carry Deka toward their camp.

Before long they arrive at an earthen mound rising above the grasses, like the one they used as a lookout just one sun ago. The vegetation covering its top and sides helps it blend into the surrounding steppe, except for a dead tree that sticks out of one side of the mound. Its bent and twisted trunk lies prone across the grass, but its roots are still firmly planted in the mound.

"This isn't much of a camp. Where's the shelter?" Keena mutters.

"There's no sign of a hearth or food." Shinoni views the open grassland uneasily.

Fadin and Seezel stop at the edge of the mound and beckon the girls to join them. The grandmothers wrestle with the brush and slide a woven mat of shrubbery to one side. An opening appears, leading into the curved side of the mound. Seezel slips inside, and Fadin helps Deka into the hole, gently pushing her, then coaxing her to lie down and wriggle through.

"Hurry, we must close the entrance," Fadin urges. Shinoni and Keena each take a deep breath and disappear inside the earth mound.

SHINONI SLITHERS THROUGH the narrow opening, Keena's feet pushing her from behind. They
emerge into a much wider chamber hollowed out of the
mound's underbelly. Overhead, long-dead tree roots,
gnarled and matted, provide a partial ceiling and ex-
tend down two sides of the chamber. The air smells of
decaying vegetation and damp earth. Still, it's a safe
place, hidden from view.

"Ho, Grandmother. Did you dig out all this dirt?"
Shinoni asks, awestruck.

"It was partly dug out when we found it, but we
made it bigger." Seezel has a fire started and tends to
Deka on a bed of woven grass. She offers her a rolled
deerskin to prop herself up and water to sip from a
small stone bowl. Seezel then rubs Deka's belly and

chuckles. "I can feel the new one moving under my hand."

"This place has saved our lives more than once." Fadin grunts as she pulls the mat of vegetation back across the entrance behind Keena. "Don't dawdle, girl. We need to close the entrance." She rolls a large stone to block entry from outside.

Shinoni opens her pouch and brings out the leaves and red berries. "You can make a drink with these to help Deka push out the small one."

"Belly plants? Where did you come by these?" Fadin asks.

"My grandmother was a healer." Shinoni bows her head. "She sent me to gather these for a woman of our band who was ready to give breath to her young one."

"Your grandmother and the woman didn't need these belly plants, then?" Fadin places the leaves and berries in a stone bowl full of water and sets it by the fire.

"They're both in the spirit world," Shinoni says.

Fadin looks at her. "Well, it's good the plants will be used now," she says. "This is probably the Dark One's first small one. The drink will help her."

Fadin joins Seezel, who is now walking Deka around the small chamber. They rub her arms and back and sing in soft voices. Then they guide her back to the grass bed to see how the birth is progressing.

"This one's strong, Seezel. It's good you had her walking. It'll make the young one come faster." Fadin nods.

"They make a good team," Keena whispers.

"Yes, I think Deka will be safe with them," Shinoni says.

"We must be on our way now," Keena says. She looks at Shinoni and nods toward the entrance.

Shinoni knows that Keena is right, but she's torn. It feels good to help the grandmothers like she used to help Reza. She's proud she could help Deka with the belly plants she'd gathered. Fadin was impressed she knew how to make the drink that was helping Deka's contractions.

"Aaaiiiieeee!" Deka cries. Shinoni and Keena turn around to see her crouching on the grass bed clutching her belly. Seezel pulls her into a squatting position and squats in front of her, demonstrating how to breathe in and push down, helping the new one come out. Fadin kneels behind her, putting pressure on the small of her back. Another belly squeeze grips Deka's abdomen, and with a great effort, she pushes her small one out into Fadin's waiting hands. The two grandmothers examine the baby and announce it's a girl. Shinoni moves closer and hugs Deka, then helps her lie down on the grass bed. Fadin places the baby on Deka's breast to nurse, then cuts the umbilical cord with a flint knife.

Shinoni and Keena crowd close to get a good look at the small one. She's tiny and wrinkled, with brown skin and wavy black hair on her head. Her fingers and toes are pink on the undersides and she clutches on to her mother's long tangled hair as she nurses hungrily.

Seezel and Fadin move to the fire to rest and gut the hares for roasting. Shinoni and Keena grin at Deka cuddling her small one as they collect their belongings and prepare to leave.

"You're not leaving, girls? Come and rest, eat. You must be tired and hungry." Fadin makes room by the fire.

"You must spend the night," Seezel calls. "Tell us why you travel together with the Dark One who carries a young one in her belly."

Shinoni looks at Keena, knowing she is eager to leave. Keena shrugs, and the girls sit by the fire.

Shinoni hopes they settle for the short version. "Keena and I have travelled a long way together. A cruel Krag hunter named Haken took her from her family. He also killed the people from my band. We escaped from his camp together and now he's tracking us."

"If this Haken is dangerous and he's following you, why did you travel with the Dark One?" Fadin asks. "She must've slowed you down."

"A lion killed her mate and she was alone, so we took her with us," Shinoni explains. "Now we must leave quickly so Haken doesn't find us."

"Deka and her small one can't travel with you. What will you do with her?" Seezel's face wrinkles with concern.

It hadn't occurred to Shinoni that the grand-mothers might not want to keep Deka with them. "Where are your people? Can Deka and her small one stay with them?"

"We have no people here. There's just the two of us," Fadin says.

"How can that be?" Keena asks. "You have no hunters, or women and young ones?

"Many suns ago a great snow came as our people hunted ibex in the high country. Our leader was young and thought the snow wouldn't come so soon. We weren't prepared." Seezel shakes her head.

"We found a small cave in the hills you came from," Fadin adds. "It wasn't large enough for all of us. Our leader was afraid the snows would stay and lock us in this area. He decided the hunters and younger people would try to make it through the snow into the valley below."

"We knew we'd slow them down," Seezel says. "Maybe even cause the deaths of young ones, so we offered to stay behind and survive as long as we could."

"My sons and Seezel's daughter didn't want to leave us, but they had small ones to think about." A tear trickles down Fadin's cheek and her voice quavers.

"It's best we stayed. And now we're here to help Deka," Seezel says.

"The Dark One and her little one can stay with us." Fadin wipes away her tears. "We can move back to the cave, and we have other hiding places here in the grass where we hunt."

"The Sun Spirit smiled on us after our people left. We've been able to snare hares and gather nuts and other foods. The snow times will be hard, but it'll be good to have Deka with us. If she wants to stay." Seezel beams.

"Yes, it'll be good to have young ones with us." Fadin hugs Seezel.

"You can help each other, then," Shinoni says, relieved.

Keena takes one last look at Deka, then turns to the grandmothers. "Haken and his hunters will kill you and Deka and the young one if they find you. It'll be safest not to go to your cave for a few suns. He's likely travelling that way."

Seezel nods grimly. "We've hidden from many predators and survived."

"It's best if Deka rests. We'll stay here for several suns," Fadin assures them.

Keena takes the leftover deer meat from her pack and looks at Shinoni, who nods agreement. "We'll leave this meat so you won't have to hunt for a while."

"Thank you for your help." Shinoni hugs the grandmothers. "Take care of yourselves and Deka and her small one. Perhaps we'll meet again."

"I'd like that," Fadin says. Then she and Seezel roll the stone away from the entrance and pull back the woven mat of vegetation. They peer outside and suddenly freeze.

"Aiiii-yiiii! What's this?" Fadin shrieks. Over the grandmothers' shoulders, Shinoni and Keena see Tewa stand up from the shrubbery. She yawns and stretches as Seezel reaches inside for her spear.

"Don't fear the wolf." Shinoni holds Seezel's arm. "She travels with us."

"She's our friend and guardian," Keena says.

"You're truly strange young women," Fadin marvels.

Seezel nods her agreement. "Go safely and swiftly with your wolf guide."

The sun's rays slant halfway between day and night as Shinoni, Keena, and Tewa leave the earth mound. They resume their journey, quickly moving through the grass parallel to the hills, looking for a stream to follow into the high country.

—— 30 ——

SHINONI AND KEENA RACE along a dry creek bed, chests heaving and legs aching with each pounding step. Their fear of Haken goads them on. How close is he? Have they stayed too long with Deka? The constant strain of being prey is draining.

Finally, when their path connects to a stream, they stop to fill their drinking bags. Tewa laps the water, then rubs against both Shinoni and Keena before bounding away into the grass.

"Where do you think she's going this time?" Keena asks as Tewa's tail disappears from view. She misses Tewa now when she leaves. It's strange how having this predator near makes her feel safer.

"Perhaps she's lonely for her pack and visits them," Shinoni says, "but I wish she would stay with us."

"You said we're her pack now," Keena reminds her.

"We are, but we're still looking for our families. Maybe she is, too."

Scudding clouds cover the sun, whipped into a frenzy by the wind rushing down from the high country. Shinoni closes her eyes.

"Are you all right?" Keena asks.

"Every muscle in my body is tired," Shinoni says. "And I'm so hungry. We need to find food soon." She takes the sling from her pouch and they scour the windswept steppe, but nothing moves among the rustling grasses.

"Perhaps we should've kept some of our meat." Keena scoops a handful of dried purple berries off a bush and into her mouth.

"It's best we gave it to Deka and the grandmothers. They'll be safer if they stay in." Shinoni stares down the creek bed they've just left. "How far behind us do you think Haken is?"

"He could be close. We've been off the trail with Deka, so maybe he's even ahead of us." Keena pops more berries into her mouth, grimacing at the bitter juice.

"Do you think so?" Shinoni shivers. "I feel like there's someone watching us from every bush."

"Maybe they'll set a trap for us." Keena gulps, almost choking on the berries, her nerves now on edge, too. "We'd better get going in case they're close."

Shinoni and Keena pull their cloaks tighter around themselves as they leave the stream. A light dusting of snow coats the grass and shrubs, and frost bites their noses and ears. They walk close together, drawing warmth and strength from each other. *Together is better*, thinks Keena, remembering her father's words.

"Do you think they'll make it?" As Shinoni exhales, her breath forms vapour in the air.

"Haken and his hunters?" Keena asks. "They can travel through anything."

"No, Fadin and Seezel — and Deka. Will they make it through the snow time?"

"Deka and the small one won't survive without the grandmothers' help," Keena says. "I don't know where her people are, and I've never seen anyone else like her."

"Well, we saw her mate, but he was dead," Shinoni says.

"Yes, he was certainly dead," Keena says.

They trudge through the snow for awhile, each deep in her own thoughts.

Keena breaks the silence. "The grandmothers are tough and smart. I don't understand why their group left them behind. They're Kula, like you. Did your band leave grey hairs behind?"

"I never saw that happen, but the snow times are hard," Shinoni says. "Fadin and Seezel offered to stay behind to save the young ones. They're very brave."

"We Krags honour our grey hairs. They carry our knowledge. Even if they can't hunt or chew their food, we help them and care for them," Keena says. "We say a lone Krag is a dead Krag, so we stick together."

"Is that why you stick with me?" Shinoni asks.

"You chose to stick with me, too." Keena nudges her. "We're good together."

Shinoni and Keena lapse into silence. It's harder now to lift their feet or hold their eyelids open as fatigue and hunger settle in. The curtain of falling snow masks the sky and the trail under their feet. Keena concentrates on taking one step at a time. It's difficult to tell if they're still heading toward the hills or how soon darkness will overtake them.

"Ho, Kula, what's that?" Keena stops abruptly and points. The snow has stopped swirling, and ahead of them lies a frozen pond surrounded by trees. Something large lies stretched out on the ice. Its white feathers ruffle in the wind, blending with the snow.

"I think it's a long-necked one," Shinoni says. "It shouldn't be here now, in the snow time."

"It looks dead, Kula," Keena asserts. "I think Leeswi's taken its breath so we can eat it." They hurry to the pond and kneel beside the stiff swan.

"It's like the long-necked one just fell asleep." Shinoni touches the graceful neck tucked back toward the folded wings. "There's no blood or signs of a struggle."

"She couldn't fly. See, her wing is bent." Keena tries to move it.

Skreeeiii, skreeeiii. A piercing shriek echoes from high in a tree nearby.

"It's my father's spirit guide." Shinoni leaps to her feet. "Shazur must've sent the eagle to help us."

"The eagle wants to make a meal of the long neck. It wants us to leave." Keena watches the great bird warily as it spreads its enormous brown wings and flies to a tree beside the pond. Its massive yellow hooked beak opens again. *Skreeeiii, skreeeiii.* The eagle's sharp talons wrap around a branch as thick as Keena's arm. Its golden eyes are fixed on the forest behind Shinoni and Keena.

The girls are startled by a sudden low growl. Shinoni spins around to face the new danger. Keena, too, turns in alarm, her heart racing. She recognizes the snarls and the putrid stench of the wolverine loping effortlessly toward them.

"Quickly, Kula. Back away." Keena tugs frantically on Shinoni's tunic. "This stink bear will rip us apart."

"It can't have the long neck. It died for us. Shazur sent it to feed us." Shinoni stands her ground, knees shaking as the wolverine glides menacingly toward them. "We can drive it off, Keena. There are two of us."

"Stink bears take carcasses away from wolves. They kill hunters who get in their way." Keena pulls Shinoni farther from the swan, but it's too late. The snarling wolverine has closed the gap. Sharp claws click on the ice of the pond. Its powerful muscles ripple under its thick flowing fur. Its lips curl back and saliva drools over its gleaming teeth. The dark mask on its face emphasizes the glare of its small red eyes reflecting the setting sun. The wolverine leaps past the swan and stalks toward the girls.

Skreeeiii, skreeeiii. A terrifying scream splits the air as the eagle swoops like a spear over Shinoni's head, talons extended, raking the startled wolverine's shoulder and bowling it over and over. The wolverine recovers and leaps, jaws snapping at the eagle. Then, undeterred, the wolverine turns back to Shinoni and Keena. The eagle rakes it with its talons again, drawing blood, but the wolverine advances, eyes focused on its prey as they scramble backward.

Shinoni sends a stone flying from her sling, connecting with the wolverine's head. It stops for a heartbeat, but then snarls and stamps its feet, preparing to lunge at Shinoni.

A fierce snarl comes from behind as a large grey shape hurtles over Keena and strikes the stink bear broadside, knocking it over. Tewa enters the fray, hackles raised on her neck, and head down. She circles the confused wolverine as the eagle strikes it again from above. With one last snarl, the wolverine turns tail and races back toward the forest with the eagle following behind, swooping and screaming.

"Tewa, sister, thank you." Shinoni rubs the wolf's strong back, smoothing the hackles that still stand erect. There's blood on Tewa's fur and she whines nervously. She licks Shinoni's face, then walks over to Keena and licks her as well.

"You're a good friend, Tewa." Keena hugs the wolf. "The blood on her belongs to the wolverine. We're lucky she came when she did."

Shinoni and Keena go back to the swan. Tewa joins them, sniffing the dead bird and wagging her tail slightly. The bird is stiff and heavy, but Shinoni and Keena hoist it up together.

Shinoni takes the swan in her arms and holds it against her chest. "I'll carry the long neck first, then you can carry it when I get tired. We need to find shelter quickly."

"Yes, the light will soon fade and that stink bear could return."

"I think he's learned not to bother us," Shinoni says. "We have powerful protectors." The eagle swoops low overhead. Its sharp, clear call lingers in the twilight, then fades as it disappears into the distance.

"That may be," says Keena, "but Haken still tracks us, and he's more dangerous than even a stink bear."

Tewa pushes between them from behind. She matches her pace to theirs for awhile before loping ahead. Faintly at first, then more clearly, the shapes of trees and a hillside emerge through the twilight. Shinoni and Keena both breathe a sigh of relief. They follow Tewa's tail flag as she disappears into the shadows, trusting her instincts that shelter lies ahead.

Later that night, in a small cave behind a fallen boulder, Shinoni, Keena, and Tewa sit by a roaring fire. They've thanked the long neck for giving itself to feed them, and the swan now roasts on a spit over coals at the fire's edge. Beside the fire is a pile of sleek white plumes, and both Shinoni and Keena wear several long feathers tucked into their hair.

Shinoni holds up a thin hollow bone from the swan's wing and examines it. "I'd like to make a flute from this. My mother used to play the swan-bone flute." Her heart aches when she realizes she's speaking of her mother in the past. "I remember how nice it sounded when I was a small one. It made me feel safe because my mother was close."

"I know how to make a flute," Keena says. "The Kula hunter Sabra, who stayed with my family, made a flute for my father out of a piece of cave bear bone."

"A bear bone isn't like a swan bone," Shinoni says.

"No, it's heavier, but they both make music," Keena says. "My father loves that flute and he plays it all the time. He lets me play it, too."

"Your father must care for you a lot to let you play his flute," Shinoni says.

"I can make you a flute out of the swan bone, if you'd like," Keena offers.

"I'd like that very much." Shinoni tingles with pleasure. She looks at Keena's tattered footwear with its worn-out laces. "I could sew your foot covers together so your feet stay warmer and dry."

"I'd like that, too." Keena beams.

Then they both settle down by the fire to work on their separate tasks. Tewa lies between them, stretched out on her back. She whines and growls softly in her sleep, perhaps dreaming of the day's adventures.

31

THE NEXT MORNING Shinoni and Keena exchange their gifts. Shinoni balances the slim swan bone on the palm of her hand. An image of her mother smiles in her head as she strokes the smooth, polished surface. She admires the four holes punched along one side, then lifts it to her lips and blows several mournful, high-pitched notes.

Keena examines the carefully stitched boots Shinoni has created from her battered foot wraps. She runs her fingers over the sinew stitches, then slips her feet inside and wriggles her toes in the dried grass lining. "These are good foot covers, Shinoni. Thanks to you, my feet will be dry today."

"Thank you, Keena. It'll take some practice, but now I'm linked to my mother."

They share a hug, then pack up quickly and leave the cave just as the sun's first rays peek above the horizon.

Shinoni, Keena, and Tewa travel along the hillside and descend into a broad valley. In the distance, a herd of reindeer trek from the high country into the warmer valley below. Their greyish-white coats meld with the snow-dotted landscape. The herd spreads out across the steppe. Mothers with nearly grown young ones nimbly travel alongside males and females without young.

"There are so many, and most carry antlers," Shinoni says. "Which are the mothers?"

"You've never seen the snow walkers flowing like a river?" Keena puffs up her chest. "In their clan, all grown ones wear headdresses. We sometimes use the antlers to dig our way through the snow after storms."

"I've seen them, but not often," Shinoni says. "They aren't like the forest deer near my people's camps. Forest deer don't travel in big groups like these."

Tewa watches the herd, her ears cocked and muscles tense. She whines excitedly, then licks her lips. She turns to the girls, gives a short yodel, and lopes down the hill toward the reindeer.

"They're a long way off. Will she hunt alone?" Keena shades her eyes, trying to follow Tewa's descent as she disappears behind shrubbery.

"Her wolf spirit's restless for a chase and a kill. The snow walkers are worthy prey and there are lots to choose from."

"Maybe she'll bring us fresh meat tonight and we'll soon have full bellies again." Keena smacks her lips. "They're very tasty."

Shinoni finds a less steep trail into the valley, away from the reindeer herd. As they make their way down, the sun rises higher above the horizon. Its warming rays lift their spirits. A thin skiff of snow on the grass sparkles under their feet and begins to melt.

"Careful, it's slippery," Shinoni says. "Want me to help you?"

"I'm from the high country. I know how to get down hills." Keena chuckles and speeds up. Almost immediately, her wet foot covers slip on the icy vegetation. "Yiiiiii," she yelps as her feet shoot out from under her, knocking her backward.

"Oh yeah, you're great at getting around. Can you teach me how to do that?" Shinoni shakes with laughter.

"Glad to show you." Keena puffs to get her breath back. Then she clutches her knees and rolls head over heels, straight into Shinoni, sending her flying. They slip and slide downhill, laughing as they tumble over each other. They land in a tangle of arms and legs at the bottom of the slope.

Shinoni grins as they shake off the snow. "You sure know how to get down hills fast, Krag."

"You're a fast learner, Kula."

"Anything to stay ahead of Haken, eh, Krag?" Shinoni quips.

"We have to keep moving, because he could be anywhere. Come on!" Keena urges, her voice suddenly serious.

The mention of her dreaded uncle's name sends a jolt of panic down to Keena's toes. She and Shinoni scramble across the valley, trying to outrun their fear, not slowing down until the sun is high overhead.

A herd of woolly mammoths grazes in the distance. Shinoni gasps at the sight of them. "Have you seen these long-nosed hairy ones before? They're more powerful than even the big horn."

"I've mainly seen them dead and being cut up for our food," Keena says. "It's good to see them alive and peaceful with their clan."

Shinoni and Keena are downwind from the huge beasts, so they settle in a stand of willows to catch their breath and rest. As the herd wanders closer to their hiding spot in the bushes, their musty scent envelops Keena and Shinoni like a wet cloak.

Shinoni stares at the beasts, her eyes full of awe. Shaggy grey hair covers their bodies and their heads, which are domed like hills. The mammoths sway as their long trunks sweep the earth, searching out tasty vegetation and stuffing trunkfuls of it into their waiting mouths. Their great curved tusks gleam in the sun.

Some of the mammoths rub against each other affectionately as they graze. "They're probably all females and young ones," Keena says. "My father told me the long-nosed males travel alone."

"That big mother must be their leader." Shinoni points to a massive female. "She's probably taller than two hunters standing on each other's shoulders."

A few boisterous young ones run and play near some half-grown females. The young ones head-butt each other and wrestle with their trunks. As they tussle, two of them move dangerously close to a nearby mudhole.

"Those ones are probably supposed to watch the young ones." Keena nods at the young females. "They should watch more closely for danger." She winces as a pang of regret lodges in her chest. She should have watched Tat more closely.

"They remind me of the boys in my band, always pushing and wrestling each other," Shinoni says.

"Are they any better at it?" Keena asks.

"No, they aren't." Shinoni's voice becomes sad. "I mean, they weren't. They can't play anymore."

"I used to wrestle and play with my friend Kreel when we were young ones," says Keena. "He was often at my hearth because his father was mean to him. My father and mother liked Kreel, so he was with us a lot. I miss him sometimes." She ducks her head, hiding a tear that rolls down her cheek.

The mood lightens as one of the little mammoths tumbles into the mudhole, making the girls laugh. The tall grasses near the mudhole begin to quiver. Shinoni stares at them, shading her eyes. "Ho, look. Something's hiding there."

Keena sees the tip of a tawny tail twitching above the grass. Is that dew on the grass or a glint of eye shine? Shinoni and Keena rise up on their knees. Keena's heart pounds wildly.

The little mammoth trumpets in distress as he sinks in the soft mud. The other young one panics and runs for the safety of the herd. Right behind him, a snarling golden streak bursts out of the grass in hot pursuit.

"Oh no. Lion!" Shinoni shrieks.

"He's not going to make it," Keena screams. Terror chokes her breath like a rope twisting around her neck.

The lion is gaining on the young mammoth, now squealing for his mother. Shinoni leaps from the bushes and shouts at the lion, distracting it. A well-aimed stone from her sling thuds on the lion's skull. The big cat spins around, slipping on the muddy ground, trying to keep its balance. The snarling beast focuses on Shinoni and Keena. Its yellow eyes narrow in slits of rage above its deadly fangs.

Panic stabs through Keena's body like a spear. She freezes as the lion lowers its head and advances.

"Run, Keena!" Shinoni screams and grabs her arm, pulling her toward a sturdy tree a short distance away. Their feet take wing as the snarling lion bounds toward them. Keena, her hands clammy and slippery from fear, struggles to pull herself up the tree. Shinoni pushes her from behind and scrambles after her just as the big cat springs, shredding the bark at the base of the tree. The lion glares at them, spitting and snarling in frustration.

"Good shot, Kula. Now it's really mad." Keena pants from her precarious perch halfway up the tree.

"Let's see you do better." Shinoni struggles to wedge herself between two branches so that her hands are free. She lets loose with a barrage of stones from her pouch as the furious lion leaps below the tree. The little mammoth struggling helplessly in the mud begins to squeal more loudly, and the cat turns back toward the mudhole.

"Fine, give me the sling!" Keena grabs the loaded sling from Shinoni, twirls it over her head, and sends a rock flying through the air. A direct hit thuds on the lion's flank. "Eeeee-yaaaa, I hit it!" Keena almost falls from the tree in her excitement.

"Nice shooting for a Krag," Shinoni hoots, obviously impressed.

The cat snarls and races back to the tree. It leaps at the girls, clawing the trunk below them.

The herd lumbers toward the scene of battle. Their trumpeting and the little mammoth's squeals fill the air. The lion faces them, standing its ground and spitting, as the girls watch from their perch in horror. As the angry mammoths close in, it turns tail and runs, the hairy giants trumpeting behind it.

As the lion escapes into the grass, the mammoths turn back toward the mudhole. The matriarch rushes to the trapped youngster and runs her trunk over his little body and brushes him gently with her head. She drops to her knees, wraps her trunk under the young one's belly, and tugs. Other females join her, wrapping their trunks around the baby and tugging. Finally the little mammoth is pulled from the sticky mud and helped up the slippery embankment. The females excitedly cluster around the calf and pat him. The youngster trumpets, a high-pitched squeak from his miniature trunk.

The matriarch searches out the tree where Shinoni and Keena sit, transfixed. She stops under them, looks up, and raises her trunk. Keena shrinks back, but Shinoni bends down and touches the sensitive tip.

"She's beautiful, Keena. Feel how delicate the end is."

Keena reaches down carefully. Her eyes open wide with awe as she feels the trunk and its gentle probing tip. "It's like a hand."

Shinoni looks down on the broad hairy back of the mammoth just below her under the tree. "We've ridden a horse, Keena. Wouldn't you like to travel on such a powerful beast?"

"No, I would not!" Keena stares at Shinoni. *Not again.*

"We'd be safe from everything on her back," Shinoni says.

"Until we come off, Kula. Then she'll stomp us like bugs."

Keena can't believe Shinoni is serious. Yet there she is, already sliding off the branch, dangling her legs over the mammoth's back.

"Come on. She's grateful we helped her young one," Shinoni says.

"Let's keep it that way and not get her mad — oh!" Keena cringes as Shinoni drops onto the mammoth's back. The huge beast stands still, not seeming to notice the puny human on her back.

Keena's muscles tighten with fear, but the terror of being alone is even greater. Closing her eyes, she steps down from her branch and lands on the matriarch's back behind Shinoni. Keena gulps and clutches the coarse hair and feels the powerful muscles under her legs. She wraps her arms around Shinoni's waist. "We're going to die!" Keena moans through clenched teeth.

What would Kreel and Sabra think if they saw her now?

The matriarch reaches back with her trunk and gently touches Shinoni and Keena, then moves out from under the tree, trumpeting to her family. The young one comes to her at once, and the whole herd of six adult females, four half-grown females, and four calves moves off at a fast clip across the valley.

32

THE SUN'S SHADOWS loom long in the valley as the fast-moving mammoth herd approaches a canyon. Shinoni sits tall and proud on the matriarch's humped shoulders. Her feet grip behind the large flapping ears. "Isn't this great, Keena? We can see so far and nothing can get us up here. It's even better than riding Ulu!"

Keena rides behind Shinoni, clinging tightly to her waist. "Yes, we're certainly up high." Keena gulps. The matriarch is moving so quickly. What would happen if she slipped off her back? Better tighten her grip on Shinoni even more. Still, the wind in her face and the treetops being so close is exciting.

Suddenly, high rock walls tower toward the sky on either side of the game trail they travel on. "What's happening, Kula?" Keena asks. "Are we out of the forest?"

"Perhaps you should open your eyes, Keena, and have a look."

Keena cranes her neck to see around Shinoni to the path ahead. There are still some thickets here, with smaller trees beside the trail, but the way is narrowing.

"The long noses are travelling on a dangerous path," Shinoni mutters. "We'll soon be almost closed in by the rock walls."

Shinoni sits up straighter and points high above them. "Look! Can you see something moving up there? An ibex, maybe? Or someone hiding on the cliffs?" Shinoni turns her head, scanning the shifting shadows on the rock face. "There are people up there. Are they Krags?"

Keena squints over Shinoni's shoulder. "I can't tell from here." A shiver ripples down her spine. "If they're Krags, they'll likely push rocks down on the hairy long noses to kill them."

"If it's a trap, we'll be squashed, too!" Shinoni screeches. "Ho, mother. Go back!"

"Back. Back!" Keena screams.

Shinoni tugs at the matriarch's ears and they both kick with their heels, trying to turn their massive mount. Their shouts reach the hunters on the cliff, who leap about, calling and pointing in amazement.

"Guess they've never seen anyone ride a mammoth before," Shinoni says. "We're friends," she shouts in Kula.

"Spare us, hunters," Keena cries in Krag.

The hunters continue to jump up and down, arms flailing, in full view of the approaching mammoths. The big beasts trumpet in panic and turn clumsily around, lumbering away at a furious pace. The matriarch crashes through the thicket beside the path, toppling small trees and breaking branches as she goes.

Shinoni and Keena hang on desperately, but a swaying branch partway up a pine tree sweeps them from the matriarch's back. They grab on to the branch and climb into the tree. The girls cling to their prickly perch high above the ground, watching the herd disappear into the distance. Keena looks in the other direction to see the mammoth hunters clambering down the rock face. The first ones to reach the valley floor race toward them, spears in hand.

The fierce hunters are almost upon the tree where Keena and Shinoni cower. The bronze skin of their faces shines with oil. Black tusk-shaped tattoos decorate their chins, cheeks, and foreheads. Their dark hair is sleek and oiled and pulled back in a tail. When one hunter turns to shout over his shoulder, Keena can see that his hair is held with hide thongs decorated with ivory — from mammoth tusks, she guesses. One especially muscular hunter wears his hair high on his head in a topknot circled by an ivory ring threaded with sinew.

"We won't have to worry about Haken anymore." Shinoni wraps her long legs around another limb, trying to keep her balance.

"Why?" Keena squeaks. She clutches the tree trunk with both arms and legs.

"We ruined their hunt, so these hunters will kill us." Shinoni's eyes are wide with fear.

Keena's jaw drops. "Maybe not," she says hopefully.

The brawny and fierce mammoth hunters stretch out their hands to Shinoni and Keena in a pleading motion. They fall on their knees under the tree and place their foreheads to the ground, chanting singsong words over and over. "Aaaoooiiii aaaeetee. Aaaoooiiii aaaeeteetii."

"What are they saying?" Keena asks. "They look like your people, but their words are different."

"They are Kulas. Their language is a bit different from my people's, but close enough for me to understand. They think we're spirits, Krag. They think the Earth Spirit sent us to guard the mammoth clan."

Keena smiles in relief, and she and Shinoni shinny down the tree into the midst of the mammoth hunters. The awestruck men gingerly touch their hair, then back up to a respectful distance. The muscular hunter with the topknot speaks to Shinoni and Keena, bending low.

Shinoni translates slowly. "His name is Ruppa and he's their leader. He wants to take us to their camp to show his people that spirits have visited them."

"Do you think we can trust them, Shinoni?" Keena asks. "I really don't want to be a captive again."

"I think he truly believes we are spirits and wants to show us to his people," Shinoni says. "I don't think we have a choice, Keena. So we'll have to go with them for now."

"Tell him all right, but we can't stay too long," Keena says. "We don't want to be their permanent good-luck amulet."

The sun is setting when Shinoni and Keena, escorted by Ruppa and his men, approach the mammoth hunters' home.

"Have you ever seen a camp such as this one?" Shinoni whispers.

"Never, Kula. They must kill many mammoths." Keena's eyes widen in disbelief as she looks at the scene before her. A circle of shelters constructed of stacked mammoth tusks and bones with reindeer hides stretched over top of them cluster around a roaring fire. Several smaller hearths dot the camp's perimeter.

Ruppa blows an ibex horn to announce their arrival. Women, children, and grey hairs rush to meet them at the edge of camp. They fall back at the sight of Shinoni and Keena.

"They're probably expecting a big pile of mammoth meat, not us," Shinoni says. "As long as they don't try to eat us, instead."

Keena smiles and nods at the gathering group as Ruppa begins to speak.

"He's telling them about their hunt," Shinoni says.

Ruppa's voice booms as he gestures to some of the hunters lumbering around in a circle. Their knees are bent and they lean forward, shoulders hunched, one arm swinging in front of their faces to mimic the swaying trunks and hump backs of the mammoths. The other hunters dance and circle them, spears ready to thrust.

"Hang on, Keena, we're going for a ride," Shinoni says.

"Not again." Keena flinches as dancers hoist them into the air and onto the shoulders of two hunters, who carry them about, snorting wildly. The ground whirls dizzily below Keena as she and Shinoni cling to their mounts, now spinning around the circle. Finally, the dancers deposit them on the ground in front of Ruppa. He looks at them expectantly.

Keena tastes vomit in her mouth and gags, trying not to retch. Shinoni holds her steady as the ground continues to spin around them. The smell of sweat and mammoth fat is overpowering as the entire band pushes close. The people's faces reflect curiosity, fear, and awe.

"Say something, Kula." Keena nudges Shinoni. "You always have words."

Shinoni pauses, then rubs her stomach and speaks directly to Ruppa. He immediately bows low and makes a sweeping gesture toward the flames. The hunters hustle the girls toward the fire.

"What did you say?" Keena gasps. "They're not going to burn us, are they?"

"I just said we're hungry."

As they approach the fire, several men rise. A grey hair, one of the mammoth hunters, talks excitedly to Ruppa, pointing to the men.

"We aren't their only visitors." Shinoni grips Keena's arm tightly, and Keena looks more closely at the strangers by the fire. The hair on her neck bristles and her skin prickles as she recognizes the strange hunters.

The glow from the flames lights up the faces of the men who've risen. Their squat builds, ruddy cheeks, and barrel chests show they aren't Kula mammoth hunters. One man steps forward. The firelight highlights the twisted scar on his face. Haken smirks as he bows his head to Keena and Shinoni, who stand in shocked silence.

The mammoth hunters look curiously from the girls to Haken and back again. Ruppa haltingly exchanges words with Haken in the Krag language.

Shinoni and Keena flinch as their enemy waves his hand at them. His face crinkles in a grotesque grin.

Keena whispers to Shinoni. "He's telling Ruppa we're spirits but have come from his land." Keena frowns like a thundercloud. "He says we're lost and they have to take us back with them."

"We have to convince them otherwise." Shinoni steadies her shaking legs. "It seems these Kulas have met Krags before and are friendly to them."

"I'm sure Ruppa doesn't know how much Haken hates Kulas," Keena says. "Haken's likely afraid to attack them because they have many strong hunters. He'll try to trick them instead."

"Ruppa can speak Krag, but can Haken speak Kula?" Shinoni asks.

"No. I had to tell him what you were saying when he captured you," Keena says. "He only speaks Krag." She looks at Shinoni and smiles, signalling that she understands what Shinoni is thinking.

"Haken will soon learn he's not the only trickster here," Shinoni says. "We'll give Ruppa a message from the Earth Spirit."

Keena and Shinoni sit in a place of honour by the fire, where they eat sizzling slices of meat carved from a reindeer haunch. The hunters dance again while they eat, retelling the story of the girl spirits' wild ride on the mammoths. Young ones sit staring at them, just out of reach beyond the ring of firelight. One little girl creeps closer and touches Shinoni, smiling shyly at her. Another child gives Keena a bone flute, which she begins to play. The trilling notes float over the crackling of the flames, and more of the mammoth-hunter clan cluster around her. Obviously they've never seen or heard a Krag play a flute before. Keena lowers the instrument. Best not to attract more attention.

"They're all here," Keena whispers. "Should we give them the message now?"

"Yes, this is a good time for the spirits to speak." Shinoni claps her hands for attention. "Mammoth hunters, we're sent from the Earth Spirit. We are not lost. We've chosen to visit you because you're great hunters."

"That's good," Keena says. "Make them trust us, not Haken."

Shinoni flings her arms wide, then curves both hands to indicate tusks. "This message is about the mammoth clan." Her shout echoes in the hushed stillness. "The great Earth Spirit is concerned. Some groups kill too many of her mammoth children." She narrows her eyes as she looks at Haken.

Keena glares at him, too. How she hates him. He watches her every move like a lion waiting to pounce.

"Groups like the one led by this Krag, Haken." Shinoni points at him. "They destroy the mammoths with their greed."

Ruppa's band murmurs angrily. They look suspiciously at Haken. Keena hides a grin behind her hands as she looks at Shinoni's stern face.

"The Earth Spirit will always let you have many mammoths to hunt if you use them wisely." Shinoni pauses to let her words soak in. "You mustn't kill more than you need to feed yourselves." She stares at Haken, then looks at Ruppa. He's listening intently to her. "You must thank the mammoths for giving their lives to feed you."

The mammoth hunters nod in agreement. Again, Shinoni points an accusing finger at Haken. "This Krag's group hasn't cared for the mammoth. So we are here to help you, not to help them."

Haken looks around, scowling. He seems to be catching on that Shinoni is turning the mammoth hunters against him. He jumps up and shouts at Ruppa. Several burly mammoth hunters surround Haken, glaring at him. Ruppa frowns and translates some of what Shinoni has said into Krag.

Haken throws the girls a menacing look, but turns back to Rappa and begins to speak in a conciliatory voice.

"Earlier, Haken said we must go with them tomorrow, but now he says they really need our help to get the Earth Spirit's forgiveness," Keena says.

"They don't believe him or trust him. I can tell." Shinoni smiles and waves at the mammoth hunters.

Night has fallen, and Keena and Shinoni are sleeping beside a flickering hearth inside one of the tusk and bone shelters. Heavy hands shake them awake. Ruppa crouches beside them with a finger on his lips. He speaks in a low voice, his face serious as the firelight reflects in his eyes.

"Ruppa doesn't trust Haken. He thinks we should go now," Shinoni translates for Keena. "He says we should travel in the hills but he'll tell Haken we're travelling in the valley."

Ruppa then hands them warm fur-lined tunics and two reindeer-skin packs. "He says there's dried meat in these," Shinoni says. "He thanks us for visiting them and for bringing the Earth Spirit's message. He says they'll take care of the mammoths. These gifts are for our journey."

Ruppa lifts up the reindeer-skin flap at the back of the shelter. Shinoni and Keena both touch hands with him and wriggle out quietly. They tiptoe out of camp. It's nearly dawn and the sky is lightening. Tewa steps out of the shadows at the camp's edge and joins them, wagging her tail in greeting. Then, together again, they hurry toward the hills rising in the distance.

33

DAYLIGHT FINDS Shinoni and Keena on the ridge above the valley. They wear the reindeer-hide tunics Ruppa gave them on parting. The thick fur on the inside cuts the frigid bite of the mountain wind. They stop to drink at a stream, thirsty after their strenuous climb. The snow has melted here and their footprints show clearly in the mud.

"Haken could be close behind us. He'll be furious we escaped again." Keena scans the rocky trail they've just climbed, much of it hidden by bushes.

"If Ruppa tells him we're in the valley, he's likely not too close," Shinoni says. But she looks over her shoulder.

"Haken might not listen to Ruppa, and he's a good tracker." Keena's ears strain to catch any telltale sound of movement in the bushes.

"We'll have to hide our tracks, then," Shinoni says. "If we walk in the stream, he can't track us through the water."

Shinoni and Keena move into the centre of the shallow stream and slog on, following the water's path deeper into the hills. When the sun is high in the sky, they reach a point where the stream joins others, all merging with a fast-flowing river. The rapidly moving water is free of ice, and it splashes and bubbles over the rocks in the shallows.

Keena and Shinoni sit on the rocky beach beside the restless river. Shinoni scoops up some of the small flat stones littering the shoreline and puts them in her pouch. Keena looks at her quizzically. "Why, Kula? If your pouch isn't heavy enough, you can carry some of my load."

"You never know when a good rock will come in handy." Shinoni chuckles. She pulls out the dried reindeer meat Ruppa gave them and shares several strips with Keena.

"Do you think we should follow this river?" Shinoni asks. "You know this land better than I do. Will the river take us to your family?"

Keena looks down the river as far as she can see and takes a deep, shuddering breath. What if she leads them the wrong way? "Many rivers flow near the mountain pass that's close to my home," she says.

This might be one of them." Keena hesitates. "Maybe not, though."

"Well, let's follow it awhile. We can walk close to the water's edge." Shinoni gets to her feet. "The river narrows here, so maybe we should cross before it gets too wide."

"Why should we cross it?" Keena stammers as she watches the wildly swirling water. "We can just walk along this shoreline."

"The shore on this side disappears soon," Shinoni says. "See, up ahead there's a thicket right by the water. There could be predators there. And then there's just a steep wall of rock." She points across the river. "There are tall cliffs on that side, and that might be where your snow pass is."

"I'd rather not cross this river," Keena says. Her stomach lurches with fear.

"Can't you swim, Keena?" Shinoni asks, eyebrows raised.

"No, Kula, I can't." Keena says. "Some of my people can, but most don't. Leeswi often takes people's breath when they cross rivers or lakes."

"It's shallow here, and I'll hang on to you." Shinoni prods Keena toward the water. "Do you want to sit here and wait for Haken?"

"No." Keena sighs. Anything is better than meeting Haken again.

Shinoni walks into the water and turns, holding out her hand. Keena takes one small step and then another until she is beside Shinoni in the water. They start walking across the current, hand in hand, toward the open steppe ringed by cliffs on the far side.

Shinoni stops and reaches into her pouch with her free hand, taking out stones one by one and skimming them across the water. Her stone-throwing attracts fish, which leap high in the air, sending rainbow sprays into the centre of the river.

"We can have fresh fish tonight," Shinoni says. "It won't take long to catch some."

"The current's too fast here! You said we were just crossing." Keena, heart pounding, breaks away from Shinoni's grip. She plows blindly toward the far shore.

"Wait up, Keena." Shinoni skips one last rock.

"Come on, stop fooling around. We've got to go now," Keena yells from the beach where she sits, annoyed and shivering.

"All right, I'm coming. No fish tonight." Shinoni turns to join Keena. Suddenly, she slips and falls backward into the water. "Help me, Keena!" Her screams disappear into the roar of the river.

Shinoni flounders, desperately trying to regain her balance, but she's caught in an undertow. Keena sees her gulp a mouthful of the icy water. She sputters and chokes as she's sucked down beneath the choppy waves and carried away.

"Shinoni, Kula, no!" Keena's screams echo above the river. There's no sign of Shinoni. "Please, Leeswi, spit her out," Keena shouts. She paces on the shore, scanning the water, unsure what to do, then runs downstream. Shinoni resurfaces, caught in the swift-flowing current.

"Help me!" Shinoni manages a desperate cry as she gasps for air and fights to stay above water.

"Hang on, I'm coming." Keena runs along the shore, keeping Shinoni in view. At a shallow bend in the river, a tree, probably washed into the water during the last snow melt, is jammed against the rocks. The raging water sweeps Shinoni against the tree, and she grabs onto it, clinging frantically to its slippery, water-logged trunk. Keena runs into the water and splashes toward her friend.

Keena screams a plea to Leeswi as she paddles clumsily toward Shinoni. "Help us, Mother. Save us from the Water Spirit!" The treacherous current snatches Keena and pulls her under the swirling water, but she surfaces again, gasping for breath. The water slams her against the trapped tree trunk, knocking the breath from her body. Keena feels the rough bark against her skin and, every muscle straining, hauls herself out of the water onto the log. She reaches for Shinoni's arm and pulls her friend up beside her.

"Thank you, Mother Leeswi," Keena cries. Shinoni coughs up water, then smiles weakly.

With a fearsome tearing sound, the log is wrenched away from the rocks, almost throwing Shinoni and Keena from its back as it buckles and sways. They cling frantically to their precarious vessel as the rampaging current sweeps them downriver.

— 34 —

KEENA WAKES WITH A START, gasping for breath. *Where am I?* Shivers wrack her body, and her teeth chatter as the icy current sucks at her feet. The last thing she remembers is being on the log as it was swept away in the raging water. Rough tree bark scratches against her hand, and she realizes she's still clinging to the log. Perhaps Leeswi took her breath and then decided to spare her and spit her out?

There's no wind now, and the sun hangs low in the sky. The log is wedged on a sand bar in a narrow part of the river. Keena heaves herself more securely onto the log and straddles it as the river laps against her perch, waiting to gobble her up. Every muscle in her body aches as though she'd been stomped by a woolly rhinoceros. Keena shakes her head to clear it. There are blood splatters on her white reindeer tunic. Suddenly memory floods back, steeped in terror.

"Shinoni!" Keena screams.

"Here, Keena." Shinoni's voice is faint and muffled.

Keena crawls on her stomach along the slippery wood and peers over the side. Shinoni is in the water, clinging to a stout branch that sticks out of the log, half-submerged. Her wet hair is plastered across her bruised face but she manages a weak smile.

"Thank you, sister. I thought you couldn't swim," Shinoni says, her breath coming in gasps.

"I can't. Leeswi must've guided me across the water," Keena says. "My arms and legs moved and I didn't sink." Keena clutches the log with her legs and hauls Shinoni up beside her. She flings her arms around her. "Leeswi's spared you twice now. You should be more careful."

"I'll try," Shinoni stammers, her lips numb.

The punishing wind has started blowing again. It bites their wet skin, pressing their soaked garments close to their battered bodies.

"We aren't far from shore." Shinoni points to a rocky beach close by. "The water looks shallow." She slips carefully off the log and grasps Keena's hand.

"Can you touch bottom?" Keena asks. "Don't let go." Keena doesn't trust the Water Spirit.

"Come in. I can stand and the current isn't strong." The water laps around Shinoni's waist. "We must leave before the log moves on," she urges as Keena hesitates.

Keena slides off the log and the water swirls around her shoulders. She grips Shinoni's hand tightly and they stumble through the water together toward shore.

"The river must've carried us a great distance," Shinoni says. The jagged cliffs that had seemed so distant before now loom close enough that the girls can see them, their sides riddled with caves.

Keena's voice drops to a fearful whisper. "Yes, and there are other people on this beach." A plume of smoke rises above trees around a bend in the shoreline.

"Perhaps they'll let us dry our clothes and warm up at their fire." Shinoni starts down the beach toward the smoke, but Keena holds back.

"It could be Haken," Keena says.

"He wouldn't be sitting at a fire with the sun still shining. Besides, he's not likely to be so far ahead of us," Shinoni says.

"All right, but we will stop and see who they are before approaching them. We need to be sure they're not dangerous." Keena joins Shinoni, and they hunch their freezing bodies against the wind and move toward the inviting promise of warmth.

Before long they hear voices. Keena's heart leaps. "Krags," she says. "But women, not hunters." They look at each other and cut through a small stand of trees that blocks their view of the beach. They duck below some bushes and creep closer.

A small group of Krag women fish by the water's edge. Some of them empty fish traps made of willow branches, and others dry the fish over a ring of fires on the beach.

"Do you think they'll be friendly?" Shinoni whispers.

"Probably, but they might be cautious. Let me talk."

Keena and Shinoni crawl out of the thicket and approach the women. Their sudden appearance and bedraggled condition startle the fishers, who drop their traps and huddle together.

A grey-haired crone comes forward. Her bushy hair is bunched on top of her head, and her stormy grey eyes glitter under brow ridges. Wrinkles crisscross her cheeks like crevasses. She points a spear at them. There is a fish still impaled on its end. Then she lowers the blade and beckons them to come closer.

Keena talks to the crone, who watches Shinoni suspiciously. "She wants to know why I travel with a Kula," Keena says, and she places a hand on Shinoni's shoulder. "I told her you're my friend."

"Ask her if we can dry by their fire and if they can spare us some fish." Shinoni smiles at the crone and stretches out her hand, palm up. The old woman ignores her.

Keena speaks to the crone, who then turns to consult with the other women. They babble heatedly, but she finally nods and motions to the fire. The girls gratefully shed their wet furs and hang them by the flames. The women continue talking, voices rising as they gesture and point at them.

"They don't seem very happy to have us here." Shinoni holds her hands close to the fire and watches the women anxiously.

"They're not. They think you'll bring them trouble," Keena says. "Their men have been gone a long time hunting a big horn. They fear having a Kula in camp will anger Leeswi and ruin the hunt."

The crone leaves the others and approaches them, carrying two fur capes and several dried fish. She thrusts the furs and fish at Keena, speaking rapidly. "You must go." She points down the beach. "This cliff provides a shorter route into the snow pass, but bears dwell in the caves there." Then she gestures toward the forest, shaking her head. "Or you can go that way, but there is a tarkan in the forest. Take these furs and these fish and leave your wet things behind."

Keena bows her head to the crone, then turns to Shinoni. "She'll trade these furs for our wet ones and she'll provide us with these fish as well," Keena says.

Shinoni fingers the thinner pelts, frowning. "These aren't as good as ours." She holds them against the heavier reindeer skins drying by the fire.

"Our furs will take a long time to dry and they want us to leave now." Keena shrugs, chewing on a fish. "I don't think we have a choice."

Shinoni sighs as she wraps one of the dry furs around her shoulders. "Was she giving you some kind of directions?"

Keena is reluctant to answer. She watches Shinoni out of the corner of her eye. "She says there's a short-cut into the mountain snow pass down the beach, but bears live in the caves in the cliff."

"Why did she point into the forest?" Shinoni nods toward the gloomy-looking patch of trees beside the river.

"She says there's a tarkan in that direction, on the other side of the forest. It's a place where spirits dwell," Keena whispers, and she feels the colour drain from her face. "She says we shouldn't go there."

"Why does she care where we go?" Shinoni asks.

"Tarkans are very bad places," Keena says. The words stick in her throat. "This one's a black thicket of dead trees. It separates the water from the mountain — and the dead from the living."

"Why's that so bad?" Shinoni shrugs. "My people often set out gifts and talk with the spirits of dead kin."

"All Krags know of these tarkans and fear them." Sweat beads on Keena's brow despite the cold wind.

"All Krags know this?" Shinoni hoots. "If Haken fears this place, we should be safe from him there."

"I don't think we should go there," Keena says.

"I'd rather face spirits than either Haken or a cave bear," Shinoni says. "Don't you see this is the best way to avoid your murderous uncle? Let's just go in a little way to find shelter. If the tarkan's on the other side of the forest, we can decide not to go that far." She pulls a reluctant Keena toward the forest edge.

As they near the trees, the women cry out a shrill warning behind them. Keena feels the hair on her neck stand up and a shiver run down her spine.

A grey figure waits in the shadows near the forest fringe. Tewa slips in beside the girls, rejoining them as if she's been with them through all the turmoil of their perilous river journey.

"Oh, Tewa, you found us." Shinoni drops to her knees beside the wolf and throws her arms around her shaggy neck. She buries her face in the coarse silver fur.

The wolf's powerful presence is comforting to Keena. She breathes a little easier. "How does she always know where we are?" She strokes Tewa's face and looks into her eyes.

Shinoni studies the wolf, a puzzled look on her face. "I think she's guiding us. Perhaps our spirits are joined."

Keena stands and continues to stroke Tewa for a moment before turning to face the forest. Her fear returns, creeping over her slowly, freezing her blood, choking her breath. "She's only a wolf, and she'll be no protection in the darkness of the tarkan." Her whisper sounds loud in the stillness.

"If Tewa is our spirit guide, she can warn us of danger from spirits." Shinoni hugs Keena. "Come on, we'll be safer going ahead than going back and meeting Haken."

"I will come, but wait. There's something I must do first." Keena takes a deep breath and straightens her shoulders. Then she kneels on the ground and gathers leaves into a pile on a flat rock. "Give me your flints, Kula, and hold the wolf." She takes one of the dried fish from her cloak and places it on the mound of leaves. "I'll make an offering to Leeswi."

Shinoni gives Keena the flints, then settles onto a log, her arms around Tewa's neck. The wolf sits quietly, ears cocked, as Keena lights a spark in the leaves. Tewa whines and salivates at the scent of burning fish.

Keena calls loudly to the Earth Mother. "Ka-kwa-rau-set, Leeswi. Leeswi. Krag-nu-kik-kwac." She raises her arms to the sky and calls again. "Mother Leeswi, save us from the tarkan. Protect us from the evil spirits!" She calls until the fish is nothing but ashes, then pours water from her bag onto the small fire.

Keena stands up. "We can go now," she says. She joins arms with Shinoni, and Tewa pushes her warm, solid body between them. Then, silently, the three disappear into the deepening shadows of the trees, toward the tarkan waiting beyond the forest.

35

TEWA LEADS SHINONI AND KEENA out of the dimness of the forest and into a clearing where a full moon is rising, ghostly over the pale, silent river. Shinoni swallows hard and clutches her eagle amulet in one hand and Tewa's warm fur in the other. Across a patch of brown grass lies a thicket of trees, tangled and blackened in death. They raise jagged limbs, stark silhouettes against the moonlit sky. As the wind picks up, the bare branches rattle like the disjointed bones of a skeleton.

Shinoni turns to look at Keena, but finds she's dropped back several paces.

"It's the tarkan." Keena's eyes are orbs of fear. "We can't go in there."

The wind stops blowing. No sounds of birds or beasts break the silence. Absolute stillness blankets the clearing.

"Come, Keena, we're safer together." Shinoni startles at the sound of her own voice rippling between them.

"You go, Shinoni," Keena whispers.

"Haken won't follow us here," Shinoni says.

"I can't move. My legs are frozen." Tears cloud Keena's eyes.

Tewa looks at the girls, then turns and bounds into the dismal thicket. She disappears into the shadows.

"Tewa wouldn't go in if there was anything to fear," Shinoni says.

A deep sigh escapes from Keena's throat. She joins Shinoni and they enter the brooding gloom of the tarkan together.

Shinoni and Keena set up camp beside a large hollow tree stump. They light a glowing circle of fire around themselves. Outside the circle, the darkness surrounds them, pushing against the flames. They share their meagre meal of fish with Tewa and settle on a bed of dead pine boughs, exhausted from their long and strenuous day.

Shinoni stares into the darkness. Tewa cocks her ears as though listening to something, but there's still absolute silence around them.

"What does she hear?" Keena whispers. "There's no birds, no insects, nothing."

"Get some rest." Shinoni looks around wide-eyed. Her breath catches in her throat. She can't let Keena see her fear. "I'll keep watch for awhile."

Keena gulps and takes one last look around, then curls into a ball, covering her head with her cape. "Wake me if you see anything strange," she murmurs, her voice muffled by the fur.

Shinoni sits with her back to the tree stump, stroking Tewa. She surveys the darkness beyond the flames. Keena moans in her sleep, tossing fitfully on the pine boughs.

Despite her determination to stay awake, Shinoni's eyelids become heavy and her head begins to droop. The harrowing events since the last dark time flash in her mind's eye. She sees the escape from Haken, the river sweeping her away, the crone, the gloomy forest. Then slowly, out of the stillness, a hot wind begins to rattle the treetops, making them moan like lost souls.

Tewa whines and yips, then gets up and trots into the gloom.

Panic pounds in Shinoni's chest as the wolf disappears. "Tewa, come back!" Her call echoes in the hollow stillness as the wind fades to a whisper. A light begins to glow in front of her, dimly at first, then growing until it lights up the thicket around her. Tewa sits in the centre of the glow between two familiar figures.

"Father. Grandmother. How can this be?" Shinoni gasps as Shazur and Reza smile at her from within the golden glow. She stretches out her arms, but her body is heavy. She can't move toward them.

"Shinoni, my daughter, I've been watching you." Shazur smiles even more broadly.

"You've grown in many ways, granddaughter." Reza looks just like she did when Shinoni last saw her in the berry patch by the marsh.

"I've missed you both so much," Shinoni says.

"I know, and I'm proud of the way you've handled yourself in this time of danger." Shinoni senses her father's pride surrounding her, and her body warms.

"It seems that being able to fight and hunt has proven useful." Reza beams. "But so has healing."

"What happened to our people? Are they all in the spirit world? Am I the only Kula left from our band?" Shinoni struggles to control her tears.

"Many of our band dwell here, but others remain, scattered to the four winds," Reza says. Shinoni feels her grandmother's touch and hears her voice right beside her, although she hasn't left the glowing circle.

Shazur's voice joins in, strong and reassuring. "There are other bands of Kulas. You'll still be a great leader of our people."

"How, Father? I'm all alone." Shinoni lowers her head, overwhelmed by her loss.

"Nonsense. Hasn't the great wolf been guiding you?" Reza's voice is as scolding as Shinoni remembers it. Tewa looks at Reza and whines.

Shinoni nods, wiping away a tear. "Tewa's been a faithful guide and friend."

"Shinoni, who's been your greatest help these past days?" Shazur points to where Keena lies, still sleeping, by the fire.

"I couldn't have travelled this far without my friend Keena." Shinoni looks over at her. It looks as if a mist has spread between them.

Her father nods his approval. "The Krag woman-child is a brave and true friend. She'll also be a leader of her people. Your friendship is a powerful medicine."

"Both of you girls come from lines of strong women. You carry their knowledge." Reza smiles as her image begins to waver.

Slowly, another image appears in the light. A young black-haired woman with friendly eyes lifts a swan-bone flute to her lips. High-pitched, haunting notes trill in the silence. Shinoni's mother, Teenoni, is as beautiful as Shinoni remembers her. *Father said Mother would talk to me when I was ready to hear her.* Tears well in Shinoni's eyes and slide down her cheeks.

Teenoni lowers her flute. "Daughter, be brave. Remember, the snake is not your enemy. Control your fear and use it to your advantage." Shinoni feels her mother's embrace envelop her as it did when she was a young one.

The glow begins to fade and Shazur, Reza, and Teenoni disappear as quickly as they appeared. Soon only the flickering firelight holds back the night.

"Don't go," Shinoni whispers. "I've more to ask you."

"What would you ask me —?"

Keena peers into Shinoni's face as she shakes her awake. "It's time to leave this cursed place. Tewa had the sense to leave already."

Shinoni rubs the sleep from her eyes and sees sunlight streaming through the blackened boughs of the twisted trees. She sits up, shivering in the frigid morning air, as Keena stamps out the fires. "Did you hear anything during the night?"

"I only heard you snoring and mumbling." Keena eyes her friend. "You must've fallen asleep while you kept watch."

"You saw no one, Keena? No lights?" Shinoni looks around the camp to see if anything's amiss.

"Only you and Tewa, sleeping by the tree stump." Keena drapes her cape around herself and helps Shinoni to her feet.

"Tewa was here when you woke?" Shinoni wraps her furs around her shoulders.

"When I woke, you and the wolf were sleeping. I stayed up the rest of the night to keep watch and saw nothing. Tewa left when it got light and I woke you." Keena turns toward the path that will take them out of the tarkan. "We really must go now. We can't stay here."

The girls begin to walk through the trees, which seem less scary in the morning light. Shinoni walks in silence, remembering the sound of her mother's swan-bone flute.

Keena looks at her anxiously. "Did you see anything last night, Kula? You seem strange."

Shinoni hesitates, unsure what happened during the dark time in the tarkan. "Perhaps I did. Perhaps this is a place where the living and the dead *can* meet." She sees Keena's worried face. "It wasn't a bad thing, Keena. I saw my family."

Keena stops, looking confused and concerned. "You saw the spirits of your family?"

Shinoni hugs her friend and they walk along the trail arm in arm. "Don't worry, they like you." Her voice rises on the wind. "They said we'd both be leaders of our people."

Keena's voice also carries on the wind. "You are *strange*, Kula."

36

AYLIGHT FINDS Shinoni and Keena closer to the limestone cliffs that hide the entrance to the snow passage. Keena leaps along the trail, giddy with relief at surviving the tarkan. She can't quite believe that Shinoni's dead family spoke to her there, but still, it is a place of spirits.

Shinoni follows Keena's lead, leaping down the trail as well. Her legs take her much farther than Keena's on each bound. "It's time for a little fun," she shouts. On the next bound she playfully kicks sideways, but she catches the less-agile Keena off guard in mid-leap, knocking her legs out from under her.

"Yiiiiii!" Keena hits the ground hard.

"If you're going to be a leader of your people, you better be more alert than that." Shinoni laughs and extends her hand to help Keena to her feet.

"Leaders don't ambush their friends," Keena growls. "It takes more than leaping like a hare to be a leader." Keena dusts herself off as they continue on their way. Soon they come to a section of the trail blocked by a fallen tree.

"If you're so great, Kula, let's see you beat this," Keena challenges. She grabs a low overhanging tree limb and swings over the obstruction, landing on her feet.

"Like scooping fish from a puddle, Krag." Shinoni laughs and grasps another branch. She swings over the fallen tree and somersaults in the air before landing. "Let's see you top that." She smirks.

Keena takes a deep breath and runs at the branch, grabbing it and again swinging over the fallen tree, but her stocky body can't make the twist into the somersault. *Thud!* She crashes heavily to the ground. Keena grinds her teeth. *What a show-off.* The Kula should try carrying a log like she can. Then Keena spots something moving in the shrubbery by the trail. *Wait, this is even better!* She reaches in and pulls out a small harmless snake. The serpent is sluggish from the cold and barely moving as Keena wraps it around her neck. She grins at Shinoni. "Let's see you do this, Kula."

"That takes no strength," Shinoni says, but her voice shakes. She backs away, stumbling over her own feet.

"Surely a great leader who rides horses and mammoths can handle one little snake," Keena says.

"I could if I wanted to, but I don't." Shinoni turns and starts walking along the trail, her strides long and quick.

"It's a good thing we didn't run into a group of snake worshippers instead of mammoth hunters." Keena chuckles and releases the snake back into the bushes.

"Only Krags would worship snakes," Shinoni snaps over her shoulder. She stops and points at a large pile of brush blocking the game trail just ahead. "Bet you can't do this." She sprints toward the brush pile and sails over in one tremendous leap.

Keena hears wood splintering and Shinoni screaming, "Eeeeiiii-yaaa." Then, silence.

"Shinoni, are you all right?" Keena shouts. *Is this one of her tricks or is she hurt?* She rushes around the brush pile and finds a gaping hole half-hidden by a broken cover of woven vegetation. Keena holds her breath, heart pounding, as she peers over the edge. Her friend lies bruised and still on the floor of a deep pit.

After a few heartbeats, Shinoni sits up slowly, aching and winded. She rubs her bleeding elbow and looks up.

High above her, Keena's pale face appears at the rim. Her voice floats down with the debris. "It's a trap. Someone set a trap to catch anything stupid enough to jump the brush pile."

Keena's voice seems to be coming from a great distance. Shinoni's ears are ringing, and the walls of the pit spin wildly around her.

"You're lucky." Keena sounds both relieved and angry. "Hunters sometimes put sharp spikes in these pits to kill animals that fall in."

"I certainly feel lucky," Shinoni says. She struggles to stand up, then uncoils the rope from her pouch and tosses one end up toward the rim. "Take this, but be careful not to fall in." The rope falls back into the pit, coiling uselessly at her feet. She bends over to pick up the rope, but pauses as she's overcome by dizziness.

"You'll have to throw higher so I can reach it." Keena wriggles closer to the edge and leans over.

Shinoni looks up quickly as Keena's shadow looms large in the pit. "Don't get too close!" Her warning is too late. The crack of breaking vegetation claps in Shinoni's ears.

"Aaaaa-yeeee!" Keena's shriek of terror announces her free fall into the hole. She lands with a thud beside Shinoni.

Keena moans as Shinoni pulls her up to a sitting

position and looks her over. Shinoni gingerly pokes and prods Keena's arms and legs.

"You're all right — but now what do we do? Who knows when whoever dug this pit will be back?" Dangling strands of broken vegetation sway mockingly out of reach.

"Yes, and *who* did dig this pit?" Keena squints anxiously up at the rim. "They'll be angry we wrecked their trap."

Shinoni and Keena get back on their feet and examine the four walls of their prison. They're slippery clay, mixed with shale, and cut at a steep angle. The girls gouge footholds on the wall with their hands. Blood drips from their fingers and the shale crumbles under their feet as they try to climb.

"These walls are higher than the tallest Kula hunter's reach. Who could dig such a deep hole?" Shinoni sits on the floor, which is strewn with brush and plant debris from the broken trap cover.

"Perhaps it was already here and they just made it bigger." Keena flops down beside Shinoni. "I've seen hunters set such traps before in pits that Leeswi provides when she shakes the earth."

Shinoni stares at the pit walls. There must be a way out. "Get up, Krag. We'll show them their trap can't hold us," she says. She stands up, her face smeared with dust and sweat.

"I think it *is* holding us, Kula. Are you going to fly?" Keena asks.

"Get up. I'll stand on your shoulders and try to reach the opening."

"Why will you stand on my shoulders? Perhaps I should stand on yours." Keena gets up slowly, her bruised body aching.

"Oh, you're difficult, Krag. You're heavier than me and I can stretch farther. That's why I should stand on you."

Keena gives in. She squats with her back against one wall while Shinoni steps onto her broad shoulders, facing the side of the pit. Keena braces herself against the slippery shale and clay. She slowly pushes her body upright and lifts Shinoni high in the air.

"Can you reach it?" Keena gasps for breath in the dusty, stale air. She struggles to hold Shinoni steady against the wall.

"No, can you push me higher? Maybe jump or stand on your toes?" Shinoni stretches as high as she can but is still an arm's length away from the edge.

"I can't. I can't even breathe." Keena's legs buckle and both of them land in a pile back on the floor of their prison.

Several failed escape attempts later, Shinoni sits on the floor of the pit, head down, shoulders slumped. Keena sits a short distance away, resting her head on her arm. They're both exhausted.

"The sun's going down." Shinoni's voice trembles as the light dims in the pit.

"The beasts will prowl soon." Keena stares up at the opening. "Do you think we're safe here?"

"Well, if anything jumps in, it won't be able to get out," Shinoni says.

"That's a comforting thought." Keena moves closer to her.

Just then a shaggy head looms over the opening. Tewa looks down at them. She cocks her ears and whines.

"Tewa, I knew you'd come," Shinoni calls.

"What will she do, Kula? Lower her tail and pull us out?" Keena asks.

"She'll stand guard and warn us if something comes."

"That'll be a comfort as we starve to death."

"We won't starve by going without food for one night, and by morning we'll find a way out." Shinoni rubs Keena's back. "You'll see." The girls huddle together and drift into sleep.

257

Outside the pit the trees and brush rustle with movement as the evening dance between predator and prey begins. The drawn-out, haunting call of an owl floats on the evening breeze, and a rabbit screams somewhere in the forest. A wolf howls in the distance. Another answers, and another, as the pack gathers for the hunt.

Tewa stands near the forest edge, sniffing the tantalizing messages borne on the air, her ears cocked toward the music of the hunt. Reluctantly she ignores the invitation and lies down near the rim of the pit, her eyes alert and glowing in the gathering dusk.

Shafts of muted morning light filter in through the dusty air when Shinoni and Keena waken to Tewa's growls. The wolf looks over the edge and whines a sharp warning. Then she draws her head back and disappears.

"What's going on?" Keena mumbles in a sleepy voice.

"Tewa's warning us. Maybe someone's coming," Shinoni says. If it's hunters, Tewa will be no match for them. Shinoni hopes she has found a safe place to hide.

The sounds of snapping branches and gruff male voices drift in through the opening. Shinoni and Keena rise stiffly and back up against the far wall, trying to disappear into the crevices.

Shadows block out the light. Ropes snake down from the edge, and dirt falls into the pit. Keena and Shinoni stare up into the leering faces of Haken and his hunters.

37

TWO OF HAKEN'S hunters shinny down the ropes, filling the pit with the stench of their brawny bodies. Their faces are twisted into fierce snarls and their eyes are wild beneath brow ridges painted red and black. The bear and wolf teeth tangled in their hair and around their necks clatter as they hang over Shinoni and Keena. There's nowhere to run, nowhere to hide.

"Keep away, monsters!" Shinoni screams. A hunter seizes her. She bites him and spits out blood. He slaps her to the ground, and Keena leaps on his back.

"Leave us be. Leeswi will take your breath if you harm us!" Keena shouts.

The threat of vengeance from Leeswi stops the hunter for a heartbeat, but Haken's angry cry echoes from above. The men roughly pin Keena and Shinoni on the floor of the pit and bind their hands behind their backs.

Shinoni struggles as one hunter wraps a climbing rope so tightly around her waist and chest she can hardly breath. She sticks her foot out and trips the hunter tying Keena with the other rope, sending him sprawling. Haken's furious henchmen jerk the ropes. It feels like Shinoni's ribs will crack. The girls are hoisted up, scraping and banging against the rough rock walls to the top of the pit, where six more hostile hunters wait.

Sunshine blinds the girls after the dim light below. They squat on the ground, surrounded by the fur-covered legs of Haken's men, who mill about them.

"Aaaaawiiiiyayaa!" Haken howls and dances with glee, thrusting his spear into the air. Some of the hunters start to dance and shout as well, and as they move, the girls can see behind them.

"Look, they have other captives," Shinoni whispers.

Two bound figures sit at a distance. One looks over at them and struggles to sit up straight. "Keena. Keena. It's me, Kreel," he shouts. He's knocked to the ground by a spear butt. Raucous laughter erupts from the hunters.

"What did he say? Do you know the captives? One's a Kula!" Shinoni exclaims.

"It's Kreel and Sabra! I told you about them. They're friends." Fear and joy mix in Keena's voice. She is overjoyed to see them, but she knows Haken doesn't keep captives alive unless he has a use for them.

"They must've been searching for you. Maybe your band's nearby."

Rough hands grab Shinoni and Keena and pull them to a standing position. Haken swaggers toward them with a nasty grin twisting his scarred face. He towers over them and utters a string of threats. Shinoni, her eyes pools of fear, turns to Keena. Keena looks back helplessly, her voice stuck in her throat. Haken pushes her close to Shinoni.

"He wants me to tell you they'll find a place to build a fire. They'll force you to tell him your hunting magic. Then they'll sacrifice all of us to the cave bears. Haken will gain power from Leeswi for his bravery."

"That doesn't sound very brave to me," Shinoni mutters.

Haken roars and pushes the girls apart. Hunters surround all four captives, and Haken leads the group into the valley at a fast pace. The hunters swagger and laugh, shaking their spears and chanting fiercely.

Shinoni and Keena are bruised and dirty from their fall into the pit and the rough way Haken's men hauled them out of its depths. Their hands, tightly bound behind them, pull on their aching muscles, and walking is difficult. Keena looks over her shoulder as best she can. She and Shinoni are in the centre of the group and hunters march behind them, separating them from Kreel and Sabra, but she can see between the men. Both boys have cuts and bruises and stagger as they try to keep up. They came for her. Kreel came. Now they might die because of her.

Haken's hunters laugh and threaten all four of them with their spears and clubs. Keena stumbles against Shinoni and whispers a warning. "They're laughing about how they'll make you tell Haken your magic."

"Ah, the magic again. I thought they'd just kill us." Shinoni sighs, then grinds her teeth.

"They will, but they want to have some fun first," Keena says.

A hunter pushes them apart again, striking Keena with his spear butt and knocking her to the ground. Shinoni flies at him and kicks him in the groin, sending him reeling backward. Shinoni bends to help Keena up. The shocked hunters raise their clubs, but Haken shouts angrily at his men, pushing them away from the girls.

He brings his face close to Keena and Shinoni, fixing them with his fearful glare. At this distance, his predator scent is overpowering. Shinoni pulls back, gagging, and turns her head. Keena lowers her eyes, her heart racing. Haken sneers and spits out a threat. The hunters roar with laughter as he swaggers away.

"He says they can kill us after he has the magic. Then they'll feed us to the cave bears and take our skulls back as trophies." Keena shudders.

"Walk behind me," Shinoni whispers as she helps Keena stand. Shinoni has that look on her face that means she's got a plan.

Keena nods and drops back a few paces to move behind Shinoni. Her heart pounds. *What does the Kula want me to do?* Keena looks at Shinoni, who carries nothing to fight with, just her cape and her pouch. Of course! She must block the hunters' view of Shinoni so she can move her pouch into a position where she can reach her knife with her bound hands.

A sudden wild trumpeting blares in the distance, stopping Haken and his men in their tracks. They gesture wildly, shouting with surprise and fear as a herd of beasts races across the valley floor, headed in their direction. The earth shakes with the tromping of dozens of heavy feet as the mammoths gallop toward them. Keena gasps when she recognizes the young one she and Shinoni saved a few suns ago. He is running alongside his mother at the head of the herd. The matriarch raises her trunk and blasts another warning.

The hunters stand their ground, spears ready, but Keena can see their nerve starting to waver as the long noses advance ever closer. Panic sets in! The hunters scatter and flee in all directions as the huge beasts reach them.

Sabra and Kreel scream in terror and grovel on the ground, trying to cover their heads with their bound hands. Shinoni and Keena leap in front of them, standing between them and the mammoths.

"Be quiet and stay still," Keena shouts at them. "They won't hurt you if they see you're our friends."

"Friends!" Sabra shouts, struggling to free his hands from their tethers. "They'll smash us!"

"Be still if you want to live," Shinoni orders. "We'll cut your ropes as soon as we're free." Shinoni's hands are still tied behind her back. She uses her fingers to push and pull the strap that holds her pouch around her waist. Finally the pouch is at her back, but she still can't reach to open it. "Keena, hurry," she calls above the din. "Help me get my knife."

Keena stands back to back with Shinoni, keeping a wary eye on the huge animals milling about so close to them. She grasps the pouch and pulls out the stone blade, transferring it into Shinoni's hands.

"Good work." Shinoni saws at her bonds, which quickly fray and fall apart, then cuts Keena free. They exchange triumphant glances as they rush to help Kreel and Sabra.

"Keena, we've come to save you! To bring you home," Kreel shouts.

"Perhaps we should untie you first." Keena chuckles.

Shinoni quickly frees them with her knife. A huge shadow falls over them, and they look up into the beady eyes of the matriarch. She trumpets and Kreel and Sabra scream. The long nose extends her trunk to Shinoni and Keena, gently touching their heads.

"Come on, Haken will be back soon." Shinoni steps gingerly onto the matriarch's trunk and the mammoth boosts her onto her back.

Kreel and Sabra stare, open-mouthed and shaking. Keena grabs their arms. "You're safe. We've ridden her before."

The mammoth reaches out her trunk again and encircles Keena, boosting her up to join Shinoni. Kreel and Sabra cling to each other, still trembling.

"Please, mother long nose, help the foolish boys. They're friends," Keena pleads. The matriarch eyes Sabra and Kreel, then feels their heads with the tip of her trunk. She picks them up, first Kreel and then Sabra, and tosses them onto her back.

Keena cheers. "You see, she's not smashing us — we're safe." She can't believe Kreel is sitting behind her, his arms hugging her tight. She leans back and smiles at him.

"Hang on or you might fall off and be trampled," Shinoni snaps at the boys. "She cares for us — she's our friend — but she might not care for you." She shoots Keena a look, then turns back and rubs the mammoth behind her hairy ear. "Thank you, big mother. Eeee-haa. Take us away."

Keena looks at Shinoni's rigid back. Could she be upset because Kreel and Sabra are here? Keena feels a pang as she realizes that she now has her two friends here while Shinoni has no one. But at least they're safe. She settles back against Kreel, ready to enjoy the ride.

The matriarch trumpets and the herd rallies behind her, moving off as rapidly as they came. Keena takes one last look back. Haken and his hunters stare, eyes wide in disbelief, from behind the boulders where they've taken refuge. Haken's furious wail echoes as Shinoni and Keena disappear in the distance.

— 38 —

F AR FROM HAKEN'S FURY, the mammoth herd stops to drink at a river that meanders through an open plateau. Golden and brown grass and shrubs line the riverbanks and sway in the wind. Nearby, the limestone cliffs Shinoni and Keena have been seeking tower over the landscape. Their steep slopes are criss-crossed with a dark network of caves.

Shinoni and Keena slide off the matriarch's back as she grazes by the water's edge. Shinoni stretches. It's so wonderful to be free of the pit trap and away from Haken and his hunters.

"Come join us, Kreel, Sabra," Keena calls. "I want to hear about home."

"Do you want me to catch you, boys?" Shinoni grins and spreads her arms.

Kreel and Sabra hesitate, then slide off the mammoth. Still grazing, she begins to amble off as they do, sending them tumbling sideways. They hit the ground hard.

"Ha, did you see those cowards run?" Sabra shouts. "Haken's no braver than a girl."

"You should be careful what you say, since it was a girl who cut you free." Shinoni extends her hand to pull Sabra up, but he ignores her and gets up by himself.

"Who is this?" Sabra asks Keena, who's helping Kreel to his feet.

"She's my *friend*. Her name is Shinoni," Keena says.

Shinoni looks at Sabra and Kreel, both bedraggled and covered in bruises and cuts from their encounter with Haken. They don't look like much, but they *did* come to find Keena — and nearly lost their lives for it. Maybe she'll give them another chance.

"It's good to see a Kula," she says. "Keena and I have come a long way since we first escaped from Haken."

"You escaped from Haken, too?" Sabra's eyebrows rise.

"It's a long story." She doesn't want to share this yet, even if he is a Kula. "Keena, we must go now," she calls.

But Keena is hanging on to Kreel and doesn't respond. "It's good to see you! How's Ubra? Did she send you?"

"I wanted to find you, Keena," Kreel says. "Ubra and Atuk wanted to come and bring you home, too, but they weren't strong enough." He hugs her.

"Atuk wanted to find me?" Keena asks.

"Yes, your father was so sad," Kreel says. "He tried to make it through the snow pass for you, but his leg gave out."

Keena turns away to hide her tears.

"I don't want to break things up," Shinoni says as she pulls Keena away from Kreel. "But we need to find food or we'll be too weak to travel much farther."

"She's right. Come on." Keena wipes away her tears and rubs her belly. "I'll feel better after we eat something."

They walk toward the mammoth herd to say good-bye. Many of the giant beasts are drinking from the river, and the young ones shove and spray each other. One of the youngsters fills his trunk, then rushes toward them, trunk raised, ears flapping. The little long nose circles them playfully, spraying each of them with icy river water.

"Eeeyaaa, little brat!" Keena shrieks. She shakes herself.

Shinoni gasps with the shock of the frigid water but can't help chuckling at the indignant, soaked Keena hopping about and shivering in the cold wind. "It's not as bad as being carried away by the river," Shinoni says.

"You were swept away by a river, Keena?" Kreel's face puckers with concern.

"We need to start a fire or we'll all freeze." Sabra shakes water from his tunic.

Shinoni takes Keena's arm as they start to walk along the river bank, turning briefly to raise their hands in a salute to the long noses as they leave. Kreel, smiling from ear to ear, and Sabra follow close behind them. The young mammoth starts to follow them, too, but returns to the herd at his mother's trumpet call.

Before long, fast-moving clouds smother the sun and ice crystals glisten in the air. They flush a hare from bushes beside the trail as they near the cliffs. Shinoni drops it dead in mid-leap with a stone from her sling. She smiles as Kreel and Sabra exchange shocked looks.

"She's good with that sling, for a girl," Sabra gasps.

"You're a good hunter, Shinoni!" Kreel pokes Sabra in the ribs.

"How do you think we've been eating?" Shinoni rolls her eyes. *You boys have no idea what we can do.* She grins at Keena and hands her the firestones from her pouch, then takes out her knife and starts gutting the hare.

"I'll make a fire," Sabra calls.

"No need," Keena laughs as she scoops up twigs and dry grass into a pile. "I can do it!" She sits and expertly strikes sparks with the flint and firestones, fanning them into flames. "See!"

"Keena, when did you learn to build a fire?" Kreel asks, his eyes full of surprise. Shinoni looks at her friend with pride. *They really are a good team.*

Shinoni and Keena finish their tasks, then share

the meat with Kreel and Sabra. They all fill their bellies as they dry out near the fire.

A rustling in the shrubbery as they're finishing their meal announces Tewa's arrival. The wolf steps into the open. There's blood on her face and head, and her tongue dangles over her sharp fangs. She pants as if she's travelled a long way.

"Wolf!" Sabra leaps to his feet and grabs a stick. "The beast must be tracking us."

"Keena, get behind me. There might be a pack." Kreel reaches for Keena, but she's calmly scooping up the entrails of the hare.

"What're you afraid of? She's only a wolf." Keena offers the bloody guts to Tewa, who snaps them up in one gulp.

"She's our friend and guardian." Shinoni ruffles her silver fur as the wolf rubs against her. Tewa turns with a yawn and settles down in the bushes.

"But there's blood on her head," Kreel says.

"She hunts and brings us meat sometimes," Keena says.

Sabra scoffs. "The wolf provides for you?"

"She travels with us, and she's saved our lives more than once," Shinoni says.

"We're her pack," Keena adds proudly.

Sabra lowers the stick he still clutches and exchanges shocked looks with Kreel.

Shinoni and Keena put out the fire and start back toward the riverbank. Tewa bounds after them, pushing her body between them as they walk together. Kreel and Sabra hustle to catch up but are careful not to get too close to the wolf.

"Where are we going?" Sabra asks. "There's just cliffs in this direction."

"Can you see the caves up there?" Shinoni points to openings in the steep sides of the cliff.

"Yes, but why go there?" Kreel asks. "There are surely some lower than those, and closer." He and Sabra hesitate, heads together, murmuring.

"If we stay down here, it'll be easier for Haken to track us," Shinoni says.

"We met women fishing by the river, and a grey hair told us those caves hold a shortcut into the mountains," Keena says.

"If that was the same old crone we met, I wouldn't trust her words." Sabra spits. "She's the one who turned us over to Haken."

"We were trading for fish to eat when Haken and his men came by," Kreel says. "We hid in the bushes, but she showed him where we were."

"She likely had no choice if she wanted to live," Keena points out.

"The crone said there are cave bears up there," Kreel says.

"The bears are likely all sleeping now for the snow time. They probably won't even notice us," Keena says.

"Haken was going to sacrifice us to a bear so Leeswi would give him the bear's power," Sabra says. "He must not have thought the bears would be sleeping."

Kreel nods. "That's where Haken was taking us when we found you in the pit."

"It's dangerous going that way, but it's even more dangerous going back and meeting Haken," Shinoni says.

"I agree with Shinoni," Keena asserts. "It's our best chance to ever get home, too. The snow pass through the mountains is likely up there."

Shinoni, Keena, and Tewa start walking along the rocky beach toward the cliff, but Sabra and Kreel still hang back. Shinoni sighs. It was so much easier when it was just their little pack.

"Kreel, Sabra," Keena calls. "Do you want to be Haken's captives again?"

"Come on, brother, she has a point." Kreel nudges Sabra. They rejoin Shinoni and Keena, and they all head for the dangerous escape route through the gap yawning in the cliffside.

— 39 —

THE SUN ON HER downward path still fills the sky with warming rays as Shinoni, Keena, and the boys reach the lowest cave. The steep climb up the cliffside trail has left them winded. Tewa ran ahead, likely following an enticing scent trail left by a small herd of ibex that the travellers later passed. Now she rises from the cave entrance where she's soaking up the heat reflected by the rock. She stretches and yodels a greeting. She mouths Shinoni's and Keena's hands, then sniffs Sabra and Kreel. They stand stiff and still as she inspects them. Tewa yips, then flops down again in the sunshine.

"She's accepted you into the pack," Shinoni says as she lights a fire.

"I suppose that's a good thing," Kreel says.

"Yes, or she'd likely rip out your throats." Shinoni chuckles.

"The wolf's lazy." Sabra waves toward Tewa dozing in the sun. "She doesn't look like she'd be much protection."

"She had to run a long way to find us." Keena frowns at Sabra. *He's still as annoying as he used to be.* "The long noses carried us a great distance, and her legs are much shorter."

"There's still a tough journey ahead. We'll need light in the cave to search for the passage into the mountains," Shinoni says. "We need to make torches." She scrapes resin from a pine tree with her knife and brings it to the fire to soften over the embers.

Keena breaks four stout branches from trees growing on the hillside and smears the end of each with resin to create a torch. Everyone takes one and lights it in the fire before Keena stamps out the flames. The hole in the cliffside beckons her. Is it really the way back to her family?

Tewa gets up and bounds into the cave. Shinoni follows closely behind the wolf, and Keena is right behind her. Sabra and Kreel follow them into the yawning mouth of the mountain. Once inside, the light from their torches pushes back the gloom. A faint draft from deep in the cave makes the flames flicker.

Shinoni moves along the back wall, feeling for an

opening. "There's a break in the rocks here. I think it's a passage. Come on."

"How do you know it leads out?" Sabra asks. "We could get lost in there."

"Would you rather wait here for Haken?" Keena demands.

"She's right, brother." Kreel moves next to Keena. Keena sighs with relief. She can still depend on Kreel.

"I'd like a fair chance to fight Haken and destroy him." Sabra makes no move to follow.

"Haken never fights fair," Shinoni calls over her shoulder. "You couldn't win."

"You don't know me," Sabra snaps.

"I'll *never* know you if you don't come quickly." Shinoni turns back to the passage in the wall.

Shinoni is not going to wait for Sabra to make up his mind. Tewa looks back toward the cave entrance and growls, then lopes into the tunnel. Shinoni swiftly follows the wolf. Keena's scent wafts close behind her and she hears the boys murmuring farther back. The passage is just high enough to allow her to walk upright, and so narrow she can touch the smooth rock walls on each side. Shinoni looks back over her shoulder. The torch flames throw dark shadows across the hills and hollows of the faces behind her. Living masks in this eerily silent place.

Tewa sets a brisk pace, and Shinoni follows close on her tail as she leads them out of the passage into a large rock chamber. They all skid to a stop, mouths agape. The flickering light dances on cavernous rock walls, revealing lifelike pictures of woolly rhinoceros, mammoths, horses, reindeer, bears, and lions. Handprints and geometric patterns painted in red and yellow ochre loom out of the shadows around the pictures. Shinoni can barely breathe with the excitement flooding her chest. Her voice is a reverent whisper.

"It's a sacred chamber like the one my father painted and held ceremonies in."

"Is it a place of hunting magic?" Kreel reaches toward the beasts spread out before them, then pulls his hand back into the shadows without touching them.

"Only hunters can attend ceremonies in such a place as this. How do you know of it?" Sabra asks.

"I know many things," Shinoni replies. "My father was a great shaman."

"We'll all join him in the spirit world if we don't move on quickly," Keena says, taking Shinoni's arm.

"I'll paint pictures like these someday." Sabra touches the belly of a horse protruding from the rock wall.

Shinoni silently moves along the rock wall, searching the floor for any sign of the artists' tools. She spots a flat piece of slate an artist used as a palette to mix coloured pigment. Several stubs of red and yellow ochre lie beside it. She bends and picks up two small chunks of red ochre and slips them into her pouch.

Tewa's sudden furious growl draws everyone's attention. There's an answering rumble from the passageway, deeper and more menacing. They all turn to the opening in the rock.

A cave bear's huge head looms into the chamber. Shinoni and Keena back up against the wall, scanning frantically for another way out. The skin on Shinoni's face tingles as a faint movement of air flickers her flame. She scrambles along a line of dancing horses that lead into a darker space.

"Quickly, there's air blowing," she calls. "There must be another opening behind us."

"Back up slowly. Don't run," Kreel says.

The bear steps into the chamber, its immense presence overpowering in the enclosed space. It's as if a giant painting has leaped from the wall and walks among them. The bear moves slowly and deliberately toward them. Its knife-sharp claws click menacingly on the smooth stone of the floor. The bear doesn't charge, but its massive head is lowered and threatening. Its small eyes, red in the torchlight, hold them in a steady stare. The heavy, musky scent of bear surrounds them, assaulting their noses and stinging their eyes.

Tewa whines loudly and disappears into the wall. Keena backs up, following her. "Here's the passage," she cries. "There's light at the end."

Shinoni, Kreel, and Sabra also back into the narrow passage, then turn and desperately head for the light at the end. Behind them, they can hear the bear's heavy breathing and the scrabbling of its long, curved claws as it squeezes into the tunnel. The bear's deep, rumbling growls feed their panic, pushing them to use every ounce of their strength to struggle up the narrow tunnel. They stoop over, torches at their sides, as they scramble, scraping exposed skin on the rough rock walls. A sudden gust of air blows out their torches as the tunnel widens and an opening beckons ahead of them.

Keena, Shinoni, and Kreel stumble out of the opening and tumble down a small incline. Tewa is already at the bottom of the hill. Sabra emerges from the cave with the bear's head right behind him. A mighty paw catches him and sends him flying down the hill. The bear stands regally in the opening. It woofs, nodding its head up and down and sniffing the air before turning back into the cave.

Shinoni, Keena, and Kreel run to Sabra and help him to his feet. His heavy fur leggings have deflected some of the bear's blow, but his thigh underneath is bleeding where two of the deadly claws sliced through the fur into his muscle. Shinoni cuts strips of hide from her cloak and wraps them tightly around the wound to slow the bleeding.

Sabra is pale and dazed as Kreel helps him stand.

"Listen to me," Shinoni says. "The bear marked you and chose not to kill you. Now you, not Haken, will have the bear's power." She helps Kreel support Sabra's weight as they slowly start down the hillside.

"If anyone has the bear's power, it'll be you," Sabra says. "You brought us through the cave."

"I think Keena and Tewa had a big part in that, too." Shinoni smiles. "Maybe we'll all have the bear's power now."

"That's good," calls Keena, who is walking ahead with Tewa. "We're all going to really need that power to escape from Haken."

"We must go faster to put distance between us and Haken," Shinoni urges Sabra as he limps beside her. "You're a strong hunter."

She looks for Keena and feels a twinge of longing to be walking beside her and Tewa, facing head on whatever comes their way, as they've done so often. She looks at the strange young hunters who've joined them. They're Keena's friends. Perhaps they're safer together, but Shinoni yearns to have things as they were.

She leaves Sabra with Kreel and slips in beside Tewa and Keena. Together again, they travel down the hill and into the mountain pass beyond.

— 40 —

THERE ARE FEW CAVES in the ravine, and day is ending by the time Shinoni, Keena, Sabra, and Kreel locate a shelter for the dark time. They're exhausted, and the entrance, partially hidden behind thick shrubs, is a welcome sight. This cave seems to have not had human occupants for a long time, but a pile of dry brush along one wall near the entrance was possibly once a kindling pile. Wolves, foxes, and bear have used the cave and left their pawprints and scat. Still, the shelter is dry and empty now.

"Kreel and I will get some wood from the forest for a fire," offers Keena.

They walk outside together and begin to gather tree branches broken by the wind, and limbs from dead trees. As they both reach for a downed sapling, their hands collide. Kreel smiles shyly and squeezes Keena's hand gently.

Keena smiles and squeezes his hand back. "I've missed you Kreel. I thought I'd never see you again."

They gather more kindling, working side by side. "We have enough wood. We should go in now." Keena straightens up, and the ibex-tooth pendant Kreel made her slips out from under her tunic.

"You still have it." Kreel beams.

Keena nods. "It makes me feel safe."

They share a smile and carry the wood they've gathered into the cave. Exchanging small glances, they quickly get to work starting a fire.

Shinoni is tending to Sabra's injured leg. She mashes up the remaining fever plants and applies the healing herbs to the gashes.

"Ouch. That stings." Sabra winces and pulls back.

"Come now, you're a hunter. You'll have a scar to be proud of here." Shinoni holds his leg firmly and continues applying the herbs and re-wrapping the wound.

The wind moans outside their shelter as night descends over the frigid land. Keena walks over to the brush pile in the corner. "I'll build up the fire. Who knows what might be lurking outside." She carries an armful of kindling to the fire.

Tewa cocks her head and whines as she stares at the brush pile.

"What's wrong with the wolf?" Sabra asks.

Tewa gets up and paws at the dry vegetation, growling deep in her throat. Then she backs off, hackles raised, and disappears out the entrance.

Shinoni goes over to the pile to investigate. As she reaches forward, she hears a faint rustling from deep in the mass, and the pile begins to tremble from within. She hesitates, a warning tremor sliding down her spine. *What's hiding here?* She withdraws her hand, overcome with a feeling of reluctance to touch the brush.

Keena steps beside her and lifts a clump of the dried vegetation. Shinoni freezes. Brown-and-grey-dappled coils wriggle deep in the brush. There are too many coils to be one snake. The pile trembles in several places. Shinoni gulps and steps backward, smothering her scream.

"It seems snakes curl up in this brush for their sleep during the snow time." Keena carefully lowers the vegetation and moves away from the pile. "Our fire has warmed them, and they think it's time to wake up."

"We should look for another shelter before they come out of their bed." Kreel moves toward the back of the cave, away from the pile. "I don't want to sleep with snakes."

"I agree. Even the wolf won't stay here." Sabra speaks in short breaths. Pain and fear twist his face. "One snake can be handled, but several won't make good sleeping companions."

Keena looks at Shinoni with anxiety in her eyes. Shinoni stands frozen, staring at the brush pile. She feels like she will never be able to move again.

Remember, the snake is not your enemy. Control your fear and use it to your advantage. Shinoni's mother's words from the dream world echo in her head.

"It's too late to look for another shelter." She takes a trembling breath. "It would be more dangerous to be out of the cave with the night hunters than here with some sleepy snakes."

"We can take turns sleeping so we know where the snakes are," Keena says.

"We could take the pile apart and kill the serpents, or catch them and throw them outside," Sabra offers.

"We're only here until sunrise, and the snakes need to stay in the cave to survive the snow time," Shinoni says. "We can share the space for one dark time."

"Yes," Keena agrees. "They'll only bite if we frighten them or try to harm them. We can all stay here tonight."

"All right, but I don't think I'll close my eyes," Kreel says.

"I'll stay awake, too," Shinoni says. "Haken may find us here, and I want to be ready for him. The snakes might be able to help us if he comes."

"The wolf could help us if he does, but she's gone. We've lost her protection because of the snakes." Sabra hoists himself up with a stick and limps to the entrance, staring into the night.

"Tewa needs to hunt. She doesn't always sleep with us, but she's nearby if we need her." Shinoni settles down by the fire and beckons the others to join her. "Come and sit. I'll tell you how the serpents can help us."

The moon hangs low in the sky when Shinoni and Keena wake, stiff and cold by the dying fire, the hot flames now only glowing embers. The dim light outside grows brighter, but a chill wind blows sleet and snow through the entrance. Shinoni's breath hangs in the air as she starts to rebuild the fire. Keena, carrying brush from the pile in one hand, clutches her cape tightly around her with the other. The chill in the cave has cooled the snakes' blood, lulling them back into their winter sleep.

"It was their turn to keep watch." Keena looks at Sabra and Kreel sleeping under their furs, restless in their dreams. "We're lucky not to wake up to a bear or lion attacking us."

"Or Haken." Shinoni lets out a deep sigh as protective flames spring from the embers, burning bright and hot once again.

"Let them sleep a bit more. They're exhausted and we have a hard climb ahead."

The girls sit down by the hearth. Shinoni looks fondly at her friend, who smiles as she watches Kreel sleep. He snores, then flinches and moans deep in the dream world.

Shinoni turns to stare at the cave wall. As the flames shoot higher, paintings on the wall begin to dance, wavy lines with forked ends and circles, all drawn in red ochre. *My paintings!* She painted them during the night, as she and Keena took the first watch.

Shinoni's heart swells with pride as she admires her artwork, the first paintings she's ever done on a cave wall. They won't be the last. And if Haken does show up, hopefully these painting will help save their lives!

Keena yawns. "The fire is so warm and I'm so tired, but we don't dare sleep."

Just then, a faint scrabbling on the rocks outside snaps Shinoni and Keena to attention. Shinoni's nerves jangle a warning and she strains to hear sounds of danger. Keena's nose quivers as she searches for the intruder's scent.

"Perhaps it's the wolf returning." Keena grips Shinoni's arm.

"It's not Tewa." Shinoni rises slowly to her feet, her voice catching in her throat. A formidable shape blocks the faint dawn light at the entrance. The chill wind brings a stink the girls know all too well, and the hairs on Shinoni's neck prick at the smell of this deadly predator. It's the stench of Haken.

Keena leaps to her feet and shakes Kreel and Sabra awake. "Haken's here!" she says, her voice tight and urgent. "Remember, stay back for now."

Shinoni moves in front of the others, facing the entrance. She breathes deeply, focusing on what she must do. The shape moves closer and the flickering flames illuminate a face, terrifying in its hatred. Haken's broad lips, drawn back in a sneer, emphasize the blood-red scar slashed across his face. His eyes are wild, reflecting the firelight like the eyes of a beast. Wolf and bear teeth clatter in his tangled red hair as he moves around the fire, his spear raised high and ready to thrust.

"Ah, pups, I have you in your den. I'll enjoy killing you." Haken throws back his head and howls, then grins at their startled reaction.

"Great Haken, you've found us." Shinoni addresses him in the Kula tongue and Keena rapidly translates the words into Krag. "But don't you want to know the hunting magic before you kill us?"

"Why should I trust you?" Haken's lips curl in a snarl.

"You're a great hunter and should have the magic." Shinoni bows her head. "It's good you didn't bring your hunters, for only you, the great Haken, are allowed to know the hunting magic."

"Yes, my hunters don't deserve the hunting magic — only I do! Haken is killer of men and beasts." He points his spear at them. "And killer of insolent pups and tricksters."

"You see these marks?" Shinoni points to the wavy lines with forked tips painted on the wall. "Kulas call the great snake spirit to bring the animals to our spears and do our bidding."

"How do you call this spirit?" Haken furrows his brow, watching Shinoni closely.

Shinoni braces herself and moves toward the brush pile.

"Where are you going, devil girl?" Haken snarls, and he leaps toward her, spear outstretched. "You can't escape."

"Don't you want to learn how to call the snake spirit?" Shinoni forces a smile. "I can show you what must be done to convince the snake spirit you're worthy."

Haken lowers his spear and Shinoni approaches the brush pile. She forces herself to push aside the top layer of vegetation. There they are. The coiled brown and grey bodies, now starting to move as the air warms. Dread twists her guts into knots as the vipers uncoil beneath her fingers. She struggles with the frantic urge to flee and swallows the terror that chokes her breath, then wills her frozen hands to move.

"*Be brave. The snake is not your enemy.*" Shinoni hears her mother's words in her ears and she breathes deeply.

"Show me the magic, girl, or I'll kill you where you stand." Haken's growl cuts like a knife, focusing her on her task. It's clear now. The snake isn't her enemy. *Haken is.*

"*Control your fear. Use it to your advantage.*" Her mother's words again fill her mind. Shinoni holds her breath and grasps one of the adders behind its wedge-shaped head, lifting it out of the pile. She exhales slowly and walks over to Haken, who recoils as she holds the serpent out toward him.

"Take the snake and hold it so the spirit sees you're brave." The adder blinks its blood-red eyes, its pupils as black as the night. "You see its eyes are like fire. Move close to the flames so the snake spirit sees you clearly."

Haken takes the reptile and holds it clumsily as it begins to wriggle, its blood warming. Keena steps next to Shinoni with another serpent, which Shinoni takes and holds out to Haken. He looks, but does not reach for it.

"The more snakes the spirit sees you hold, the more hunting magic he'll give you," Shinoni says. Keena, still translating, hands her yet another adder. Shinoni stretches her long arms, holding both snakes close to the fire. "You aren't Kula, so you must hold many snakes to show the spirit you're worthy of hunting magic."

Haken places his spear under his foot and takes the serpents. They coil around his arms and onto his shoulder.

"Good. Be sure you're close to the fire so the spirit clearly sees how brave you are." Shinoni backs away slightly. She raises her hand and waves. "Spirit, come *now!*"

Keena twirls Shinoni's sling over her head and sends a large stone flying through the air, striking Haken's head. He lurches forward, roaring in anger as he tries to drop the snakes. Kreel and Sabra shout loudly and pelt him with more rocks.

Feeling threatened, the snakes react with alarm. They tighten their coils around Haken's arms, then sink their fangs deeply into his face and neck.

"Arrrgh! Raahhrr!" Haken twirls around wildly, trying to dislodge the snakes. He roars and flails his arms and legs in a grotesque dance around the fire.

Patricia Miller-Schroeder

Shinoni, Keena, Kreel, and Sabra stare at the spectacle for a moment, then rush out of the cave entrance. They race along the trail leading out of the ravine and up toward the mountain pass as fast as Sabra's injured leg allows. Haken's shouts echo in their ears.

41

THE RACE TO LEAVE HAKEN and the snake cave behind them slows as Shinoni, Keena, and the boys climb higher. Giddy laughter rings in the crisp mountain air. They've defeated their deadly enemy!

"Haken rat-kap! As-ni-gip!" Kreel shouts in Krag. Keena laughs and repeats the phrase, and Sabra, who knows some Krag, chuckles, too.

"What's so funny? You should share," Shinoni says.

Keena puts her arm around Shinoni and translates the insult. "Haken's a coward! He has no power!"

Shinoni smiles and nods. "I want to insult the monster in Krag, too!"

Keena, Kreel, and Sabra all shout the Krag words several times. Shinoni joins in the furious rant that echoes from the rocks all around them. At last they return to speaking Kula.

"Ho, Haken. Where's the great hunter, now?" chortles Kreel, slapping Sabra on the back.

"Sleep well with the snakes, Haken." Sabra picks up a stick from the trail, shaking it in the air before using it as a crutch.

"Thank you, Leeswi. Haken didn't deserve the bear's power." Keena throws her arms wide, embracing the wind.

"You're too stupid to outwit a Kula, Haken," Shinoni boasts. She hastily adds to Keena and Kreel, "Of course, not all Krags are stupid."

"Come, wise Kula," Keena grins. "We'd better get going. It's still a long way through the mountains."

The challenge of the journey ahead sobers their mood and turns their attention back to the winding trail. Tewa rejoins them toward the middle of the day. She playfully greets Shinoni and Keena, brushing against them and wagging her tail. She gives Sabra and Kreel a friendly sniff, then bounds ahead. Her tail, coated with ice crystals, waves in the wind, a silver banner leading them ever higher and closer to the glacier.

"The wolf greets you like her pack members," Kreel marvels.

"She thinks she's the leader," Sabra says.

Keena nods. "She comes and goes as she chooses, but she seems happy to see us today. Perhaps she's sorry she wasn't there to attack Haken."

"If Tewa had attacked him, we couldn't have tricked him into holding the snakes." Shinoni laughs with relief. "It's good to finally be rid of him."

"Yes, the great Haken, killer of men and beasts, is no more," Sabra shouts.

Keena voices a nagging doubt. "Haken is powerful. He's survived many things that should've killed him. We didn't see him dead, only fighting off the snakes."

"Surely he's dead. I saw him bitten by three snakes. The bite of just one killed my mother." Shinoni can't bear to think Haken might still live.

"One thing's sure. If Haken isn't dead, he'll be looking for our blood," Kreel says uneasily.

Much later the sky has cleared, but the wind still howls. The group climbs to a ridge high above the path, overlooking the mountain pass. The ridge drops off steeply on the far side to a boulder-strewn river valley far below. They climb back down from the precipitous lookout and rest under a rock outcrop near a bend in the trail. They are exhausted after their escape.

Sabra and Kreel flop down for a nap under the shelter of the rock, but Shinoni and Keena sit with their backs against the stone wall to keep watch. Tewa sits with them, but she's restless. Before long she growls and jumps to her feet, hackles bristling. Then she disappears into the trees by the trail.

"Ho, get up. Tewa's warning us." Shinoni jumps to her feet. She fits a stone to her sling.

"Something's coming." Keena shakes Kreel, who's dozed off. "Quickly. Protect yourself." She scrambles to collect rocks for Shinoni's sling.

"Is it a bear?" Sabra winces as he gets up, leaning on his crutch. He steadies himself and hoists the crutch over his shoulder as a club. Kreel brandishes a stout branch. They back up against the rock wall, straining to see what the wolf sensed.

"Where's Tewa?" Keena's eyes are full of fear.

"She'll be here for us, Keena. We'll be all right," Shinoni says. Shazur's face smiles in her mind. She hears her father's words again. *You will be a leader of our people, Shinoni. Be strong.* Shinoni swallows her fear. She strains to see or hear any trace of Tewa, but only the sound of their anxious breathing mingles with the shrill cry of the wind.

"Something's coming," Keena whispers.

Shinoni hears the heavy, shuffling footsteps, barely audible. She sniffs the wind and gasps. There it is, the scent of the predator on their trail.

To their horror and disbelief, Haken rounds the bend in the trail, his face swollen and purple from the snake venom. His steps are unsteady, but he holds his heavy spear flexed and ready. A triumphant grimace spreads across his face when he sees them.

"Ha, we meet again. This is the last time, I assure you." Haken's howl echoes from the rock walls, trailing in the wind.

"How can this be? I saw the snakes bite you." Kreel's words are barely a whisper.

"You're a dead man. You can't hurt us." Sabra grips his crutch, his voice quavering as Haken advances toward them.

"I've been bitten by snakes before and lived." Haken lunges toward Shinoni.

"Leeswi must've given him power," Keena cries. She clutches Shinoni's arm and they sprint up the slope to the ridge towering above them.

"No one escapes Haken when he's on their trail." Fuelled by his fury, Haken lurches unsteadily after them, slipping on the loose shale in his relentless pursuit.

"Leeswi wouldn't give power to one as worthless as Haken," Kreel shouts. He and Sabra pelt him with a barrage of rocks.

"Leave them alone, coward." Sabra forgets his injury and bounds up the slope after Haken, striking him in the back with his crutch.

Shinoni and Keena hide behind large boulders scattered near the top of the ridge and watch the ensuing battle between Haken and Sabra and Kreel. The boys outnumber Haken two to one, but they're no match for the powerful hunter, even though he's half-blinded and unsteady from the venom.

Haken growls and turns to face them. He swings his spear in a wide arc and seizes Sabra by the arm, flinging him against a tree. His back slams into the trunk with a thud. Sabra gets up bruised and winded. As Kreel runs to help his friend, Haken charges up the slope toward Shinoni and Keena.

Shinoni holds her breath as Haken moves past her hiding place. His eyes must be foggy but some of his senses must work. *Oh no.*

Haken leaps behind another boulder, screaming in triumph. "Eeeyaaaiii!" He drags Keena by her braid from her hiding spot up onto the ridge.

Kreel races after them in a frantic effort to free Keena. He throws rocks at Haken and pounds the hunter's massive arm with Sabra's crutch, but Haken is unfazed. He strikes Kreel with the heavy shaft of his spear, sending him flying backward.

"Kreel!" Keena screams and buries her teeth in Haken's hand. Haken shakes her off and holds her at arm's length.

"Come out, devil girl, or I'll throw your worthless friend over the cliff." Haken places his spear blade against Keena's throat. "She'll make good meat for the lions in the valley."

Shinoni steps from behind her boulder and shouts at Haken. "Haken rat-kap! As-ni-gip! Coward. You have no power." With a lightning-fast movement Shinoni sends a stone from her sling smashing into Haken's arm, causing him to loosen his grip on Keena. She kicks free from his grasp and runs to the fallen Kreel.

Roaring with rage, Haken lurches unsteadily toward Shinoni. A silver streak of savage fury bursts from the trees. Tewa races toward him. Fangs bared, snarling, the wolf gains on Haken, and with a leap she strikes him from behind, sinking her teeth into his arm and pulling him down. The force of the impact sends both Haken and Tewa hurtling over the ridge into the steep drop beyond.

"No. Not Tewa!" Shinoni screams as she races to the edge of the cliff, afraid of what she'll see. She moans as she searches frantically for a trace of Tewa on the ground far below. A wild tangle of trees and bushes fills the narrow crevice between this mountain ridge and the adjoining one. Broken shrubbery and jagged boulders dot the sheer rock cliff.

Keena and Kreel rush to Shinoni and peer over the edge. "Look, something's moving down there." Keena points to some shrubs growing tenaciously on a small rock outcrop a short distance below them. Tewa's head and front legs protrude from one of the bushes. The wolf whimpers and slides a bit as she struggles to get free, but she catches herself. "She's alive."

Sabra joins them on the ridge. "She must be a spirit to survive that fall."

"Ho, Tewa, stay calm, sister." Shinoni soothes her as she uncoils her rope.

"I can go and get her," Sabra offers.

"Thank you, Sabra, but your leg is hurt and Tewa trusts me. I'll get her and you can use your strong muscles to help pull us up." Shinoni ties the rope around her waist, and Sabra, with help from Kreel, lowers her to the outcrop where Tewa waits precariously, whining. The scent of her fear as she dangles over the abyss mingles with that of Shinoni's fear of losing her faithful friend and guide.

"Aiii, aii ... ho, ho ... aii ... hoho ... Stay calm, sister ... We'll do this together," Shinoni chants softly. She reaches around Tewa under her forelegs. The biting wind freezes her hands and stings her eyes, but she keeps her voice low and steady. "It's me, Tewa. We can do this, sister."

The wolf stiffens and growls deep in her throat, then suddenly relaxes and settles into Shinoni's arms.

"Pull us up. She's all right." Shinoni's voice is calm as she calls to Sabra.

Together, Sabra, Kreel, and Keena pull Shinoni and Tewa to safety, struggling with their combined weight.

Tewa strains against Shinoni's arms, but the girl hangs on. Working as a team, slowly and painstakingly, the three friends haul Shinoni and Tewa safely up onto the ridge.

"I thought you were gone, sister." Shinoni's arms remain tightly clamped around the wolf, tears freezing on her face. "You saved me, Tewa."

"Thank you, Leeswi, for sparing our brave wolf friend," Keena shouts into the wind. Then she throws her arms around both Shinoni and Tewa. She buries her face in the wolf's fur, her voice muffled. "Thank you, Tewa. You've freed us from Haken."

Kreel and Sabra join in, gingerly rubbing their hands over Tewa's back and sides as her tail slowly waves. Then they all look back over the ridge, searching for any sign of Haken's broken body. The wailing wind whips between the rock walls, stirring the dense shrubbery far below them.

Kreel and Sabra step back from the edge and sit on the ground, propping each other up. "I have never been so sore and exhausted," groans Kreel.

"I can't believe we all survived that," gasps Sabra.

Keena and Shinoni still peer over the edge. Their view of the cliffside blurs as a veil of sleet and snow descends over the crevice. Shinoni struggles to keep her eyes open as the icy needles sting her face. Soon the white curtain closes in, burying whatever lies below.

It seems as if Haken's howl of rage echoes in the shrill howling of the wind.

"He must be dead," Keena says. "But my fear of him remains."

Shinoni, chilled to her marrow by the furious wind, turns and guides both Tewa and Keena from the ridge. She, too, struggles to shake her uneasiness. They've seen no sign of their enemy, but it's a long way down. No one, not even the mighty Haken, could survive such a fall.

42

SNOW CONTINUES TO FALL, hiding the signs of battle on the mountain ridge. Shinoni, Keena, and their friends huddle together for warmth behind the shelter of a boulder, trying to regain their strength before continuing their search for the snow pass.

"We must find shelter." Shinoni rouses the others. "We'll freeze if we don't build a fire and get out of the wind." Tewa shakes the snow from her body and stands beside Shinoni.

"You're right." Keena brushes her hand across her eyelids, which are freezing shut. She gets up, brushing the snow off her tunic. Sabra and Kreel rise painfully, nursing their injuries.

Suddenly they're startled by shouts coming through the wind. Keena's stomach lurches. Who could this be? Surely Haken or his hunters aren't returning?

The wind slows its howling blast and they can see people emerging on the cliff across from them. More people join the others, shouting and waving from the far ridge.

"Who are these people?" Shinoni asks.

"I can't tell from here." Keena squints and struggles to shield her eyes from the snow. *There's something familiar about them.*

To the friends' dismay, as the blowing snow begins to clear, a connecting bridge of land between the two ridges is revealed. "They can reach us. They might be more enemies." Shinoni begins to load a rock into her sling.

Keena puts her hand on Shinoni's sling hand. "I don't think these people are enemies, Shinoni." She peers across the distance. Yes! She's not mistaken! Happiness shoots through her as she recognizes her father's distinctive limp. "Mother, Father. You're here!" she calls in disbelief. Her shouts echo joyfully from the rock walls.

Atuk, Ubra, and members of Sabra's band have arrived through the snow pass. They wave frantically as they struggle through the freezing snow showers to cross the bridge between their two ridges. Keena, Kreel, and Sabra rush to meet them. Shinoni and Tewa follow more slowly. The snow showers end and the sun peeks out from the clouds and smiles on the reunion.

Keena's heart leaps in her chest as her parents rush toward her. Sobbing with joy, she runs to meet them.

"Keena, daughter." Ubra embraces her. The mother Keena has been seeking for so many suns is now hugging her tightly in her arms.

Keena's father, Atuk, is clearly troubled as he stands beside her. She looks at his lined face. He doesn't look like the powerful leader she knew as a child. He's the father who sent her away with the hated and feared Haken.

"Father, you sent me with Haken, but I couldn't do what you wanted and stay with him," Keena says. "I've travelled a long way to come home. Will you have me back at your hearth now?"

"I'm so sorry, Keena. I never should have sent you with that savage bear." Atuk stretches out his mighty misshapen arms. "You're my daughter and now a strong Krag woman. You can stay at any hearth you want, but you're always welcome at ours."

Keena nods and blinks back tears. Kreel hovers nearby. He touches her shoulder. "It'll be good to have you home, Keena." He smiles his huge sunshine smile.

Shinoni watches Keena's joyful reunion with her parents. Her heart is heavy and she wonders what she will do now, with no home and no people of her own.

Keena links arms with her parents and pulls them toward Shinoni. Sabra and his father, Luka, come and stand with them. The other Kula band members gather around.

"This is Shinoni, my friend. Haken destroyed her band. Without her I'd never have escaped or survived." Keena throws her arm around Shinoni, drawing her friend close to her parents.

"How can we thank you?" Ubra looks into Shinoni's eyes. She touches her large brow to Shinoni's smooth forehead.

"I wouldn't have escaped or survived without Keena's help as well." Shinoni squirms a bit under the scrutiny of the strangers surrounding her.

"You travel with a wolf?" Atuk looks doubtfully from his daughter to Tewa.

"She's our friend, Father," Keena responds quickly. "She's helped us many times."

"You're lucky these fine young hunters were able to find you and bring you to us." Luka beams at his son and Kreel, placing one hand on each of them.

"Father, it was they who saved *us* from Haken," Sabra says.

"They travelled most of the way themselves and faced many dangers before they found and rescued us," Kreel says.

"These are indeed remarkable young women,

then." Luka shakes his head, his weathered face puzzled as he looks at the two females. "They may be smaller than you, but they must be strong."

"You've helped my daughter, and if your people are gone you're welcome at our hearth as long as you would like to stay," Atuk says.

"You're welcome to stay with our band, too, Shinoni," Luka says. "I don't have daughters and would be happy to have you at my hearth."

You'll be a great leader of the Kula people one day. Shazur's words echo in her ears. She looks from Keena's familiar, smiling face to the brown faces of Sabra, Luka, and the other Kulas. Hazy images of their journey float in Shinoni's mind's eye: Keena's joy at lighting a fire, their riding the mammoth and running from hyenas together, Keena's face smiling over the edge of the pit, Keena calling her *friend*.

Shinoni hears her father's voice again in her head. *The Krag woman-child is a brave and true friend. She'll also be a leader of her people.*

Everyone stands respectfully waiting for Shinoni's answer.

"Luka, I'd like to live with your band for awhile, but I must be free to visit Keena and her people whenever I wish," Shinoni says.

"Then you'll be like Sabra, who spends half his time with Kreel," Luka says.

"Tewa must be free to join me when she wishes — wherever I go." Shinoni takes a deep breath as she realizes how important this is to her.

Luka hesitates, but only briefly. "Such a brave beast will be welcome."

"If Keena says the wolf's a friend, she's welcome." Atuk shakes his head at the wonder of this relationship with a beast.

"There may come a time when I want to leave and travel to search for my lost people. I must be free to go when the snows have melted under the sun, if I choose to."

"If that time comes, I'd like the challenge of travelling to a new land with you," Sabra says.

Shinoni smiles but ducks her head. She's not willing to commit to taking any companion with her on her travels except Keena.

Snow begins to fall, spiralling down lazily at first, then faster and heavier, cloaking the hillside in a frigid white blanket. The soft flakes turn to icy pellets, stinging exposed skin and freezing eyelashes. The ominous reality of their present situation sinks in and pushes all else from the minds of the group clustered at the glacier's foot.

"We must get into shelter while we can still see." Luka points in the direction of the trail that he, Atuk, and Ubra took through the snow pass. "There's a large cave back there where we can spend the night and re-gain our strength before travelling home."

The group moves as one, Krags and Kulas, through the snow. That night they share stories around glowing hearths, and in the morning they gather for the dangerous return journey into the high country.

Before they leave, Shinoni, Keena, and Tewa walk to the back of the cave for a moment alone. Shinoni takes out her precious red ochre and mixes it with water from her bag. Both girls prick their thumbs and mix drops of their blood into the pigment. Tewa cocks her head and watches as first Shinoni, and then Keena, places a hand in the pigment and presses it onto the stone. They smile at the red handprints floating high on the rock wall.

Shinoni draws two red circles underneath the handprints, then dips her finger into the pigment again and outlines the pointed ears, eyes, and snout of a wolf. She smiles at Keena. "When we return here, we'll see our marks and know this is our cave."

"When will that be, Kula?" Keena asks as they turn to leave.

Shinoni smiles. "Only the spirits know."

Shinoni of the Kulas and Keena of the Krags link arms and follow Tewa out of the cave to continue their journey.

AUTHOR'S NOTE

SISTERS OF THE WOLF is set in prehistory, a time for which we have no written records. However, we do have other types of evidence about prehistoric peoples, and this record is growing all the time. Scientists have found traces of them in ancient rocks, fossils, and artifacts. They've even found DNA in some of the fossil bones of our ancient relatives. We now know that modern humans have the same DNA as the early modern humans called Cro-Magnons. Recently, we've discovered traces of Neanderthals and Denisovans, two other prehistoric human species, in our own DNA. Some fossils with DNA from more than one group have also been found, which leads us to think that some of them had families together. We weren't always the only humans on the planet.

Cro-Magnons, Neanderthals, and Denisovans were named for the places where we first discovered their fossils. They are all in the genus *Homo*, which means "human." As scientists found more fossils, the Cro-Magnon people were called *early modern humans*. They and the Neanderthals split from a common ancestor and evolved in different places. Neanderthals developed in the cold of Ice Age Eurasia, and early modern humans developed in the heat of Africa. They first met in the Middle East, and by 48,000 years ago, several waves of early modern humans had travelled north and then west. In *Sisters of the Wolf*, Shinoni is from the Cro-Magnons and Keena is from the Neanderthals. The areas they live in represent the places where the original fossils of their peoples were discovered. *Kula* and *Krag* are made-up names for what they might have called themselves.

The early modern humans were hunter-gatherers. They depended on the animals they hunted, following them into the fertile plains, steppes, and mountain valleys of Eurasia. By 40,000 years ago, they were in what we now call France, Spain, and Italy, as well as in other European countries. In many of these places, they met the indigenous people who had lived there for hundreds of thousands of years. These, of course, were the Neanderthals, who were also hunter-gatherers.

At that time, the climate was erratic, swinging between long glacial periods and milder periods. The Neanderthal people were shorter and heavier, and their bodies were adapted to the cold. They had distinctive brow ridges, broad noses, and light-coloured skin. They had various eye and hair colours, and at least some had green eyes and red hair like Keena. The early modern humans were taller and slimmer, with long legs and arms. They had dark hair and brown skin and eyes. Even though the Neanderthals and early modern humans looked somewhat different, they were, in fact, very similar to each other — and to us today.

As mentioned above, there is evidence that these two peoples had a third relative, another species of human they sometimes interbred with. They are called Denisovans, named after the cave in Russia where their fossils were first discovered. We know they had dark skin, eyes, and hair. In *Sisters of the Wolf*, Deka is likely a Denisovan.

Scientists sequenced the Neanderthal genome in 2010, and since then there has been an explosion of discoveries about the Neanderthals and early modern humans and how they lived. We have learned how they made and used fire, sophisticated tools, and bedding. We know they had spoken language and they used body decorations, symbols, and cave paintings. They also used plants for medication and to make thread. We are learning more about them all the time.

We also have evidence that humans and certain wolves made their first connections about 40,000 years ago. These early relationships would lead to the close bond between humans and domestic dogs that we enjoy today. In *Sisters of the Wolf*, Tewa is one of these wolves.

We'll never know for sure what happened when the different groups met each other. We can assume that at least some meetings were friendly and the groups traded knowledge and customs. At other times, they may have avoided each other, or even fought and killed each other. There's evidence that Neanderthals and early modern humans competed with each other for caves, and both groups competed with cave bears, cave lions, and cave hyenas. Fossil bones of Neanderthals and early modern humans show that some died violent deaths. However, some skeletons were intentionally buried, showing signs of care during their lives and after their deaths.

Sisters of the Wolf incorporates many of the most recent discoveries about our ancestors into its storyline. Since it is a work of fiction, it imagines what the interactions and relationships of Keena, Shinoni, and the other characters would have been like, and it lets us look into the lives of our ancient ancestors.

ACKNOWLEDGEMENTS

I'M OF COURSE GRATEFUL that Shinoni and Keena chose me to write their story. From the first day they appeared, one sat on each of my shoulders and they guided my writing and the development of their story.

However, there are many people I want to thank for help, guidance, support, and inspiration along the way. I first thought about writing a prehistoric fiction novel when I read Jean Auel's *Clan of the Cave Bear* in the early 1980s, and her Earth's Children series has remained an inspiration to me over the years. *Sisters of the Wolf* is set in roughly the same time and place as Ms. Auel's stories unfold.

I started researching and writing Shinoni and Keena's journey when I was a graduate student in biological anthropology at the University of Calgary, and all three of my children were born during that time. I was nine months pregnant when I walked across the stage to get my degree. Without the help and encouragement of my family I would not have been able to keep writing and researching during this time.

A big thank you to my husband, Curt, and my children — Michelle and her husband, Nathan; Hartley and his wife, Kristy; and my writer son, Winston — for their support and encouragement over the years. You enriched my life and inspired my writing. Also, thanks to Curt for sharing his knowledge of bushcraft and tracking and our trips to wilderness areas in Banff, Jasper, Vancouver Island, Haida Gwaii, and Yellowstone (the best place to observe wild wolves in winter). Those images and experiences enriched my writing.

A special thank you to my friend Judith Silverthorne, who always encouraged me and helped me delve into my family links in parts of Europe where Neanderthals and early modern humans lived. I appreciated you travelling with me in the Ukraine and sending me links to articles and information on Neanderthals and prehistory.

I'm proud to be a member of the Children's Round Robins' Writing Group. You provide me with support, readings, advice, critiques, retreats, and friendship. Thanks to: Judith Silverthorne, Alison Lohans, Sharon Hamilton, Sandra Davis, Dianne Young, Anne

Patton, Myrna Guymer, Paula Jane Remlinger, Linda Aksomitis, and Gillian Richardson.

When doing research, I visited some of the actual caves where Neanderthal people lived in France. I had an exceptional guide, Bart Vranken, who took me on a private tour of several caves in the Les Eyzies area, which is a UNESCO world heritage site. I saw firsthand the cave painting, etchings, symbols, and, in one, cave bear sleeping beds hollowed out of the cave floor. It was magical for me. I can't speak French, but Bart spoke English and we were able to have good discussions about our views on Neanderthals and early modern humans and the links between them. Bart also provided me with English translations to the displays in the National Museum of Prehistory, with its wealth of displays, bones, and artifacts. It was a wonderful and inspirational experience and important to my research for *Sisters of the Wolf*. Thank you, Bart.

Two people instrumental on the journey to get my book published were my agents from Transatlantic Literary Agency. Marie Campbell saw me pitch my manuscript at a CANSCAIP Saskatchewan Prairie Horizons conference. She felt it had potential and took me on. When Marie retired, my present agent, Amy Tompkins, worked hard to find a home for *Sisters of the Wolf*, which she did at Dundurn Press. Thank you both!

Good editors are worth their weight in gold. I've had the honour of working with three editors during different stages of writing *Sisters of the Wolf*: I want to thank Carla Jablonski and Emma Dryden, both in New York, who helped me start off in the earlier stages of writing in a good way. A special thank you to Susan Fitzgerald, my substantive editor, who really got inside my characters and their world to the extent that she even dreamed about them.

Dundurn Press is the publisher where *Sisters of the Wolf* found its home and it's been an honour to work with their professional team. A special thank you to Kathryn Lane, associate publisher; Jenny McWha, project editor; Heather Wood, publicist; and everyone who has welcomed me and Shinoni, Keena, and Tewa into their fold. It's an honour to work with you.

ABOUT THE AUTHOR

PATRICIA MILLER-SCHROEDER is an active member of the Saskatchewan writing community and an active member of the Canadian Society of Children's Authors, Illustrators, and Performers (CANSCAIP). She has written seventeen children's non-fiction books about nature, science, and the environment. Two of her books, *Bottlenose Dolphins* and *Japanese Macaques*, were nominated for the Saskatchewan Book Awards and another, *Blue Whales*, was nominated for the Hackmatack Children's Choice Award. Her book *Gorillas* received the Canadian Children's Book Centre Choice Award.

Patricia has also written several children's educational films and television scripts. She has a master's degree in biological anthropology and has developed and taught university classes in gender, the environment, and evolution. She lives in Regina, Saskatchewan.